kamikaze l'amour

also by richard kadrey

METROPHAGE

COVERT CULTURE SOURCEBOOK

COVERT CULTURE SOURCEBOOK 2.0

SIGNAL:COMMUNICATION TOOLS FOR
THE INFORMATION AGE (CO-EDITOR)

kamikaze l'amour

a novel of the future

richard kadrey

ST. MARTIN'S PRESS ❧ NEW YORK

Kad
cl

A PORTION OF THIS BOOK APPEARED PREVIOUSLY, IN SLIGHTLY
DIFFERENT FORM, IN *OMNI BEST SCIENCE FICTION ONE* (OMNI BOOKS).

DESIGN BY SARA STEMEN

Library of Congress Cataloging-in-Publication Data

KADREY, RICHARD.
    KAMIKAZE L'AMOUR / Richard Kadrey.
        p.   cm.
    ISBN 0-312-13100-3
    I. Title.
PS3561.A3616K36   1995
813'.54—dc20   95-9978
                                                  CIP

FIRST EDITION: JUNE 1995

10 9 8 7 6 5 4 3 2 1

FOR PAT M., PIRATE OF LOVE

Acknowledgments

I'd like to thank the following people who helped me in various ways to finish The Book That Would Not Die: Steve Brown, Ellen Datlow, Merrilee Heifetz and Charles Platt for advice and encouragement; Jeanne Carstensen for playing tour guide in the cloud forests of Costa Rica; Steve Doberstein for the low-down on plant hormones; my editor, Gordon Van Gelder, who beat my scattered manuscript into submission. And for inspiration and reminders of why we put up with the nonsense it takes to write books, Pat Murphy, Eva Restrup, Mag/Tiff, Kristi Olesen and all the boys and girls at Martini Monday.

And for the background music, thanks to Holger Czukay, Brian Eno, Jon Hassell, Bill Laswell, and Ingram Marshall.

"SELF-ORGANIZATION PROCESSES IN FAR-FROM-
EQUILIBRIUM CONDITIONS CORRESPOND TO A DELICATE
INTERPLAY BETWEEN CHANCE AND NECESSITY,
BETWEEN FLUCTUATIONS AND DETERMINISTIC LAWS."
—ILYA PRIGOGINE

"THE DIFFERENCE BETWEEN A MAD MAN
AND ME IS THAT I AM NOT MAD."
—SALVADOR DALI

"BREAK ON THROUGH TO THE OTHER SIDE. . . ."
—JIM MORRISON

i. Sensitivity to Initial Conditions

Fame is just schizophrenia with money.

I died on a Sunday, when the new century was no more than four or five hours old. Midnight would have been a more elegant moment (and a real headline grabber), but we were still on stage, and I thought that suicide, like masturbation, might lose something when experienced with one hundred thousand close, personal friends.

I don't recall exactly when I accepted the New Year's Eve gig. The band had never played New Year's Eve or Madison Square Garden before, but they both became inextricably tied up with my decision to kill myself. I simply couldn't bear the idea of a twenty-first century. Whenever I thought of it, I was overwhelmed by a memory: flying in a chartered plane over the Antarctic ice fields on my thirtieth birthday (the trip, a gift from my manager, Nikki). A brilliant whiteness tinged with freezing blue swept away to a hard, crystal horizon. It was an unfillable emptiness. It was death. It could never be fed or satisfied—neither the ice sheet nor the new century. Not, at least, by me.

No one suspected, of course. Throughout this crisis of faith, I remained true to fame. I acted out the excesses that were expected of me. I denied rumors that I'd invented. I spat at photographers, while making sure they always shot my good side when I appeared at the chicest places with the chicest people.

The suicide itself was a simple affair, rather dull

and anticlimactic. The police had closed the show early after the audience started a bonfire with their seats during our extended version of "Auld Lang Syne." Back in my room at the Pierre I swallowed a bottle of pills and most of a bottle of Stolichnaya. I felt stupid and disembodied, like some character who had been written out of a Tennessee Williams play—Blanche Dubois's spoiled little brother. I heard later that it was Nikki who found me swimming in my own vomit and got me to the hospital. When I awoke, I was in Oregon, tucked away in the Point Mariposa Recovery Center—where the movie stars come to dry out. There wasn't even a fence, just an endless expanse of lizard-green lawn. Picture a cemetery. Or a country club with Thorazine.

The media had picked up the story by then. Several prominent newspapers claimed that I'd died before reaching the hospital; a tabloid television news program, that I'd suffered permanent brain damage. MTV had a one-hour special detailing the most imaginative reports, the ones in which I'd been murdered by the CIA, a Satanic cult, Muslim fundamentalists, or possibly a conspiracy among all three. Mez, our guitarist, was all over the place, drooling after the press like Pavlov's dog in spandex. He told them that I was taking a well-deserved rest. When asked about solo projects, he was vague, having learned the value of controlled confusion. From my bed, the distant chatter of the media comforted me, and convinced me that I'd been right all along. At its first opportunity, the public had opted for my destruction: The most popular rumors had me dead or in an irreversible coma. A possible corpse, the public loved me all the more, thrilling to my ambiguous silence.

I left the sanitarium three weeks later, without telling anyone. I went out for my evening walk and just kept on walking. Point Mariposa was housed in a converted mansion built on a bluff overlooking a contaminated beach near Oceanside. I had, until recently, been an avid rock climber; inching your way across a sheer rock face suspended by nothing but your own chalky fingers is the one of the few highs comparable to being on stage (death, spiritual or physical, being the only possible outcome of the wrong or false move in either place). It took me nearly an hour to work my way down the granite wall to a dead beach dotted with Health Department warning signs and washed-up medical waste. Then, squatting among plastic bags emblazoned with biohazard stickers and scrawny gulls holding empty syringes in their beaks, I picked up a rusty scalpel and slit the cuffs of my robe. Two thousand dollars in twenties and fifties spilled out onto the gray sand.

As I made my way down the beach to the highway, the sounds of the ocean were transformed by my brain into a thin haze of colorless static, like a television station that had just gone off the air. I left my robe on the sand, following the freeway shoulder in sweat pants and a T-shirt, the money stuffed in my pockets and sneakers. I was thinking about silence.

It hadn't sunk in until I was actually on the beach scooping up the money that I'd really left the band. And my home. And my name. This last was the easiest to lose because over the years, in the grand tradition of artists and criminals everywhere, I'd used a lot of names, and some of them were still out there. And some of them were attached to bank accounts.

In Cannon Beach I bought a coat and a ticket on a cargo ship bringing supplies to the occupation forces in Los Angeles. My ticket, however, only took me as far as San Francisco.

It was a slow, fog-bound passage down the coast. The few other passengers aboard were, like myself, cautious and unlikely to strike up any unnecessary conversations. We reached the city two days later during the dark hours of the early morning. As we sailed in through the Golden Gate, San Francisco was aglow like some art nouveau foundry, anesthetized at that hour beneath dense layers of salt fog. Far across the bay, on the Oakland side, I could just make out the tangle of mangrove swamp fronting the wall of impenetrable green that was the northernmost tip of the rainforest.

2. Indeterminacy

Six weeks later, I left my apartment in the Sunset District and headed for a south of Market Street bar called Cafe Juju.

A jumble of mossy surface roots, like cords from God's own patchbay, had tangled themselves in the undercarriages of abandoned cars on the broad avenue running along the southern border of Golden Gate Park. Here and there hundred-foot palms and kapoks jutted up from the main body of the park land, spreading their limbs, stealing light and moisture from the smaller native trees. The Parks Department had given up trying to weed out the invading plant species, and concentrated instead on keeping the museums open and the playgrounds clear for the few tourists who were brave enough or crazy enough to come to the city. Downtown, the corners buzzed with street musicians beating out jittery sambas on stolen guitars, and improvised sidewalk markets catering to the diverse tastes of refugees from Rio de Janeiro, Mexico City, and Los Angeles. Trappers from Oakland hawked marmosets and brightly plumed jungle birds that screamed like scalded children. In the side streets, where the lights were mostly dead, golden-eyed jaguars hunted stray dogs.

Overhead, you could look up and watch the turning of a new constellation: *Fer-De-Lance,* made up of a cluster of geosynchronous satellites. Most belonged to NASA and the U.N., but the Army and the DEA were up there too, watching the progress of the jungle and refugees northward. Months later, when I was less sure of my sanity, I would ask Frida if she, too, saw these things. She would smile sweetly. "This is all Amazonia now, dear," she would say. "And beyond the equator, everything is permitted."

6   At Point Mariposa I'd been diagnosed as manic-depressive, and suffering from exhaustion. I was prone to hallucinations and fits, quick and random episodes of violence. At night, scarlet ibises would makes their nests in my hair, while caimans grunted to each other from under my bed. When my doctor refused to prescribe it, I purchased lithium from some of the nurses. The drug helped smooth out some of the bumps in reality, but left me feeling slow and unreal, like a walking Xerox of myself. The pills ran out suddenly a couple of weeks after I left the sanitarium, and the world slowly regained it edges, losing the pulpy smoothness that made everything I touched feel like rotten fruit.

My father had been the first person to call me "insane." That is, in fact, my last memory of him. Him pronouncing me crazy, my mother crying, and him walking away (his face instantly forgotten; I could never remember it when he wasn't looking right at me), feet shuffling and shoulders bent with the bitter knowledge that all that would survive of him, all that his feeble DNA had led him to in this life, was the production of a single lying, scramble-brained monster: me.

My brain isn't like yours. Somewhere, a circuit was misconnected; the blueprints were read upside down; the gears didn't quite mesh. Depending entirely on your perspective, I was either crippled or blessed at birth with a neurological condition known as "synesthesia." My senses are, in many ways, unique. When I eat, I sometimes taste shapes. Good pasta has the flavor of curved ceramic; the sweet and sour folds between a woman's legs are a rain of ball bearings. There are other things. Opium smells like A sharp. Mahler is a boiling red fog; Steve Reich is long silver rods; and the Velvet Underground's first album is black wax floating in a pool of mercury. As a child, I was too simple and naive to understand how disturbing my worldview could be to those not similarly blessed. My father beat me, not for knowing the shapes of sounds, but for talking about them. I was ten years old when I tried to shoot myself with my father's gun. He had just abandoned my mother and me. The pistol was a .44 magnum, a weapon best suited for psychopaths or shark hunters, and much too heavy for me to hold properly. I lost my right eye to the barrel flash. For as long as I can remember I have understood one important thing—that sound is nothing more than light waiting to happen.

After all that, you see, the twilight city that San Francisco was in those last days was, finally, easy to accept. Why worry if the jaguars are real if you've spent the first thirty years of your life having people tell you that you're mad as a weasel on crack?

I was walking to a club called Cafe Juju.

Inside, a few heads turned in my direction. There was some tentative whispering around the bar, but not enough to be alarming. I was thinner than when I'd left the band. I'd let my beard grow, and since I'd stopped bleaching my hair, it had darkened to its natural and unremarkable brown. As I threaded my way through the crowd, a crew-cut blonde pretended to bump into me. I ignored her when she said my name, and settled at a table in the back, far away from the band. "Mister Ryder," said the man sitting across from me. "Glad you could make it."

I shook the gloved hand he offered. "Since you called me that name so gleefully, I assume you got it?" I said.

He smiled. "How about a drink?"

"I like to drink at home. Preferably alone."

"Got to have a drink," he said. "It's a bar. You don't drink, you attract attention."

"All right, I'll have a screwdriver."

"A health nut, right? Getting into that California lifestyle? Got to have your vitamin C." He hailed a waitress and ordered us drinks. The waitress was thin, with close-cropped black hair and an elegantly hooked nose sporting a single gold ring. She barely noticed me.

"So, did you get it?" I asked.

Virilio rummaged through the inner recesses of his battered Army trenchcoat. He wore it with the sleeves rolled up; his forearms, where I could see them, were a solid mass of snakeskin tattoos. I couldn't be sure where the tattoos ended because his hands were covered in skin-tight black kid gloves. He looked younger than he probably was, had the eager and restless countenance of a young bird of prey. He pulled a creased white envelope from an inside pocket and handed it to me. Inside was a birth certificate and a passport.

"They look real," I said.

"They are real," Virilio said. "If you don't believe me, take those down to any DMV and apply for a driver's license. I guarantee they'll check out as legit."

"It makes me nervous. It seems too easy."

"Don't be a schmuck. The moment you told me your bank accounts were set up with names from the *Times* obituaries, I knew we were in business. I checked out all the names you gave me. In terms of age and looks, this guy is the closest match to you."

"And you just sent to New York for this?"

"Yeah," Virilio said, delighted by his own cleverness. "There's no agency that checks birth certificates against death records. Then, I took your photo and this perfectly legal birth certificate to the passport office, pulled a few strings, and got it pushed through fast."

From the stage, the guitar cut loose with a wailing Stratocaster solo, like alley cats and razor blades at a million decibels over a tense *candomblé* backbeat. I closed my eyes as turquoise fireballs went off in my head. "You never told me why you needed this," said Virilio.

"I had a scrape with the law a few years ago," I told him. "Bringing in rare birds and snakes from south of the border. Department of Fish and Game seized my passport."

Virilio's smile split the lower part of his face into a big toothy crescent moon. "That's funny. That's fucking hysterical. I guess these weird walking forests put your ass out of business."

"Guess so," I said.

The waitress with the nose brought our drinks and Virilio said, "Can you catch this round?" As I counted out the bills, Virilio slid his arm around the waitress's hips. Either she knew him or took him for just another wasted homeboy because she didn't react at all. "Frida here plays music," said Virilio. "You ought to hear her tapes, she's real good. You ever play in a band, Ryder?"

"No," I said. "Always wanted to, but never found the time to learn an instrument." I looked at Frida the waitress and handed her the money. From this new angle I saw that besides the ring through her nostril, Frida's left earlobe was studded with a dozen or so small jeweled earrings. There were more gold rings just above her left eyebrow, which was in the process of arching. Her not unattractive lips held a suppressed smirk that could only mean that she had noticed me noticing her.

"That's interesting," Virilio said. "I thought everybody your age had a little high school dance band or something."

"Sorry."

Frida folded the bills and dropped them into a pocket of her apron. "They're playing some of my stuff before the Yanomamö Boys set on Wednesday. Come by, if you're downtown," she said. I nodded and said "Thanks." As she moved back to the bar, I saw Virilio shaking his head. "Freaking Frida," he said.

"What does that mean?"

"Frida was okay. Used to sing in some bands; picked up session work. Now she's into this new shit." Virilio rolled his eyes. "She sort of wigged out a few months ago. Started hauling her tape recorder over to Marin and down south into the jungle. Wants to digitize it or something. Says she's looking for The Music of Jungles. Says it just like that, with capital letters." He shrugged and sipped his drink. "I've heard some of this stuff. Sounds like a movie soundtrack, 'Attack From the Planet Whacko,' if you know what I mean."

"You ever been into the rainforest?" I asked.

"Sure. I've been all up and down the coast. They keep one-oh-one between here and L.A. pretty clear."

"L.A.'s as far south as you can get?"

"No, but after that, you start running into government defoliant stations, rubber tappers, and these monster dope farms cut right into the jungle. Those farms are scary. Mostly white guys running them, with Mexicans and Indians pulling the labor. And they are hardcore. Bloody you up and then throw your ass to the crocodiles just for laughs. Which reminds me—" he said, pulling a vial of pills from his coat and setting them on the table. "This is a present. It's Fansidar. The instructions are on the bottle. You're in a malaria zone now, so you ought to be careful. Not that these pills are going to do you much good since the local bugs are mostly immune to it, but it's better than nothing, which has sort of become the motto of our little town."

I almost didn't ask the question knowing how it would sound. "How long have things been like this?"

The kid just laughed. "What am I, the NB-fucking-C?" he asked. "Where the hell have you been?"

Between the damp and spectral thighs of America,

I wanted to tell him, leaving a seed of strange dreams. I remembered a morning mixing our third album at the Power Station in New York. Between touring and a cocaine romance with a gangster's daughter in London, I'd mislaid a year of my life somewhere. I'd had some sort of mini-breakdown during the mix. I couldn't listen to the music anymore. I didn't recognize a note of it, and I knew that I couldn't have played it or recorded it. Listening to it was like having ants build their nests along my spinal column.

I found a liquor store nearby and bought a pint of Stoli, which I kept in my jacket for quick hits between takes. It seemed that I'd punched a hole in my head, and everything important was draining out. The vodka didn't plug the hole, but it helped me not to miss the lost parts so much. "I've been kind of preoccupied," I said.

"Did you know they serve *masato* here?" asked Virilio. "Local Indian homebrew. The women chew up manioc, spit it into these big pots, and let it ferment for a few days. Supposed to knock you on your ass. A very happening drink with the local fashion victims."

"You want me to buy you one or something?"

"Christ, no. I don't drink hag spit. I thought maybe you'd be the one to try it and tell me how it is."

"I don't even like French mustard."

The kid grinned. "Like I said before—this is a malaria zone. There's a lot of sickness, a lot of crazies, and the hills are always covered in fog. When you ask a question like, 'Where'd the jungle come from?,' I wouldn't take any answers you get too seriously."

"Okay, so give me something I can laugh at."

"The *Santeros* say it's revenge. The forest is getting back at all the stupid, greedy bastards who've been raping it for years."

"That's a pretty harsh judgment," I said. "Are you always so Old Testament?"

"I told you not to take this shit seriously. Besides,

how can I be upset? L.A.'s gone. They finally got something besides TV executives and mass murderers to grow in that goddamned desert."

"You seem to know a lot about this," I said.

"I don't live in a complete fucking fog, if that's what you mean."

The band finished their set and left the stage to a silver haze of applause. I stood and dropped a jiffy bag on Virilio's side of the table. "I've got to go now."

"Aw, don't go away mad."

"Thanks for the ID," I said. Virilio slipped some of the bills from the end of the bag and rifled through them. "They're nonsequential twenties," I said, "just like you wanted."

He smiled and put the bag in his pocket. "Just to prevent any problems, just to short-circuit any second thoughts you might be having about why you should give a person like me all this money for some paper you could have gotten yourself, I want to make sure you understand that the nature of my work is facilitation. I'm a facilitator. I'm not a dealer, or muscle, or a thief, but I can do all those things, if required. What I got you wasn't a birth certificate; any asshole could have gotten you a birth certificate. What I got you was *the* birth certificate. One that matches you, close enough so that getting you a passport, letting you move around, will be no problem. I had to check over two years of obituaries, contact the right agencies, grease the right palms. It's knowing which palms to grease and when that you're paying me for. Not that piece of paper."

I slid my new identity and the Fansidar into a pocket of my jacket. "Thanks," I said. "I've got to go now."

"Think of me as your guardian angel," said Virilio. "You have any other requests, any problems, any desires unfulfilled, give me a call."

"I've got to go now."

Outside Cafe Juju, the warm, immobile air had taken on the quality of some immense thing at rest—a mountain or phantom whale, pressing down on the city, squeezing its Sargasso dreams from the cracks in the walls out onto the streets. I pulled out my emergency hip flask and took a drink.

There's a region of windless ocean known as the Horse Latitudes, called that in remembrance of the Spanish galleons that would sometimes find themselves adrift in those dead waters. The crews would strip the ship down to the bare wood in hopes of lightening themselves enough to move in the feeble breeze. When everything else of value had been thrown overboard, the last thing to go were the horses. Sometimes the Horse Latitudes were carpeted for miles with a floating rictus of palominos and Arab stallions, buoyed up by the immense floating kelp beds and their own churning internal gases. The Horse Latitudes weren't a place you visited, but where you found yourself if you allowed your gaze to be swallowed up by the horizon, or to wander on the map to places you might go, rather than where you were.

I'd walked a couple of blocks up Ninth Street when I realized I was being followed. It was my habit to stop often in front of stores, apparently to window shop or admire the beauty of my own face. In fact, I was checking the reflections caught in the plate glass, scanning the street behind me for faces that had been there too long. This time I couldn't find a face, but just beyond a wire pen where a group of red-faced *campesinos* were howling at cockfights, I did see a jacket. It was bulky and black, of some military cut, but decked out with slogan buttons and bits of silver. Just to make sure it wasn't simply paranoia, I went another block up Ninth and stopped by the back window of a VW van full of caged snakes. The jacket was closer. I cut to my right,

down a side street, then left, back toward the market.
When I checked, the jacket was still back there.

I ran down an alley between a couple of closed
shops and kept going, taking corners at random. The
crumbling masonry of the ancient industrial buildings
was damp where humidity had condensed on the
walls. I found myself on a dark street where the warehouses were lost behind the blooms of pink and purple
orchids. The petals looked like frozen fire along the
walls. Behind me, someone kicked a bottle, and I
sprinted around another corner. I was lost in the maze
of alleys and drivethrus that surrounded the rotting
machine shops and abandoned wrecking yards. Sweating and out of breath, I ran toward a light. When I
found it, I stopped.

It was a courtyard or a paved patch of ground
where a building had once stood. Fires were going in a
few battered oil drums, fed by children with slabs of
dismantled billboards, packing crates, and broken furniture. Toward the back of the courtyard, men had
something cooking on a spit rigged over one of the
drums. Their city-issued mobile shelters, something
like hospital gurneys with heavy-gauge wire coffins
mounted on top, were lined in neat rows against one
wall. I'd heard about the tribal homeless encampments,
but had never seen one before. Many of the homeless
were the same junkies and losers that belonged to every
big city, but most of the tribal people, I'd heard, were
spillovers from the refugee centers and church base-
ments. Whole villages would sometimes find themselves abandoned in a strange city, after being forcibly
evacuated from their farms in Venezuela and Hon-
duras. They roamed the streets with their belongings
crammed into government-issue snail shells, fading
into a dull wandering death.

But it wasn't always that way. Some of the tribes
were evolving quickly in their new environment,

embracing the icons of the new world that had been forced on them. Many of the men still wore lip plugs, but their traditional skin stains had been replaced with metal-flake auto body paint and dime-store makeup. The women and children wore necklaces of auto glass, strips of Mylar, and iridescent watch faces. Japanese silks and burned-out fuses were twined in their hair.

Whatever mutual curiosity held us for the few seconds that I stood there passed when some of the men stepped forward, gesturing and speaking to me in a language I didn't understand. I started moving back down the alley. Their voices crowded around me; their hands touched my back and tugged at my arms. They weren't threatening, but I still had to suppress an urge to run. I looked back for the jacket that had followed me from Cafe Juju, but it wasn't there.

I kept walking, trying to stay calm. I ran through some breathing exercises a yoga guru I'd known for a week in Munich had taught me. After a few minutes, thoughts of the tribesmen fell away. And when I turned a corner, unexpectedly finding myself back on Ninth, I discovered I was alone.

On Market, I was too shaky to bargain well and ended up paying a gypsy cab almost double the usual rate for a ride to the Sunset. At home, I took a couple of Percodans and washed them down with Stoli from the flask. Then I lay down with my clothes on, reaching into my pocket to hold the new identity Virilio had provided me. Around dawn, when the howler monkeys started up in Golden Gate Park, I finally fell asleep.

3. The Butterfly Effect

The walls of my apartment were painted the same restful shade of green as the rooms reserved for violent patients at Point Mariposa. A coincidence? I wondered. Or had I been drawn, on some deep and truly twisted level, by the apartment's antiseptic charms?

None of the windows closed completely, so the place was always damp. Some previous tenant had stuffed the open spaces between the frames and glass with old shirts and socks, so that from the street the windows looked like traps for slow ghosts. The building had been all but abandoned by the man who claimed to be the landlord. I still don't know if it was really his building or not. It was common at the time for buildings in San Francisco literally to collapse into the street from lack of maintenance. Other buildings, like Frida's, were overrun with landlords. Every week or two someone, a fat man or a tall woman (it was never the same person twice) would ask for rent. The amounts they wanted could range anywhere from twenty dollars to several hundred. Like most people, Frida usually paid because it was easier and because with things the way they were, it was almost impossible to confirm things like building ownership.

The city was always with me in the apartment. The movement of traffic shook the walls. Small lizards and insects from the park worked their way in through the windows, under the doors. I'd set up a small recording studio in the bedroom, but the sound of the city's steady breathing sometimes filled my brain with so many colors that I couldn't see my hands. Despite this, I mostly liked the random lights. In New York, I'd slept and sometimes worked in an anechoic chamber, a soundproof and vibration-free fiberglass womb that afforded me black and silent dreams. In San Francisco I slept on a sofa in the front room, over the street, hoping (I realized later) that some random combination of sounds would trigger in my head the particular light that I'd been looking for all my life.

The French composer Olivier Messiaen wrote and performed his first great work, *Quartet for the End of Time,* in 1941 while a member of a small orchestra at Görlitz, a German POW camp. Messiaen was also a synesthete, but during his most productive years, no one had named or described the syndrome thoroughly. Not understanding the interchangeable nature of his senses, Messiaen was at their mercy. Any external noise could end up being incorporated into his music. Every morning before he began to work, he would send his family outside to chase the birds from the nearby trees; otherwise their songs would take over the new piece.

In some ways I was luckier than Messiaen. After my father took the Big Walk, I tried to shoot myself with his gun. I lost my right eye and eventually ended up in a King's County psych ward. While I was there, a clever young intern diagnosed my synesthesia, and even explained it to me. Until then, I had always seen the strange lights, but I'd learned to be ashamed of them. Suddenly, I'd a name for what I saw and I knew that it was all right. I began to explore the radiant world inside my skull. This lead me to another discovery, the one that made me rich and loved and almost killed me: All songs contain cylinders—golden cylinders that spin along their vertical axes and move in the chaotic butterfly-wing patterns of a Lorenz Attractor. The closer the movement of the cylinders to the Attractor, the more successful the song would be. Almost any song, I learned, could be worked and reworked until the light it gave off was the color and shape that would make it a hit. After the doctor named my mind, it was inevitable that I would write my own songs, to amuse myself with the lights I wanted to see, just as it was inevitable that other people would love my songs, even if they couldn't see the lights.

I wrote my first album in a third-floor walk-up in Brooklyn, my second and third in a forty-eight-track home studio in Soho, my fourth, mostly on private jets.

I liked to work in my little San Francisco studio at night, when it was quieter. I was using a Yamaha music workstation patched through a clone computer and some cheap Korean effects boxes, a no-name mixer whose noise wasn't too annoying, and a Fostex eight-track reel-to-reel. All supplied by some college kid on his way out of town. All, no doubt, hot.

When I worked, I sat on a hard wooden chair that shed scales of yellow paint, revealing previous layers of blue, red, and green, like the cross-section of a body in an anatomy book. Occasionally, the sudden, silver-grid sounds of a night kill would come from the park. I drank Stoli neat when I worked. If I got the buzz just right, it helped cut my depressions and let me focus the lights in my head. I played melodies on the synth; sometimes I typed notes or numbers directly into the computer keyboard and played them back through the sequencer on the synth. I was experimenting with a simple program I'd written to generate chaos music.

It was a homely little iteration code, something I'd stolen from the back of a PC magazine. As I played a melody through the synthesizer program in the work-station, the program scanned each note, its relative position on the staff line, and its duration and assigned it a number. Then it ran each number through a simple formula, like $X - X^2$, each X being the number assigned to the note. The program then plugged the result back into the equation and repeated it until I told it to stop.

I generated dozens of these chaos compositions in my clandestine studio. Every one of them was shit—glittering digital farts. The light they gave off was random and pathetic, lightning bugs on laughing gas. Night after night I sat in the green room staring at the cursor on the VDT while insipid computer melodies flashed their wretched light. Time seemed elastic during those sessions. The room was infinite, circumscribed by faint vibrations, a region of negative space, made terrifying by the relentless hum of the fan in the back of the PC.

What would lie at the heart of a note, I wondered, if you could split it apart like an atom? Life, maybe. Time. I was trying to invent something new, Open System music, and capture the sound of period-doubling chaos in notes. This was the only thing that mattered. The way to find the city of light was through that sound. Listen—

Music is a nonlinear thermodynamic system, stable only on a macrolevel (the level at which we hear it). Certain types of music—early rock, blues, Baroque and most pre-Romantic symphonies—can be seen as Closed Systems. The structure of these musics is fairly rigid, laid out in advance by the writer deciding on a single note.

Other musics, like free jazz, can be seen as Open Systems because their structures are more flexible and less predictable. Open System music allows for the free exchange of ideas between the performer, the local environment, and the notes themselves. This music operates like a biological system, evolving over time, rather than being written in the usual way; like most biological systems, it is highly complex (though not necessarily containing many notes) unpredictable, and nonlinear. A score for this type of music would probably look more like a Twin Dragon fractal or a Lyapunov jellyfish that the standard black and white dots you see in cheat books. Really, though, true Open System music couldn't be written down, or, if written down, couldn't be played the same way twice. Because it's dynamic, the action of one Open System can't exactly duplicate the action of another Open System. The slightest change in the piece—the holding of a note, or a difference in breath—would result in minute internal changes that would multiply throughout the piece until, at the end, it would become a wholly different piece of music.

What this music would sound like, I didn't know, but I heard snatches of it in a recurring dream. In the dream, I awoke just before dawn in a recording studio in Hollywood. The skyscrapers glowed pale pink outside the window. Through some trick of the light, the buildings along Vine seemed to be moving toward me and away from me at the same time. I was falling down some long transparent shaft among the buildings. The traffic overhead moved like a colony of termites across the rainforest floor. Chromed offices opened up like rows of metallic lotuses along Hollywood Boulevard, and the substance of the city had been transformed, giving off light and sound. And I was at the center of it all, falling toward a black vortex that branched off into beetle-shaped islands and spiral archipelagos. Sound and rhythm sizzled like lightning in and around a central attractor. They formed the skyline of a city of light, a consuming fractal light made up of sound. It was the light of my own botched suicides. It was home. I had to get inside the city. I'd been trying since I first discovered my synesthesia as a child. The way to the city was through music or my death. I'd realized after much self-abuse that the former was the place to start the search. The latter would always be there.

I wondered sometimes if my garage band gear was up to the journey. I kept reminding myself of the nobility of haiku, of seeing a thing's restrictions as its strengths, and of the karmic brownie points to be gained from a life of simplicity. The truth is that I was afraid to show my face in any of the few music shops left in the city. My name still made the front pages of the papers. Rumors had me jamming with rural tribesmen in Ghana; blind and covered with sarcomas in New York; brain-dead and on life support in a Swiss clinic next to James Dean and John Kennedy. The public preferred me dead, clearly. Dead or inaccessible, which is the same thing in show biz. And why shouldn't they? Dead heroes don't fuck up. They don't suddenly go electric when you're used to them acoustic. They don't puke on stage or release lame collections of B-sides because they've run out of ideas. A dead hero's only job is to make the living feel better about themselves. Understanding that, I was happy to stay dead.

4. Strange Attractors

Sometimes, on the nights when the music was especially bad or I couldn't stand the random animal lights
of the park anymore, I'd have a drink, and then walk.
The squadrons of refugees and the damp heat of the
rainforest that surrounded the city made the streets
miserable much of the time, but I decided it was better
to be out in the misery of the streets than to hide with
the rotten music in my room.

 I was near Chinatown, looking for the building
where I'd shared a squat years before, when I first saw
the sleepwalkers. At first, I didn't recognize them, so
complete was their imitation of wakefulness. Groups of
men and women in business clothes waited silently for
buses they had taken the previous morning, while merchants sold phantom goods to customers who were
home in bed. Smiling children played in the streets,
dodging ghost cars. Occasionally a housewife from the
same neighborhood as a sleepwalking grocer (these
night strolls seemed to be a localized phenomenon,
affecting one neighborhood at a time) would re-enact a
purchase she had made earlier that day, entering into a
kind of slow-motion waltz with the merchant, examining vegetables that weren't there or weighing invisible
oranges in her hand. No one had an explanation for the
sleepwalking. Or rather, there were so many explana-
tions that they tended to cancel one another out. The
one fact that seemed to be generally accepted was that
the night strolls had become more common as the rain-

forest crept northward toward San Francisco, as if the boundary of Amazonia was surrounded by a region compounded of the collective dreams of all the cities it had swallowed.

I followed the sleepwalkers, entering Chinatown through the ornamental gate on Grant Street, weaving in and out of the oddly beautiful group pantomime. The streets were almost silent there, except for the muted colors of unhurried feet and rustling clothes. None of the sleepwalkers ever spoke, although they mouthed things to one another. They frowned, laughed and got angry, reacting to something they had heard or said when they had first lived that particular moment.

It was near Stockton Street that I heard the jittery pastel sound of looters. Then I saw them, moving quickly and surely through the narrow alleys, loaded down with merchandise from the sleepwalkers' open stores. The looters took great pains not to touch any of the sleepers. Perhaps they were afraid of being infected with the sleepwalking sickness. More likely, though, they were simply afraid of waking someone while in the act of emptying his or her store. The looters seemed to be organized into a kind of human chain. The runners moving in and out of the shops took their booty to the nearest corner and gave it to someone, usually a skinny teenager, who moved off, and was replaced by another adolescent. They were taking food, mostly, but I also saw televisions, cameras, and CD players making their way down the chain. I watched the looters loading the goods into their rolling mobile shelters, moving full shelters away and bringing empty ones in. What the groups of homeless were going to do with the electronic gear baffled me. Living in the streets, they had little access to electrical power, and they would be taking a terrible risk if they tried to sell the stuff—the penalties for looting having turned draconian during the first wave of refugees from the poorer Americas (and included deportation and hard labor clearing the rain-forest).

Cop paranoia got hold of me then, and I started back the way I'd come, out of Chinatown. I was almost to the gate, dodging blank-eyed Asian children and ragged teenagers with armloads of bok choy and video tapes, when I saw it out of the corner of my eye: Coming out of a darkened dim sum place, peeling the paper away from a cold *cha siu boa,* was the jacket. Same military cut, same cluster of pins on black that had followed me from Cafe Juju the week before. The jacket must have spotted me too, because it darted back into the restaurant. I followed it in.

A dozen or so people, mostly elderly Chinese couples, sat miming silent meals inside the unlit restaurant. Cats, like the homeless, had apparently figured out the pattern the sleepwalking sickness took throughout the city. Dozens of the mewing animals moved around the tables, rubbing against sleepers' legs, and scrounging for leftovers in the dim-sum trays. I went back to the kitchen, moving through the middle of the restaurant, trying to keep the sleepers around me as a barricade between me and the jacket. I wasn't as certain of myself inside the restaurant as I'd been on the street. Too many sudden shadows. Too many edges hiding between the bodies of the dreaming patrons. I had to go slowly; working with only one eye, my depth perception was never great, and in the flat underwater light of the restaurant, dodging cats and sleepers, I was just about blind.

There were a couple of aproned men in the kitchen, kneading the air into dim sum. Cats perched on the cutting tables and freezer like they owned the place. Whenever one of the sleepwalking cooks opened the freezer doors, the cats went berserk, crowding around his legs, clawing at chunks of pork and raw chicken. There was, however, no jacket back there. Or in the restroom. The rear exit was locked. I went back out through the restaurant, figuring I'd blown it. I hadn't had any medication in a couple of weeks, and decided I'd either been hallucinating again, or had somehow missed the jacket while checking out the back. Then from the dark she said my name, the only name she knew me by. I turned in the direction of the voice.

I'd walked within three feet of her. She was slumped at a table with an old woman, doing a good imitation of the narcotized pose of a sleeper, only revealing herself when she shifted her gaze from the tablecloth to me. She motioned for me to come over and I sat down. Then she pushed a greasy bag of cold dim sum at me. "Have one," she said, like we were old friends.

"Frida?" I said.

She smiled. "Welcome to the land of the dead."

"Why were you following me?"

"*I* was scoring some food." She reached into the bag and pulled out a spring roll, which she wrapped in a paper napkin and handed to me. As she moved, I caught a faint glimmer off the gold rings above her eyebrow. "*You,* I believe, were the one who was pinballing through here like Blind Pew."

"Glass eye. I don't do well in the dark. Do you always steal your dinner?"

"Whenever I can. I'm only at the cafe a couple of nights a week. And this town isn't what it used to be. Tips nowadays wouldn't keep a poodle in Milk Bones."

The old woman with whom we shared the table leaned from side to side in her chair, laughing the high, fake, wheezing laugh of sleepers, her hands describing arcs in the air. "So you weren't following me tonight," I said. "Why did you follow me the other night from Cafe Juju?"

"You remind me of somebody."

"Who?"

"I don't know. Your face doesn't belong here. Where it should be, I can't say. But I know I've seen you before. Maybe you're a cop and you busted me. Maybe that's why you look familiar. Maybe you're a bad guy I saw getting booked. Maybe we went steady in the third grade. Maybe we had the same piano teacher. Ever since I saw you at the cafe, I've got all these maybes running through my head."

"Maybe you've got me mixed up with someone."

"I don't think so," said Frida. She smiled and in the half-light of the restaurant I couldn't tell if she knew who I was or not. She didn't look crazy, but she still scared me. I'd gone to the funeral of more than one friend who, walking home, had turned a corner and walked into his or her own Mark David Chapman. Frida's smile made her look strangely vapid, which surprised me because her eyes were anything but that. Her face was pockmarked and had too many lines for someone her age, but there was a kind of grace in the high bones of her cheeks and forehead. Sitting with her in the dark I never quite got past my suspicion of her, but I didn't want her following me around anymore either.

"You're not a cop or a reporter, are you?" I asked.

Her eyes widened in amusement. "No. Unlike you, I'm pretty much what I appear to be."

"You're a waitress who tails people on her breaks."

She shrugged and bit into her spring roll, singing, "Get your kicks on Route Sixty-six."

"Now you're just being stupid," I said. "Virilio didn't tell me that part. He just said you were crazy."

"Did he say that?" She looked away and her face fell into shadow. I leaned back, thinking that if she was crazy, I might have just said the thing that would set her off. But a moment later she turned back, wearing the silly smile. "He's one to talk, playing Little Caesar in a malaria colony." She picked up a paper napkin from the table and, with great concentration, began wiping her hands, a finger at a time. Then she said: "I'm looking for something."

"Right. The Music of Jungles?"

"Jesus, did he tell you my favorite color, too?"

"He just said it was something you'd told him."

"Red is my favorite color," she said and shrugged. "I am looking for something. But it's kind of difficult to describe."

"California is a dead issue. If you want to play music, why don't you go to New York?"

She reached down and picked up a wandering cat. It was a young Russian Blue. The animal curled up in her lap, purring. "What I'm looking for isn't in New York," she said. "I thought from your face you might be looking for something, too. That's why I followed you."

"What is the Music of Jungles?" I asked.

She shook her head. "No. I think maybe I made a mistake."

I slid the hip flask from my pocket and took a drink. "Tell you the truth, I am looking for something, too."

"I knew it," she said. "What?"

"I barely have a name for it. It's a color and it's made up of sound. I've only seen it twice, but I think it's what my whole life's been leading me toward."

"You're a musician?" she asked.

"Yes."

She picked up the flask, sniffed, and took a drink, smiling and coughing a little as the vodka went down. "What's your name?" she asked.

"You already know my name."

"I know *a* name," she said, setting down the flask. "Probably something store bought. Maybe from Virilio? Not that I have anything against having more than one name. Frida's not my original name, either."

"What was your name?"

"Catherine."

"Why did you change your name, Catherine?"

"I didn't. It came with the job and the apartment, but you wouldn't know that kind of thing unless you had to work," she said. "The only reason San Francisco is still here is because of handouts from Washington. They don't like the idea of all this unoccupied territory. But people are nervous, you know? Daddy's not going to keep up our allowance forever. If someone with a job gets sick or dies or moves on it's no big deal, because there's lots of people around who'll take any job. Only if you're a boss, you don't want the state employment boys to find out the job's open, because maybe they'll say it doesn't need filling and you'll lose part of your subsidy. So, anytime anyone gets a job, more than likely they also get a new identity. I'm Frida now. With Frida's apartment and clothes, her photo albums and dishes. I don't know how many other Fridas there've been before me, but I'm her now. My name was Catherine, but now I'm Frida."

I put the flask in my pocket. "Listen, Frida," I said, "the atmosphere in here is definitely not growing on me. Would you like to go someplace?"

"Sure. I don't live too far away." She paused and said, "Maybe I could play you some of my music."

"I'd like that," I said. The cat jumped down from her lap as she stood. At the door she said: "You know, you managed to still not tell me your name."

I looked at her for a moment. An old man shuffled between us, nodding and waving to sleeping friends. Welcome to the land of the dead, I thought. And told her my real name. She hardly reacted at all, which, to tell you the truth, bothered me more than it should have. She just looped her arm in mine, and we strolled out of Chinatown. In the quivering light of the mercury vapor lamps, the activity of the looters was almost indistinguishable from the sleeping ballet of children and merchants.

5. The Thermodynamics of Nonlinear Systems

We walked to Frida's apartment. She lived near China-town, in an unlit rat's maze of old brick buildings skirt-ing the edge of the financial district, like some corrupt border town. The area was called the Tenderloin, tra-ditionally a departure point for immigrants on their way up and locals going the other way. I followed her past corners where the sewers were blocked by lush growths of jungle flowers, school yards where iguanas fed on blue grasshoppers, and abandoned Vietnamese cafes whose walls were marked not with the tags of streets gangs, but with tribal and *Santeria* talismans. Frida was living in a loft above a shuttered porn house; one floor below her, squatters shivered with malarial fevers among the racks of mildewed magazines. Con-siderately, she left the bag with the dim sum by the porn shop door, and opened the gate to the stairs that lead to her apartment.

Perhaps it was the smell of the damp wood that did it, but walking up the dark staircase to her loft, I had the sudden feeling of being back at Point Mariposa. It didn't get any better when she opened the door at the top and we entered a long windowless corridor. I fol-lowed her to the end of the hall and around a corner where several doors led off an open area, reminding me of the entrances to the fake-comfortable rooms the attendants would lock us in at night. When Frida opened one of the doors, I was half-expecting an exam-ining table or a nurse's station, and I found myself wondering nervously where I'd left my medication, when I realized we were in her apartment.

I couldn't see anything at first. I just stood there by the door. In the absence of light, the sounds from the street and the delirious murmurs of the squatters beneath our feet seemed amplified. Their light was a snowfall of multi-colored phosphenes that settled, burning, into the floor. "You don't have to just stand there," she said from somewhere in the room. "Come in." I took a step and kicked something. Froze. I hadn't really had a bad episode of depression or manic behavior since I'd blown Point Mariposa, and I'd long since stopped taking lithium. But standing there in the blackness, something turned over in my belly, a cramped giddiness, like an orgasm or panic. At that moment, I was back in the clinic, sweating in my bed as animals moved in the shadows of my room. "Oh, right," Frida said, "You don't like the dark." She turned on a light.

Her loft looked more like the hideout of a rainforest cargo cult than a place where someone lived. Microphones, gutted tape recorders, and soldering gear covered nearly every horizontal surface amidst a clutter of plants, butterfly collections, and animal bones. There weren't many things that looked like instruments: a laptop steel guitar, an ancient lacquer-peeling trombone fitted with a MIDI pickup over the bell; a battered Fender Rhodes electric piano, its top off, the tines removed, bird skulls scattered across the keyboard. Two of the loft's walls were taken up by gray industrial shelving that held stacks of audiotapes and computer diskettes labeled things like "Storm over mangrove swamp," "Vultures fighting over carcass," and "Caiman swimming—jaguar and copter in background." In the corner, near a window and a small unmade bed, was a somewhat more orderly area holding a battered laptop computer, a digital sampler, and a portable Sony ODR—an optical disc recorder. I stood there nodding, overwhelmed by the alienness and familiarity of the place. It could have been a shrine preserving half the things that had come to horrify me. Frida was sitting on the arm of a battered green easy chair, watching me. I pointed to the ODR machine. "That looks new. Where'd you pick it up?" I asked.

"Bought it from a friend," she said giving me a look that was partly lust and partly distant curiosity—the kind of look she might give to some unknown insect or parasitic plant.

"How much?" I asked.

She shrugged. "A hundred, I think."

"Must be a good friend. That's a two-thousand-dollar recorder."

She swung a leg out, stretching. "People leave town. Things get jettisoned. Food, gas, plane tickets north, that's what most folks care about now. Stuff like this—" she aimed the toe of her tanker boot at the ODR—"is worthless to them." She sat up suddenly, as if remembering something. "Hey, you want something to smoke? A drink?"

Those magic words. "A drink would be nice."

"What do you want? I have everything."

"I'll drink anything I can see through," I told her. She went to a small kitchen just off the main room. I listened to her rummage around in the cupboards, and then run water in the sink. I smiled, thinking, No clean glasses.

The recorder was an ugly find, full of nasty memories, unresolved fear and anger. Worse yet, seeing it had started me down a road of self-pity and nostalgia. These were dangerous feelings, evil emanations from the most base and coke-laden parts of my brain. They led to depression and worse. I'd been administering myself careful doses of Stolichnaya these last few weeks, trying to maintain some sort of equilibrium; I craved more medicine now.

I turned back to the clear area by Frida's bed and saw that the amber control display on the sampler was lit. I pushed the eject button on the disk drive and looked at the diskette. Written on it in smeared magic marker was, "Howler monkey—dawn." I reloaded the disk and pressed middle C on the keyboard. There were studio monitors bracketed to the ceiling at either end of the loft. A split second of white noise, and then the monkey's call erupted from behind the speakers' tight black mesh, filling the room. The sound started as a pale gold, low and from a distance, like some mad thing coming through the walls; then it rose quickly in pitch and volume, expanding into an ice blue fist that exploded, shaken apart by its own internal vibrations.

"That's something new," Frida called from the kitchen. She reappeared a moment later, coming around the gray shelves. As she turned, her profile stood out for a second, caught in the low light, blending with the caiman skull and discarded monitors stacked behind her. She had a glass in each hand and a bottle tucked under her arm. "I hope vodka's okay."

"Vodka's lovely," I said, and took a gulp, feeling the liquor's healing juices warm my stomach.

"That recording is still raw," she said defensively. "You probably heard that little blip of white noise at the beginning of the sample. Sometimes it's hard to find a good loop point for some sounds, but you probably know all that. . . ." Her voice trailed off. She turned to the shelves of recordings. "When the sound's clean, I'll add it to the others," she said. "That monkey came out all right. Some of the others aren't as good. Anything from the canopy's a problem because that means climbing, and that's a bitch. But it's easy enough to go back and try again."

"To Marin?" I asked.

"Yes."

"It sounds dangerous. How do you get there?"

"Stroll right across the bridge. No one's going to stop you."

"I thought there were guards."

"Not for months."

"Do you go there alone?"

"Sometimes," she said. "But usually I bring along my good buddies, Mister Smith and Mister Wesson." She reached under her jacket and slid out a blue-black .45 caliber automatic. "The gift that keeps on giving," she said. "Actually, I've never even had to pull it, but having it makes everywhere feel like home. So tell me—" Frida said, setting the gun down next to the sampler, "why aren't you dead?"

I shrugged. "It's not for lack of trying."

"That's sad," said Frida, taking a gulp of her vodka. "If I was in your position, I'd have gone for it all. All the music and craziness I could swallow."

"But you aren't me," I said. "And the truth is, you don't know a goddamn thing about my position."

She frowned and I immediately regretted saying it. "I've read your interviews," she said.

"You can always trust interviews. I mean, the press has me autopsied or jamming with Elvis on Mars."

Frida smiled wickedly. "But you liked parts of it, didn't you? The adulation. The power. The drugs. The sex."

"Those are all nice things."

"What didn't you like?"

"Everything else," I said, and finished the drink. "Look, anything you do, no matter how stupid or destructive, can be laughs for a while. I'm sure Hitler, before he ended up gibbering in his bunker, was basically having a good old time with his Tiger tanks and U-boats. But even a crazy old fuck like him couldn't keep the party rolling forever. How many countries can you walk over before it gets old? How many hotel rooms can you vandalize? How many citizens' daugh-

ters can you chew up? The truth is, it takes as much
energy to burn something down as it does to make it.
And after a while breaking things just isn't fun anymore."

"And there're rumors that Hitler is still alive, too."

"We have a lot in common. We're both failed
artists." She laughed at that, which made me feel better
because I hadn't meant it to be that funny. Despite my
inevitable suspicions of her, I found myself oddly
touched by Frida's assumption that I was being ironic
and not merely self-pitying.

She poured me some more vodka from the bottle
she'd left on the floor. "So why'd you do it? As one
crazy person to another, tell me, straight up, no sea stories—why did you try to kill yourself?"

On a shelf above her head was a small Mexican
Day of the Dead sculpture, a simple papier-mâché cari-
cature of a woman playing a guitar. Her grinning skull
was attached to her body by a short silver spring. "I
don't like people demanding things of me. That's one
of the reasons." I took the bottle out of her hand and
refilled her glass, avoiding her eyes. "It was kind of you
to invite me here, to let me see where you live and how
you make your music, but don't go expecting payment
for things I didn't ask for."

Something shifted in her face; the neediness I'd
seen there just a second before sharpened to something
hard. I thought that she might try to slap me or throw
me out. "Fine," she said. "Why did you fucking do it?"

I stared at the drink in my hands. "It was the light,"
I said. And I drank some more vodka, trying to think of
something else to say, only coming up with "Oh fuck
it." Then, "Just before our last tour, I woke up one day
and was sure that I'd died. I was sure that I'd died and
been replaced by a machine and that I was the
machine, only no one would tell me. We'd be in a limo
or a jet and I'd hear the sound of the engine and think it

was coming from inside my head, the sound of gears working my hands and eyes." I kept on talking, a little drunk. I told her my greatest secrets: that sound was nothing more than light waiting to happen, and that light revealed the patterns that lead to songs. I told her about my first suicide, about my father, and about how, when I was a child, I'd lost my eye. Frida didn't say a word, didn't smile. She just kept looking at me or down at the bottle. I told her about the city of light. My head ached, but when I started talking, it all just boiled out. I'd never told anybody these things before, not even the doctors. By the time I stopped talking I was shaking and couldn't stop.

"It's okay, baby," she said, moving closer and putting her arms around me. "You're a cheap date. I like that. Little vodka and you're gone."

I wanted another drink, but I couldn't move. Frida stayed there with me, and holding me for no other reason than that I was there and hurting. It sank in then how much she must be hurting, too. What I'd first taken as the strange hate/love game of an addled groupie, had been a genuine attempt to communicate with someone she thought could understand the things she did. For the first time in many years I felt ashamed of myself. Then I asked her to play me one of her tapes. Frida hesitated. She kept one arm around me, not as a comfort any more, but as an anchor for herself. Finally she got up and dropped a disk into the ODR. She went over and sat on the unmade bed, and I sat next to her.

At first there was just the rainforest, a pleasantly strange sound full of effervescent colors, but a creaky old trope of the New Age crowd. I kept waiting for the entrance of the synthesizer playing the mandatory too-sweet melody, but the forest rasped and growled and squawked on until—it changed. Subtly. She had dubbed in a second track of the same recording so that the two tracks were playing identical sounds, slightly out of phase with each other. The light in my head changed too, moving from staccato globes of ochre and gold to a procession of lines that flickered into moiré patterns. The rainforest sounds grew dense as she piled up more tracks and introduced new sounds: metallic tree frog calls, a storm off the Farallons. The light moved with the sound, flowing like the surface of an oily lake, sometimes breaking up into moving vortices of individual pixels, like one of Dali's paintings of sub-atomic particles. And then I wasn't hearing the music anymore (and, yes, it was music I was hearing. The real thing). I was in the city of light. But not quite the same city. This was a parallel place that pulsed with the same heat and light as my city, but carried with it the imprint of the woman who sat beside me.

When the music was over I lay down on the bed, exhausted, drawing my knees up to my chest. My head was full of bugs: the low buzz of vodka, and the last few fireflies of the music. I couldn't move, and Frida didn't ask me to. She didn't say a word, just got up and put on a CD. When she came back to the bed, she took off her clothes and lay down, curling her body around my back. Her mouth was near my ear, and as the music came up she explained that this was a recording of a tribe she sometimes used in her music. The recording had been made by a French anthropologist travel-ing through Brazil. *"Recit du vieux chef,"* she said. "Song of the old chief." Then, *"Chant des hommes peints;* Song of the painted men." And, *"Chant de chasseurs;* Song of the hunters . . . Song of the jaguar . . . Invocation of the moon . . ."* Frida's voice and the music washed around me as I drifted in and out of sleep, replaying fragments of the city of light in my head. She didn't ask me to leave and I was grateful.

6. Phase Mapping

In my dream I was back in the clinic, standing by the cliffs overlooking the ocean. The water was clean and calm, its sound a milky jade. I was holding an acoustic guitar. Santa Ana winds blew extravagantly toward the sea, vibrating the guitar strings. The sunlight on the ocean was brilliant. Things moved in the light, slithering through the waves. The wind picked up and I heard the sound of a siren. I took a step toward the light.

Frida had to work early the next day. When I refused to leave her bed she said I looked like a dead bird, whereupon I leaned back my head and began a series of gagging, gasping sounds that I believed approximated an expiring pigeon. She pushed a pillow down on my face, and I wrestled her to the bed and spanked her fast, which I guessed she would like. She did. Unfortunately, it didn't go any further because she had to get to the bar.

When she had gone, I began looking for the clothes that I'd tossed on the floor sometime during the night. I tuned her radio to static at the low end of the dial; some days, when the ionosphere was just right, the static produced a pleasing orange and blue snowfall in my head. Somehow my socks had become buried under a pile of Frida's jeans and shirts. A ghost of music drifted into the static band and for a moment, I was back a few years, digging through another woman's underwear looking for my clothes.

I'd known even then what a bad idea it was to sleep with business associates, but Nikki Price had been as lovely as she was stoned, and I was rather compulsive about getting laid during that first big rush of success. I can't remember if we made it before or after I decided to dump my old manager and go with her, but for ego's sake I like to think that it was before and that she was at least a little responsive to my charms. I wondered where Nikki was now. Working on damage control in Manhattan, no doubt, in the office she loved so much. She left the polarized windows in opaque mode all the time and worked under custom track lighting. "Sunlight is overrated," she used to say. "It causes cancer and damages the follicles." We called her office the Abattoir, she kept it so cold. Since my untimely death, she would be busy. There would be contracts to juggle, money to move round, angry calls from record execs and promoters, T-shirt sellers and tax people. Above everything else, Nikki looked forward to these calls. She loved any kind of professionally related telephone abuse. It confirmed for her not only her place, but her importance in the grand scheme of things.

She had been a singer of sorts when I met her, having fled her Virginia old-money roots to tour prominent biker bars throughout the Southwest. Her band was mediocre, but her voice wasn't and I remain convinced that had she worked at it, she could have been a contender—not a superstar perhaps, but a good and respected blues singer. Even then, though, she'd been restless, bored by backstage chatter and the process of recording and touring. She took a small inheritance, my name, and together with her unnatural energy, parlayed it into her own management mega-corp—while still in her twenties.

By then she'd gained a whole new history, dismissing her own musical career, even coming up with amusing little stories about how bad her singing had been. That failure seemed important to her somehow. Obliquely, she seemed to be asking for permission to live in the thing she had been searching for back when she'd sung—the raw power of the beat. I would come back from a tour, three months in buses and planes piled high with boredom and anonymous skin, and look at her and see America there in her eyes. As if, in her transformation from musician to manager, she'd become the restless distillate of the road, the whole country boiled down to one brilliant, stiletto-thin, almond-eyed package. I still think of her that way: as America. Reinventing herself daily. Living in limos— using motion as a kind of self-induced amnesia, digging into the beat, working it in under her skin so deep that her bones lit up like burning phosphorus.

Maybe she was another reason I walked away from the clinic. Sometimes she'd come with us for a few nights on the road. There was a savage electricity to those times. Nikki played leader. Not a moment was wasted in testing our limits, snorting more, going harder, chewing our way through the androgynous tides of comely groupies. It was a game, I later understood. I won, and she probably hated me for it. I died first.

Fog was rolling in off the ocean, one of those blinding salt-fogs that burned the inside of your nose, corroded everything it touched, and turned every object into a surprise. It was just after sundown; in the morning when the sun rose, the fog would lift for an hour or so and the city would shine; a sprawling ice sculpture, unreal and glittering beneath a layer of crystallized brine. Tourists, God's roving masochists, loved that kind of misery. A few dozen of the Singaporean variety were milling around a brightly lit tour bus on Market Street. Some were buying blankets and jewelry, while others took snapshots, trading cameras and positions every few seconds so that each could have his picture taken with the fake Indians the local tour agency hired for just such occasions. The bogus tribesmen were an assortment of undernourished Mexicans, blacks, and pasty whites, but their feathers were mainly in place, and the tourists either didn't notice or didn't care. I tried to despise them, but they all looked so earnestly happy, I couldn't do it.

It was the early evening crowd at Cafe Juju. The music pulsed with the metallic spheres and pyramids characteristic of European synth-pop. Virilio was at a table in the corner, wearing his Army coat with the rolled sleeves, showing his snakeskinned forearms. He smiled when he saw me, leaned across the table and said something to the woman with dragons tattooed on her scalp. She got up and moved off without looking to see who was taking her place. I sat in her empty chair. Virilio crooked a finger at a drink the woman had left on the table. "Julie was having vodka. She wouldn't mind if you finished it."

"No, thanks. I can pay for my own."

"You sure? She's probably not coming back, and it'll go to waste."

"Still."

Virilio smiled, then shrugged broadly. "Suit yourself," he said. "You don't look too good. You taking that Fansidar I gave you?"

"Yeah. I'm just running a little low on sleep today."

"Is that all it is? When I saw you just now I thought that maybe you shouldn't be here, in San Francisco. I said to myself, 'Now there's a man who needs a vacation in the sun.' "

"The sun is overrated," I said. "And it ruins your hair. What I need is some lithium." Virilio nodded minutely. He was wearing shades, but the angle of the lights was such that I could just make out the outline of his eyes behind the lenses. His gloves were immaculate, as was his coat. When he smiled, there was an air of cultivated depravity about him that I hadn't pegged on our earlier meetings. It was as if each of his expressions had been rehearsed before the mirror in some motel bathroom, constructed piece by piece from memories of movies, videos, and magazine covers. A face in search of a close-up. When I met him a few weeks back he had reminded me of someone, and now I knew who it was—myself, a decade earlier when I was playing the bar circuit.

"Is this some kind of high I don't know about?" Virilio asked. "What, do you do it with poppers or something?"

"Nothing that exotic. Lithium is something I realized I liked having around for emergencies."

"Of course I can get the stuff, I can get anything you want. But it's not like picking up some of grandma's hash brownies," he said. "It'll take a couple of days." I told him that would be all right.

"So what's going on that you need lithium for? Frida didn't give you the brush, did she?" Virilio asked.

A waitress removed Julie's discarded drink from the table. I ordered a vodka martini, and Virilio another Dos Equis. When I looked at him, Virilio was staring off into the crowd. "Have you had me followed?" I asked.

"You paid last time. When she brings the drinks, they're on me."

"Don't fuck around."

Virilio turned back to the table and finished the beer. "This was never a big city," he said. "And the more crowded it gets, the more like a small town it becomes. There are no secrets here."

"I like her music," I said.

"You like her because she's crazy. I think you're crazy, too, but she's crazier. That's good for you, though, because you can feel like you're in charge," said Virilio, setting down the empty bottle. "And her music is shit. I expected you to have better taste than that, considering your background." He said my name then. The name I'd abandoned to become Ryder.

The fact he had said it didn't register at first, and when it did, I wasn't sure how to react. So I applauded him. "Very good," I said. "Great show. You've been sitting here this whole time waiting to drop that on me, and you did it very well." Virilio smiled graciously. "So what are you? A reporter? I don't do interviews anymore, but don't let that stop you. Write anything you like. Tell your readers I'm dead. Tell them I'm in jail for marrying a twelve-year-old. Tell them I found Jesus and I'm weaving blankets for the homeless."

Virilio shook his head. "It's not like that. I'm not here to blackmail you or to tell a living soul where you are. I'm only interested in your music. Specifically any new music you might be working on."

The waitress brought our drinks. The luminous feathers of some rainforest parrot were woven into her hair, and her arms and forehead were dyed with *achiote* juice in the fashionable geometrics of the Akarama Indians. I raised my glass in a toast and we both drank. "I don't have any new music," I said.

"I know you have gear," Virilio said. "You bought a synthesizer and an eight-track from a kid in your building."

"Having the paints doesn't make you Leonardo. Besides, you wouldn't be interested in the new stuff. My priorities are different now. It's still very experimental, very tentative."

"That's stupid. Why mess with a style that works?"

"Unfortunately, you may be right. Everything I've recorded is shit."

Virilio slid his shades down onto the end of his nose. "I'm not sure if I trust your judgement." He said my name again. Its sound was the color of bruised skin, but with the texture of brushed aluminum.

"Don't call me that. Not in a place like this."

"I tell you what," said Virilio. "Why don't you let me hear what you have, and I'll tell you if it's shit or not."

"So now you're a record producer."

Virilio sipped his Dos Equis. "I told you before— I'm a facilitator. I was contacted by some people very interested in your sound. Frankly, I didn't believe them when they told me who you were. I just read where you were spotted playing for change outside an Indian festival in Amsterdam. These people are very interested in you. Especially in new sounds from you."

"Who are these people? Where are they based?"

"Los Angeles."

"Bullshit. L.A.'s a jungle," I said. "There's nobody down there."

"Sure there are," said Virilio, setting down his beer. "There's always holdouts. Crazies. Indians. Rock and rollers."

I ate the olive from my martini. "Tell your people that their interest doesn't interest me."

"Your interest isn't necessarily the issue here," replied Virilio. "These are legitimate business people interested in making you an offer regarding your product. Obviously you weren't happy with your previous situation. They can work out something different for you. Give you room to move around. Space to breathe. Time."

The cafe was getting crowded. I finished my drink and waved to the waitress for another one. The European pop had been replaced by a bootleg of some local band, dark rhythms of the rainforest, and vocals in a language I didn't understand. "I'm really not interested," I said politely.

Virilio leaned back in his chair holding up his

hands. "That's cool. My job is just to approach you with the offer. But do yourself a favor and think about it. You need to work again. I could see it when you walked in here. And these are very reputable people."

"Right, that's why they're going through *you.*"

"Considering your present state of mind, they thought if they approached you directly you might jackrabbit."

The waitress brought my drink. I swallowed it straight down and put a bill on her tray. Virilio said, "You shouldn't drink like that. You don't wear it well."

"Then get me some lithium."

"I'll work on it," Virilio said. I stood and he looked back into the crowd. "Think about getting your music back out there, Ryder. You're not the only one that needs some distraction. America needs it, too. We're forgetting our dreams." Julie with the dragons appeared out of the crowd and dropped into a chair on Virilio's side of the table.

I framed them in my fingers like a movie director. "You make a lovely couple. Very *American Gothic,*" I said, feeling weirdly giddy.

"You may feel differently when you've had time to think about it, so I'll drop by sometime and make you the offer again," Virilio said.

I just smiled and left. It wasn't until I was back on Market Street that the possibility of a threat in Virilio's final words hit me. I thought about Virilio the Facilitator rehearsing his moves alone in his room, smoothing his hair, thinking of Bogart and Bowie. I remembered reading about the arrest of a serial killer in Texas who used to bring along a videocam on his bloody sprees. He made a whole production out of it, posing with the corpses and all. But, of course, how much of what the media tells us are we intended to believe?

In a parking lot near Larkin Street, a group of homeless men were pushing their mobile shelters together into groups, six across and stacked six high. A small, dark-skinned woman worked around the men, using a stolen National Guard arc welder to fuse the shelters into a skeletal coffin hotel. I checked behind me, but there were nothing but ghost outlines in the fog. A damp wind was blowing in from the Bay. I walked on, thinking how odd it was that the more people knew who I was, the more alone I felt. I hoped Virilio got me some lithium soon.

I went back to Frida's, letting myself in with the key I'd taken on my way out. Her apartment was comforting in its thoughtless clutter, even beautiful in its way. Light filtered through gauzy mosquito netting, colored by quetzal feathers and Christmas lights strung across the ceiling. I felt no demands from the room, possibly because of the clutter, possibly because the space wasn't mine. I'd always felt most at home in hotels and airport lounges, at ultimate ease with the anonymity that infects the air of all such places like a colorless nerve gas. Frida's room was far from that kind of space, but in it I felt the reassuring sense of obscurity that belongs to all objects moving through space propelled only by inertia.

I powered up her sampler and amp, loaded in a disk labeled "Poison arrow frog." From the porn shop below came the barely audible sighs of the fevered squatters, drifting up from the floor as if the building itself were crying out with bad dreams. When the disk had booted, I touched the keyboard and heard the metallic chirrup of the frog's voice. It went on for several seconds then abruptly stopped. It took me a few minutes to figure out the sampler's controls. I'd played with different models in the studio, but had never considered them interesting. They'd always struck me as designed for keyboard players who really wanted to be playing something else. Frida's music, though, made the possibilities of the instrument seem more real than ever before.

In a few minutes, I figured out the Loop function, instructing the sampler to splice the end of the sound to the beginning. When I pressed a key again, the little frog chirruped endlessly, giving off a pulsing orange-red firefly light. From the mixer output, Frida had routed a pathway through a battery of effects boxes and signal processors. I added a little delay to the frog's voice, then a stereo chorus, Dopplering its call from one end of the room to the other. Each modification of the sound, added to the complexity of the light the frog's voice gave off. The firefly light came apart like sun through a prism, splitting into the fractional light of simple Julia Set patterns, then breaking up into jagged arms of lightning, the filigreed edges of a Mandelbrot Set. I tried other disks, loading in Frida's samples of cicadas, spider monkeys, and the percussive ambience of a bamboo forest. Each sound gave off its own complex and unique light. As I routed them one at a time through the effects boxes, I found I could unlock the fractal pattern embedded in each call and chitter.

I looked up and Frida was standing by the door. She was holding a paper bag blotched with grease spots. I stood there dumb for a moment, disengaging myself from the light show in my head. "Guess what," she said, tossing her leather jacket onto a chair. "I was walking up Ninth on the way home, and coming the other way was a young kid with this monster boombox blasting *The Snake Charmer's Daughter.*"

"Can I get one of these?" I asked, touching the sampler.

"Sure," she said. "They're cheap, like the rest of this stuff." Frida disappeared into the kitchen and came back with a plate on which she set the greased bag. "Did you hear me before? I heard somebody playing one of your albums."

I looked back at the keyboard. "It's no big deal. The first time, it's great. You're in an elevator and you hear a song you recognize, then you realize it's yours. It's wild. Soon though, you realize you're just part of the air, like carbon monoxide and other people's farts."

"You are so full of shit," she said. Frida removed a couple of wax-paper bundles from the greased bag and examined them before putting them on the plate. "I was hoping you'd be here. I got us some food. You like Mexican?"

"Only if it's stolen," I said, and she smiled. "I didn't see you at the club."

"Were you there? They had me in the back, schlepping booze from the basement. You could have come on back."

"That's okay. I wanted to get out of there," I said. "I ran into Virilio. He gave me a story about some people in L.A. who want to make me an offer I can't refuse."

Frida stopped, put the bag down and looked at me. "How did they find you?"

"Nobody found me," I said. "It's just a hustle. L.A.'s a goddamn swamp. Virilio thinks he knows who I am and wants to scare me so he can make a quick buck on the bootleg market."

"Maybe you should give him something, just to get him off your back?"

"No. Nothing," I said, moving to the table where she was standing. I slipped behind her and began to massage the muscles in her neck and shoulders. She relaxed and leaned back against me. "Truth is," I said, "if there was a deal to be made, it should be for your music, not mine."

"Do you mean that?" she asked. Her shoulders started to stiffen.

"Relax," I told her. "Yes, I do mean that."

She reached behind my head with both her arms and got ahold of my hair, pulling my head down so that my face was close to hers. I slid my hands to her waist and up across her belly to cup her breasts. We had just locked in on the kiss, when she leaned too far back and I leaned too far forward. We suddenly found ourselves tangled together on the floor, amidst the dust bunnies and splattered Mexican food. Frida pushed me down and straddled my waist, pulling off both my shirt and hers. Eventually, we managed to scramble into her bed where we had a little contest, seeing who could throw their clothes the farthest.

Later, when were eating the portion of the Mexican food that hadn't been rolled on, Frida said, "If you're going to use a sampler, you're going to have to learn to make sound samples. Ever been into the rainforest?"

"Not even close," I said.

"Fine. Tomorrow, I'll take you and you can watch me do field recordings." She scooped up some *frijoles* with her fingers and spread the brown beans on a tortilla.

"I'm not entirely sure I want to go there," I told her.

She took a bite of the tortilla, and kissed me lightly on the cheek. "Don't worry, dear," she said between chews. "The monkeys don't want your autograph."

7. Bifurcation Point

A few decades from now, when the jungle has overrun the defoliant lines and the government's itinerant bush-cutters, San Francisco will be just another lagoon in what will be called something like the North American Tropical Forest Zone. Wild plants will lay down a carpet of rotting leaves and stems that will nourish each succeeding generation. Insects and birds will carry seeds to every neighborhood and building in the city. From the air, nothing man-made will be visible above the jungle canopy, except perhaps for the white pinnacle of the Transamerica Pyramid, rising out of the tangle of tall trees like the nose cone of a forgotten Saturn 5.

We took a gypsy cab from the Tenderloin to Park Presidio. A young *cholo* was driving. A 3-D image of the Virgin of Guadalupe stared down at him from the headliner. I overtipped him and tried to get him to wait for us. He just took the money and roared off, laughing.

When Amazonia finally swallows San Francisco, it will try to destroy all traces of the city. Large animals will follow the smaller ones, attracted by the fresh vegetation. But here is where the city might take its revenge. The rodents will eat the city's electrical wires, choking on the insulation. Birds will build their nests in power transformers, poisoning themselves and their eggs with dioxin, perhaps even releasing it into the local environment. The snakes and burrowing animals will find the toxic waste pits. Eventually, the jungle will have to contend with all the time bombs the previous inhabitants left hidden throughout the body of the city. The jungle will probably win, but perhaps not. If that happens, if the jungle dies out, will our descendants come back to the desert that will, no doubt, be here, marked with the deformed skeletons of poisoned jaguars and shriveled palm trees, and say "We're home"?

We headed north on foot through the MacArthur tunnel near the old Presidio Army base. From the moment we stepped out of the cab, Frida was in constant motion and happy as a six-year-old. She sped ahead then looped back to run circles around me, gliding along on her rollerblades, street skates with all four wheels set in a row under the sole. Frida was in her element—perpetually short of cash; skates were her main means of transportation around the city. I, on the other hand, clattered along on conventional skates like some arthritic maiden aunt, hugging the walls and cursing, with my boots slung around my neck. We emerged quickly from the tunnel, then sped down a decline in the roadbed, around a corner, and found ourselves suddenly at the foot of the Golden Gate Bridge. Even from this side of the Bay, you could see that Marin was completely gone. What should have been scrubby coastal vegetation, was the dark, ragged edge of the jungle canopy.

Fog was billowing in through the Golden Gate, cutting visibility on the bridge down to a few feet. Frida circled back and settled in beside me, skating at my crippled pace. Above us, herons and black-winged terns wheeled on the updrafts near the hills, before disappearing into the mist. "The rain forest is the sexiest place on earth," said Frida. "It's one big orgy in there. What the forest is really about is fucking. Fucking, trying to fuck, and having babies, who will grow up fast so that they can fuck, too. The only thing that happens in the forest as often as fucking is dying, and that's just to feed the vegetation so there will be some place for the kids to fuck, and to make room for the next fucking generation."

"Why is the jungle here?" I asked. "How did it come this far north?"

"There's lots of theories about that. Global warming or global cooling. Sun spots. All kinds of theories," she said. "Personally, I think nature just hates a vacuum. And what else would you call America for the last twenty years?" Frida skated on ahead, fading into the fog. She reappeared a moment later and grabbed my hand. "We're at the first bridge support. Come on." I skated harder, trying to keep up with her. Moisture was condensing on her leathers and the piercings around her eyebrows, quivering like globs of mercury atop the gold rings.

"Careful here," said Frida as we passed the first support column. We were moving over the remains of a trampled hurricane fence. The wreckage was scattered north, away from the city; around it were cigarette butts, crushed food and beer cans, graffiti and the scraps of wood and sheet metal that were all that remained of the squatter shanties. "The National Guard came through here one night after the homeless took over the bridge," said Frida in a flat voice. "Troops knocked down all the lean-tos and shacks and tossed them into the bay. The city council and cops said it was for their own protection. A few people went over the side, too. There was talk back then of reopening the highway north, but that was just so much vapor. I don't even think the authorities were afraid of losing control. I think they were just afraid that people would find out they didn't need them." Frida let go of my hand. Her face was as tense as when I told her Virilio had called her crazy.

"You were here that night?"

"Yeah," she said. "It used to bother me a lot, remembering when they came for us, but now it's kind of like you and your music. Just static. Background noise."

As we got closer to Marin, it was hard to imagine what the powers-that-be thought they were preserving. The orange overcoating of marine paint was peeling away from the bridge's body in long strips, like pastel lianas, as if the bridge were beginning to imitate the jungle in preparation for being swallowed by it. The Marin end of the structure was completely lost in churning rolls of fog. When we finally hit the jungle it closed around us like a trap. The effect was like stepping from a lit room into a darkened one, the change was that abrupt and severe. Tough, wrist-thick vines had snaked down from the hills, completely enclosing the rusted suspension cables and the open area above the anchorage, effectively sealing in the northern end of the bridge. It was like rolling down some sea monster's sloppy green gullet. Near the top, the ends of orchid-festooned vines hung in clumps, like frozen waterfalls; gulls called to each other, resting and preening themselves wherever the vegetation had left openings to the sky.

We had to squeeze through an intact but overgrown section of fence at the end of the anchorage. Jungle succulents and gaudy flowers like deep-sea invertebrates sprouted from the roadbed. Dead fronds from nearby palm trees littered the area with obstacles. The skating grew harder, and Frida moved on ahead of me, heading for an off ramp on the Marin side.

When I caught up with her, at the base of a two-lane road that wound along the shoreward side of the hills, she had her skates off and was slipping her boots on. I dropped down onto a log beside her. "Be careful," she said. "Most of the local plants have been displaced, but there are still patches of poison oak wherever the sun can get through."

I put on my boots carefully, trying not to touch any living thing in the vicinity (poison oak was red and kind of waxy looking, that's all I could remember). Frida adjusted the ODR's strap on her shoulder, and we started up the winding road into the headlands. The wind off the ocean was blocked somewhat by the palms and rubber trees that had taken over any open space between the eucalyptus and pine. We climbed for an hour or so, lost in gray vapor, making our way around fallen trees and stands of bamboo, stumbling over the shallow surface roots of the trees that had gotten a good purchase on the sandy soil. After just a few minutes of the steep uphill climb I was sweating like a malaria patient under the heavy coat I'd worn as protection from the fog.

Every few seconds, a thinning in the fogbank would reveal San Francisco (colorless and fragile) in my peripheral vision, then the city would fade away behind the next fog sheet. It went on like that—city, fog, city, fog—all the way up the hill, like stills from a silent movie. We were up very high then, higher than the bridge. Looking down at the old fort under the San Francisco anchorage, we could catch glimpses of the shoreline almost to Fisherman's Wharf. "Nobody comes up here anymore," said Frida. "Rubber-tappers or a *santera* gathering herbs with a kid in tow, but that's about it. I pretty much have the hills to myself."

Set low between twin stony ridges overlooking the ocean was the dull concrete dome of an artillery emplacement, a relic from those nervous years when the military expected inscrutable Eastern powers to invade California through San Francisco Bay. The main structure was still solid, but the gun itself was long gone, the only trace of it being a rusted circle of two-inch-thick bolts sunk into the foundation. The raw concrete and lonely wreckage of the pillbox reminded me of Mayan ruins I'd seen years before at Chichen Itza and Tulum. They all had the same peculiar forsaken quality to them. Why, I had asked myself in Mexico and then on that artillery emplacement above San Francisco, would you pour all the energy and talent and thought into building something that massive and complex, and then just walk away? (Because, of course, walking away is the only thing that makes sense sometimes.)

I was still chewing that over when Frida said, "Look." She had climbed on top of the pillbox and was pointing down the hill. I climbed up beside her and looked around. I could just make it out through the fog: standing several dozen yards high was an FM broadcasting antenna. Frida went just inside the entrance of the pillbox, and I followed her. Near the far wall was a rotting swivel chair and a desk. A gutted switching console and video rig bloomed rust and blue fungus; lengths of coaxial cable lay beside a stack of cardboard boxes and filthy clothes. "It's a pirate radio station," I said.

"They used to broadcast into the city from here," Frida replied. "It was the last nongovernment station in the city. Used to play news, rock and roll, salsa. Stole concerts right off the satellites. They played a lot of your stuff." I started inside the station, but Frida took my arm. "You can look around that later. I want to show you something important," she said. Her voice was quiet and grave.

We climbed back on top of the gunhouse and looked inland, where the misty jungle canopy was thickest. "I don't just use rainforest sounds in my music because I think they're beautiful, although I do think they're beautiful," she said. "I use them because they're the keys to finding the Spiritlines of a place.

"Here's what it is," Frida began. "Some of the Amazonian tribes believe that the world came into existence through songs sung by certain gods. The land of a place is a map of a particular song. The contours of the hills, the plants, the animals—they're notes, rests, and rhythms in the song that calls a place into being. Over the last thousand years or so, the Indians have mapped all the songs of Amazonia, walked everywhere and taught them to their children."

Frida pointed to the land below us. "This piece of the forest, though, is different; it's Amazonia, but it's brand new. And it has its own Spiritline. That's what all my music is about. That's what I'm all about. No one has found the song of this part of Amazonia yet, so I'm going to find it," she said. "That's one of the reasons my music is so important to me."

I watched her watching the movement of fog through the trees. "When you find it, what will the song tell you?" I asked.

She shrugged, pressing her hands deep into the pockets of her black jeans. "I don't exactly know. Maybe the story of the place. What went on here in the past; what'll happen in the future. I don't know exactly. It's enough for me just to do it."

A moan from the hill below us. Immense and metallic; the birth wail of chrome. It vibrated the air around us, coming in a single long, bawling tone, shifting when the wind changed direction—a malarial orange glow, shot through with dissonant turquoise overtones. I started toward the ocean, where the sound was the loudest, Frida trailing behind.

"That's a lot to swallow," I told her. "I don't know if I'm built to believe in things like Spiritlines."

"When it's impossible to believe in anything, why not believe the impossible?" said Frida.

I was walking blind, trusting to sound. "I don't know," I said. And I didn't.

The hills quivered with neon echoes. A hawk hovered above me for a moment, plucking a macaw out of the sky. I tripped over something and fell into an array of wires strung from one side of the radio antenna and down the hill, like a steel spider's web. The moaning was all around me. The sound came from a flattened metal plate bolted to the wire. Similar plates were set at intervals along the dozens of other web strands extending all over the hillside. When the wind hit them, the wires vibrated and the steel resonating plates gave the wind harp its voice.

I recognized the wires in the harp as coax, the same type they'd used in the pirate radio station. Many of the strands were broken, snapped by rust and temperature inversions. Broken wires had tangled themselves around some of the taut ones, choking their voices. I started pulling some of the damaged wires loose. Frida came down the hill and watched me work, settling into a cradle of densely packed wire near the antenna's base. She was a funny one. She didn't look crazy. And she'd been brave to confess her obsession to me. Braver than I would have been under similar circumstances.

"Did I ever tell you about the song that just about got me thrown out of the sanitarium?" I asked.

"No," said Frida. "How did it go?"

"It didn't have any words," I said. "I'd made friends with a nurse who worked in the locked-down section of the clinic. That's where they kept the violent patients and true psychotics. Every few weeks, the clinic would have these little recitals for the families of some of the controllable patients. Mostly it was pathetic. Shellshocked vets reciting the Pledge of Allegiance; runaway kids doing little dances, hammered on Thorazine 'cause Mommy and Daddy didn't know what to do with them. A real dose of Bedlam, but it gave the folks back home an incentive to keep paying those doctor bills.

"While I was there the doctors, very gently, very politely, let me know that if I wanted to get out with a clean bill of health (and you need that kind of thing for insurance when you tour), I had better participate in their show. So I went to my friend the nurse and rounded up a dozen patients with a condition called echolalia. Echolaliacs aren't violent; they're kind of autistic. And they mimic anything they hear, like human tape loops. When a roomful of them gets going on a word or phrase it can drive you nuts. Which is kind of what happened.

"I took my twelve sweet sheep down to the performance room and sat them in a row on stage. The place was absolutely silent, like a meat locker after dark. The doctors knew something was up, but they were too chickenshit to cause a scene in front of the customers. Then I leaned near the ear of the nearest echolaliac and, very quietly, sang a note.

"She'd been a piano teacher at a private school in the Valley; she sang the note back perfectly. One other patient picked it up, then another. Pretty soon, they were all sawing away on this one note. Some of the doctors got restless, and I think they were going to stop it, but something amazing happened.

"Since most of them weren't singers, they couldn't quite hit the note right, so very soon, these strange harmonies started to develop. And as they came out, the other patients would hear the new notes and start imitating them. Of course, they couldn't sing the new notes any better. Besides, the acoustics of the room suppressed some notes and accented others. Within five or six minutes, this wheezing drone mutated into a kind of exotic round, and spontaneously generated all these complex inner rhythms and harmonies. It's almost the way a Julia Set seems to arise suddenly from a series of random points. That first note was the attractor around which all the others clustered."

"How did it end?" Frida asked.

"I lead them off stage one at a time, saving the

piano teacher for last," I told her. I tied the end of a broken wire to a crossbeam of the antenna. "It's ridiculous, I know, but I still like that song more than anything else I've ever done because I didn't know how it was going to come out. That's when I knew that chaos was at the heart of all real music. The song gave off a lovely light."

Frida rocked back and forth in her wire hammock. "Is this your way of saying you don't think it's crazy of me to be looking for Spiritlines?" she asked.

"I killed myself to look for a city of light," I said. "I'm hardly one to judge."

Frida smiled at me. "Your friend the nurse. You were making it with her, weren't you?"

I secured a couple more loose wires and went to where Frida sat. "She had all my albums, including some very expensive bootlegs," I said.

"And she wouldn't just settle for an autograph."

"What could I do? She was, after all a member of the hospital staff, and knew what was best for me." I took Frida's hand and helped her up out of the wire web, pulling her to me. I licked the condensation off her lips, and she lightly bit my tongue, drawing it into her mouth. She broke away in a moment and, taking my hand, lead me back up the hill to the pillbox. Inside, she spread my coat on the bare concrete floor, set aside her ODR, and pulled off her leather jacket. "There's something I've always wanted to do up here," she said. I knelt beside her and she slid her hand inside my shirt, massaging my nipple, then leaning over to tease it with her tongue. She pushed me back until I was flat on my coat. The wind harp wailed below us, vibrating through the floor of the gunhouse. Frida teased and bit my chest and neck. I slid an arm down and cupped my wrist to her crotch; her legs closed on me, grinding against my arm.

I didn't see the caiman until just before it lunged at Frida's leg. I pushed her clear and must have yelled something, because the thing turned and came right for me. I rolled away. Coming up with the loop of coax, I whipped it at the reptile's eyes, and the animal backed off. The caiman was thin and suffering, maybe sick, clearly starving.

Frida was in the opposite corner near the boxes, waving a short length of pipe, her eyes wide. The caiman backed into the middle of the room, cutting us both off from the door. "Shoot it!" I yelled. "Use your fucking gun!"

"It's in my jacket," said Frida.

The animal writhed on the floor, made furious by our voices, tossing its head and tail, scattering broken furniture. It started toward me, but when I whipped the wire at it, the reptile settled back, grunting and snapping. "Frida," I said quietly, "I need you to call it. Make a sound so I can get to your jacket."

"No way."

"I'm closer to the gun. Do it."

"Shit," Frida whispered. And started screaming, beating the pipe against the walls, gouging out bits of concrete and parasitic plant life. The reptile darted toward her, but when I moved, it twisted back toward me. Frida screamed even louder, throwing boxes and scraps of old clothes at the caiman. It bit and thrashed at her when a T-shirt fell across its eyes. I ran the few steps to Frida's coat. The reptile knocked off the shirt and snapped at me. I kicked the dead swivel chair in its way, and the animal backed off. Feeling inside the jacket, I pulled out the .45, and as the caiman came around the swivel chair, I leveled the gun at its head and squeezed the trigger.

Nothing happened.

"Take off the safety!" yelled Frida. "The button on the left!"

I fumbled with the gun looking for a goddamn button, hearing, in those long dead seconds, the faint echo of Nikki's voice as she scolded me for not going to the shooting range with her. Something on the gun clicked. The caiman lunged, wide jaws like bubblegum-colored chainsaws. I pulled the trigger and the gun went off, the sound of it so loud in the pillbox that I was blinded by a vermilion shock. I kept the gun down and pulled the trigger again. Metal thumped against metal. I heard Frida yell my name.

When my head cleared, the caiman was backing to the door, blood trailing under it from a wound in its tail. It hissed and snapped as it moved outside, and off into the fog. Frida pushed away from the wall, still holding the pipe, and we grabbed each other in the middle of the room.

From the pillbox's entrance, a man's voice calmly bellowed, "Exactly what the hell do you think you're doing?"

8. Intermittency

He was a large, bearded man in a battered camouflage jacket and knit watchman's cap. His face was strangely tanned, with overlapping patches of dark and light skin, as if he had been augmenting a natural bronzing with trips to a tanning parlor. Around his neck hung a couple of ill-treated Nikons, sprouting various lenses and filters, and a small 8 mm videocam. His broad shoulders filled the pillbox's entrance. He moved with the strength and self-assured grace of a linebacker or a jaguar. "I asked what you were doing," he said, scowling at us and nodding after the caiman. "Don't you know that all rainforest animal species are protected by the Department of Fish and Game?"

"None of these animals are even native to the state," said Frida. "And there's no hunting restrictions on any of them."

"There will be, if I have anything to say about it," the man replied. He came inside the pillbox and went to the old desk. His bulk overwhelmed the place, and I couldn't get rid of this feeling that I'd seen him somewhere before. He sat on the edge of the desk, feigning casualness, but he watched us discreetly out of the corner of his eye. He kept one hand in his coat pocket—perhaps, I thought, on a weapon. It was then that I realized that I was still holding Frida's gun. I decided to keep it for the moment, until we knew more about the visitor who'd told us a lie before telling us his name.

"Who are you?" I asked.

"The name's Eric Lurie," he said. Unzipping the breast pocket of his jacket, he removed a tin of stubby Danneman cigars and lit one up. His hands were tanned and chapped, but his nails were exquisitely manicured. "You didn't have to shoot that animal."

"Call a cop. It was going to take a bite out of us," I said.

"I could have scared it off without injuring it."

"You a biologist or something?" asked Frida.

"I'm a layman naturalist, working for NHK out of Tokyo. We're doing a series on this area for distribution in Asia and Europe. Acquainting people all over the world with the beauty and vibrancy of the rainforest ecosystem," he said, his voice falling into the distinctive medicine-show rhythms you hear often in places like Hollywood, New York, and London, where hustling is part of the air. His deliberate, modulated speech contrasted starkly with his appearance, which, too, would be part of the hustle. "We're the only group working to document the emergence of these neo-Amazonian species."

"Think folks in Tokyo would get off on footage of that caiman chewing our legs?"

"Truth is they'd have loved it," said Lurie. He shrugged. "It's the chance you take, isn't it? The forest is full of predators. It's your job to stay out of their way." He was still looking at us oddly, not so much with apprehension as with the detached gaze of a television producer, wondering how he might fit us into his documentary. I would be the reactionary urbanite, the ecological racist, pining away for the good old days when humans and McDonald's dominated the continent, blindly destroying that which I didn't understand. Frida would be my concerned mate, compassionate, sensing the error of my ways, but unable to stop me. She would be a source of pathos, a tragic figure, made guilty by her failure to control my worst impulses.

I remembered Lurie's name then. I'd met him once at a party on somebody's boat. Nikki had introduced us. It was New Year's and he was that month's movie golden boy, having just been nominated for an Academy Award for a documentary about cancer clusters around a West Coast nuclear power plant. There were rumors that he was floundering in his success, unable to focus on a new project. He told me he was looking to expand his horizons, and wanted to do a film about the band, follow us around on our European tour. Unfortunately for him, it was probably the one we cancelled. The last thing I remembered about Lurie was hearing about his arrest for animal cruelty. One of the members of his crew reported him for hosing down a whole herd of horses with gasoline and torching them. Apparently the film he'd been doing on southern California wildfires wasn't producing the kind of dramatic footage he wanted. I wondered back then what he might have done if he'd to come on tour with the band and we hadn't been interesting enough for him.

Frida picked up her jacket. I handed her back the gun and asked Lurie, "What did you mean when you said that your group was documenting new species in the jungle? You mean you're tracking how Amazonian plants displace the native ones?"

"No, it's much more than that." He stabbed his cigar at the fogbound hillside. "A lot of your California plant life are imports. Some of the grasses came in seeds from horse droppings when the Spanish explored the state. Most of the eucalyptus comes from groves planted by railroad companies in the nineteeth century. But what we're watching now is the development of whole new lines of plants and trees, species never seen before. They're mutating right along with the forest."

"How do you explain that?"

"I don't. I just set up photo opportunities." Lurie stood, lifting one of the Nikons up to his eye. He took a low stance, with his feet apart, moving around the pillbox, trying out different angles on the blood trail left by the caiman. "None of this is too surprising, though. Most of the plants you see around are direct descendents of mutant strains from Brazil."

"Let's go," said Frida. "This guy's a fucking liar." Lurie glanced at her and smiled, recognizing a good story hook.

"It's true," he said. "We cover it in the first episode of the series. Officially, it was hushed up by the federal government, but I've got sources in the Department of the Interior and Agriculture.

"A couple of geneticists who'd been cut loose from Stanford were working with the Brazilian government, developing a strain of fast-growing foliage to reseed burned-over areas of the Amazon. The idea was that the modified plants would grow and mature quickly, send out their seeds, and die, pumping nutrients into the soil and stabilizing it. This was supposed to go on for ten or twelve generations, then the new plants would die and the natural vegetation could move back in.

"Of course, it never happened. The modified plants lived for hundreds of generations, not a dozen, and choked out everything else." He raised his camera to snap our picture. Frida gave him the finger and I covered my face.

"Camera shy? Too bad," he said. "I can't use shy people. Now you'll never get to be a star."

"You were talking about the Amazon," I said, making sure his camera was pointed away.

"Yeah. We have a whole re-creation scenario worked out for the arrival of the plants in America. Have you ever heard of a bunch of monkeywrenchers called Gaia Now? That's their logo," Lurie said, turning to show us the patch sewn onto the shoulder of his jacket. It was an amateurishly rendered globe shot through with what could easily have been either spaghetti or neurons. "The project was pissing everybody off. Indians were forced off their land. The big ranchers were paying them and some of the local farmers to steal seed samples for them. Gaia Now paid them, too, and got a hold of fifty pounds of the seeds, which they brought back to the States. Somehow the seeds got into the environment. The story gets fuzzy here, but that's all right because we'll shoot it both ways. Either the Gaians planted the seeds and deliberately introduced the modified plants into North America, or they got paranoid and ditched the seeds, some of which took root on their own. Personally, I don't think those people are afraid of anything." He took a camera from around his neck and began rewinding the film. "Gaians don't usually fly because they believe it depletes the ozone layer, so they travelled overland back to the States. They could have been dropping seeds the whole way through Central America, all the way up into Texas and southern California."

"And the plants are still mutating?" I asked.

"Yeah," said Lurie, snapping open the back of the camera and slipping the film into its opaque protective cylinder. "It's fast-forward evolution. Darwin on speed. And where it stops, nobody knows."

Frida picked up her jacket and put it on, dropped her skates over one shoulder and the ODR over the other. "We should go. The fog's going to sock in the bridge completely. And I'm sick of this guy's bullshit."

I found my coat, tracked with dirt and blood, under some boxes where it had been kicked during our square dance with the caiman. My skates were under the gutted mixing board. Lurie leaned against the door frame as I gathered my belongings.

"This is going to be beautiful one day," he said. "Not in that pussy State-sanctioned nature-preserve sense. But beautiful and wild. Too many people, that's the problem. That's why you have inventions like nature preserves. Too goddamn many people on the land. But that's changing now, finally. The bubonic plague didn't change it; AIDS didn't change it. Nature's paying it all back herself."

"You just told us how this was a man-made phenomenon. That people created the modified seeds and then planted them," I said.

He smiled at my ignorance and blew smoke into the fog. "You ever hear of the selfish gene theory? People are often doing something different from what they think they're doing. Sometimes they do things that are completely at odds with what they believe, only they don't realize it at the time."

I picked up my skates. Frida was already outside. "Thanks for the chat," I said to Lurie.

When I was on the hillside with Frida, he said, "You'll want to avoid this area, for a while at least. There's a government defoliant team coming through here in the next few days, and Gaia Now will be staging some acts of civil disobedience."

"Going to get some good footage?" I asked.

Lurie dropped his cigar and crushed it out with his big boot. "Going to get some great fucking footage, friend." In one swift motion, he raised one of the Nikons to his eye and snapped my picture. Then he turned away and disappeared into the pillbox. His camouflage jacket, drained of color in the fog, blended perfectly with the pitted concrete and scrubby vegetation around the old gun emplacement.

Frida said nothing as we stumbled downhill through the fog. The wind was picking up, bringing in a cold drizzle from the ocean. When we reached the bottom of the hill, we stopped to put on our skates. "Are you all right?" I asked her.

"I'm fine," she said, checking her wheels. "That guy was such a fucking liar."

"Why do you say that? His story makes as much sense as anything else I've heard."

"I thought maybe you'd figured it out by now," Frida said. She stood and zipped up her jacket. "The forest isn't here because some little boys with hard-ons and flak jackets stole a bag of magic seeds. It's here because I called it here with my music." Frida turned and skated onto the fog-obscured bridge, leaving me sitting in the poison oak and wind.

9. Self-Similarity

The Hindu prophets tell us that around fifteen billion years ago, Shiva danced the universe into being by the beat of a drum, sucking in unholy tons of protonatural debris through the pores of his perfect skin and spitting out our common existence: stars, planets, fish, Pizza Huts, fax machines. Thus, through this cosmic fox-trot, music and chaos are always linked. Chaos is implicit in music. When listening to a good player or singer, minute variations in tempo, attack, and release can be heard; in the case of stringed instruments or the voice, there may be a slight sharpening or flattening of individual notes. This despite what is written on the manuscript page. These individual, unpredictable chaotic acts are what is meant by "playing music." A musician, then, is simply an organic Strange Attractor around which music swarms, like ants around sugar or vibrating sand falling into skeletal Chladni patterns.

Frida didn't come home that night. I waited at her apartment until after midnight, then went out to look for her. The evening fog was thinning, leaving the streets shining and spotted with rain, like fool's gold. The rain on the pavement smelled like frozen glass globes pressed against my throat. Fog tasted like an out-of-tune string quartet.

A young *Moreno* girl was selling small insect-eating bats from a bamboo cage outside Cafe Juju. Frida wasn't inside the bar and no one had seen her. It occurred to me that Virilio might know something, but he wasn't there either. On my way out, I bought all the little girl's bats and let them go, remembering that in Buddhist countries it was good luck to give a bird its freedom (even though we weren't in a Buddhist country. Even though bats weren't, strictly speaking, birds). Their dark bodies dissolved immediately into the flat sky, but I could see them for some time, rimmed in the metallic halo that was the sound of their high-pitched navigation call.

It was the last Friday of the month and government subsidy checks had just arrived. The suicides were out. Dozens of them stood in hushed, orderly lines watched by animal-eyed young men idly swinging *nunchakus* though perfect figure-eights. In their patient waiting, it was almost possible to mistake the suicides for sleep-walkers, but their determined isolation and restlessness always gave them away. Each of them clutched one of the orange tickets that the gangs sold. The tickets gave the holder access to the roofs of the tallest skyscrapers. Most of the tickets had gone limp in the damp air, but the holders, sometimes whole families, dared not let them out of their sight. The tickets were expensive and, in a town where money was harder and harder to come by, often represented the entire net worth of the holder. Bored children cried, fought, or played tag between their parents' legs.

The gangs were the only true entrepreneurs left in the city. Since the first groups of refugees had hit San Franciso and the first breeze of suicides became a hurricane, it was the gangs that stood up, organized the deaths and, oddly, made the streets safe again. Frida told me of a period that lasted several months when you literally had to watch the sky all the time when you were outside. If you didn't, or if you became distracted or lost in thought or were simply unlucky, you could find yourself flattened under the terminal velocity weight of some refugee screenwriter or tax lawyer. They were the types that gave the suicide business its start. The ones who had lost the most to Amazonia. It took a while for the middle class to catch on, and for suicide to go Norman Rockwell. By then, the *cholos* and the Vietnamese gangs had taken charge. Being good business men, they had even expanded their clients' options.

At that time, a very chic way to kill yourself was to take one of the gang-controlled ferries out to Alcatraz (a good-way to die whether you wanted to or not—street gangs weren't too conscientious about ship maintenance), where you were treated to a formal sit-down dinner, including all the Japanese champagne you could drink. After that, you were escorted to the shore and invited to swim the mile-and-a-half of shark-infested, riptide-laden water back to San Francisco. Nobody ever made it. If you weren't up to such an extravagant death, for slightly less money, you could arrange to be towed in a small dinghy out beyond the Golden Gate. There you would be given a paddle made of a paper-compound that dissolved in salt water. Before the ship cut you loose, you were given a bottle of some inexpensive local wine. Rumors abounded that to ensure customer satisfaction, both the liquor in the dinghy and the food on Alcatraz were poisoned.

I walked back to Frida's place. On the way, I checked reflections in shop windows to see if I was being followed. I didn't see anybody, but for some reason that didn't make me feel better. Frida still wasn't home when I got there. I took off my coat and sat down on the decaying easy chair. I looked at the watch I'd purchased from a street merchant on my first day in the city. It was a cheap Chinese thing, with a tiny liquid quartz nature scene just above the numbers. The image was supposed to change with the seasons. Mine didn't work. It fluttered feebly between winter and spring, never one or the other, but a smear of each. This was the only movement in the room. I looked at the watch and kept very still, holding my breath. I'd played the same game as a child, then later in hotel rooms in Munich and Seoul. It was called Silence. The object of the game was to hear the sound of the quartz crystals twisting themselves in and out of phase as the numbers on the watchface changed. I strained to hear the watch breathe, to detect some hint of life, shoring myself against the quivering amber dreams of the squatters moaning one floor down.

Frida came in around dawn, silently, like a postcard slipped under the door. One minute I was alone playing Silence and the next, she was standing over me, dark circles around her eyes and rain beading on her leather jacket. "You're sitting in my chair," she said. I got up. She set her skateblades and the ODR on the floor by her feet. "Get me a drink, will you?"

"What do you want?" I asked.

Frida ran a hand through her wet hair. "Anything I can see through." She rested her head on the back of the chair.

I fixed us both screwdrivers, remembering Virilio's joke about vitamins, figuring it couldn't hurt to get some juice in her. I brought Frida her drink and sat on a plastic milk crate full of oversized votive candles, red glass cylinders the size of a child's leg, with cut-outs of a wretchedly beneficent Christ, gaze turned to heaven. The cheap off-register printing made Christ look wall-eyed. Frida held her glass with both hands. She sipped her drink slowly and wouldn't look at me. Her dark eyes were half-closed, and her mouth was drawn down at the corners, a sullen gash. Sitting there then, I was surprised by her anger. Later I understood it fully—I'd betrayed her in the deepest manner possible. I was still there after she had told me her secret. The drink had been a test for herself, to see if I was real or just some rag of exhaustion or memory. I realized then how shocking and treacherous it must have seemed to her when she found me in her chair, and not gone like Virilio had been after she had told her secret to him.

"Your condition has taken a turn for the worse," said Frida.

"Worse than dead? That's bad."

She leaned back, wiping the damp hair from her forehead. "You're not dead yet, but you're hovering near it in a prestigious university medical center in Houston. Your family's been called to your bedside. You're not expected to make it through the night. That or you're having a sex change in Germany. An unnamed source revealed that you're getting ready to tour in your new female persona by performing in a number of notable Berlin drag bars."

"It's all true. Every word of it," I said. "All drag bars in Berlin are notable. My surgeon is also a Vegas showgirl. She's teaching me how to walk in those big hats. I never expect to make it through the night."

Frida set down her glass. "I think you ought to go and not come around here anymore."

"Thanks for thinking of me. But I believe I'll stay."

"Fuck you."

"You've already done that."

Frida laughed and shoved me with her boot. "You'd look a lot better without that beard."

"That's what my manager said when I grew one a few years ago."

"She was right."

"She was psychotic."

Frida shrugged. "That doesn't automatically mean she was wrong."

"You're right, and from moment to moment she could be quite perceptive, not to mention fun. However, the charms of mental derangement are fleeting. She thought I was her evil twin."

"You still think about it, don't you?" she asked.

"The twin theory? Hardly. Haven't got the breasts for it."

"Killing yourself," she said.

"It's sort of inevitable," I told her. "I sometimes think it's part of the bargain. Built right into the equation of being ridiculously famous. The need for some defining gesture at the end. In Chaotic terms my suicide would be described as 'sensitivity to initial conditions,' where an initial input leads to a vaguely predictable, but ultimately unknown result. Fame equals insanity equals what? Death? More fame? A sudden resurrection selling miracle hair products on late-night TV?

"Suicide is the best way to go, gesture-wise. There's nothing like a good flare-out to get the public all hot and bothered. Murder or accidental death can work just as well, but they have to be done with style. Jim Morrison's death was a total botch job—heart attack. Forget it. Hendrix was fine, though. Choking on your vomit has just the right ring. And Lennon, of course. There's still an air of timelessness and romance in the lone assassin. That's the key, right there. Rock and roll is, at its heart, a romance with violence. That's why rock and roll has to be played loud. We act out the murders the public can't or won't commit themselves. Then we turn the gun back at them. When that doesn't work anymore, we murder ourselves."

Frida closed her eyes. "I'm tired," she said. She stood and walked to the bed, deftly removing and tossing aside her clothes as she went, like a snake thoughtlessly crawling out of its old skin. She slid between the covers and pulled the blanket up to her chin, looking at the ceiling. I followed her over and sat on the edge of the bed. She curled her body around mine.

"I always went for the edges, too, hunting up dread and ecstasy," she said. "That's why I was so happy when I stopped being Catherine and learned to be Frida. Sometimes, though, at night I wonder how many

Fridas there have been before me, and how many will follow. When I look in the closet, Frida seems young and, I believe, happy. But there are photos—taped inside books, tucked into the frames of mirrors. Fading black-and-whites of men and women dressed in odd clothing. Baggy shirts and shapeless dresses marked with strange designs. No one ever smiles. The land in the background looks hard. The people in the photos all seem hopelessly old. There are glasses in the bottom of the dresser with smoked lenses so dark, they must be for a blind woman. In the bathroom, there are pills for heart conditions, arthritis and migraines. Sometimes I take them, because Frida would, and I get the prescriptions refilled because the Frida that comes after me might need them." She rolled over on her back, idly fingering a tattered Indian weaving on the wall above the bed. It showed an Amazonian moon deity in the form of a young woman. In the story, before the woman was transformed into the lunar goddess, she had been raped by her father and murdered by her brothers. "It's funny. When Catherine died I thought I'd found a way out. Now I find myself responsible for all the Fridas. And I can't seem to walk away from Catherine's desires."

"Who's calling the jungle north," I asked, "Catherine or Frida?"

She shrugged, her shoulders bunching under the covers. "I don't know anymore. I'll tell you one thing I do know. I know why you're here. In this city and this room. Your greatest desire was to disappear into light, in the same way that mine was to disappear into the forest. When we couldn't do it, we each did the next best thing. We killed ourselves. Really, though, we just killed the idea of ourselves. And the desires that lead us here are still walking around, independent of us."

A high, wavering moan rose for a moment from the shop below, filling the room with sparks. "I've been thinking that maybe I should go back to New York," I told Frida. "Write some new songs. Tour again. I'm no closer to finding what I'm looking for than when I got here."

"You think your epiphany is on the road waiting for you, perched in fish nets on a heated waterbed in Atlanta?"

"I used to have epiphanies all the time. I used to eat epiphanies like popcorn. On tour, my life was one constant and seamless peak experience. Of course, I was taking a lot of animal tranquilizers and ecstasy, so this may have colored my recollections," I said. Then added, "Tell me something. If you call the jungle north, you can send it back, too, right?"

Frida looked at me for a long moment. "Why would I want to do that?"

"It's messed up a lot of people's lives."

She stretched her body under the sheet. "Everything that happens messes up somebody's life," she said. "You cut down a tree, you dam a river, you eat meat, you use electricity, you smoke a cigarette, somebody gets fucked. You ever hear of the Jains in India? They sweep the ground before themselves wherever they go so that when they walk, they won't step on any insects. Well, this life just isn't that precious to me, sorry. Amazonia and I belong here, together."

I nodded as she spoke. "I'm having a lot of trouble with this. I don't believe in it."

"I know," she said. "You can always leave."

That I could, and there was a little voice in the back of my head telling me to do just that. I always had a hard time labelling anyone as crazy, but I knew myself well enough to understand my own compulsive longing for the company of lunatics. There's no escaping the fact that, in certain people, madness is very sexy. But I also knew that there was a difference between madness and simple damage, even when they looked the same. In some ways, madness was easier to deal with, since a madwoman (for instance) is at least in motion. Damaged people, on the other hand, can be frozen in place by the psychological scar tissue that builds up over years of abuse. What worried me most was that I suspected Frida wasn't truly mad, but acting out some kind of elaborate damage-control ritual. And yet I didn't leave. I didn't want to be alone anymore. I laid my hand lightly on Frida's leg.

"I bought you a present," Frida said. She pointed to the recorder. "Some sounds of your own to play with. They belong to you. I can't use them."

"Is that what you were doing last night?"

"Uh huh. Mostly I needed to be alone." Frida stretched, arching her back and making me think of a young, undernourished cat. "Bring me a drink and go play," she said.

I brought her the rest of the Screwdriver and took the ODR to the mixing board, plugging it into the special cable attached to the back. Frida was propped up on one elbow in the bed, looking out the window as morning bird chatter rose from the rooftops. I pushed Play on the recorder and listened through headphones.

Men's voices, shouting odds and taking bets at a cockfight. A drunken street corner samba jam. Hawkers and fortune-tellers (I always found listening to pure digital recordings unnerving, like having a separate reality competing for room inside your head). Coins in a parking meter. Coins in a pay phone. Boots across a polished dance floor. Din of voices at the Greyhound terminal. The tick-tick of a truck engine cooling. A hand brushing across the marble facade of a skyscraper.

I didn't know how to download into the sampler, so I routed the sounds through Frida's sound processors, adding delay and reverb, creating endless sound loops, dropping and raising sounds an octave, then slowing them down to half their speed. The lights came in colors I'd almost forgotten, rising on their own internal heat, boiling into slow motion arcs, ganglial knots trailing to crystallized solar flares.

I turned away. Frida was looking at me from the bed. I took off the headphones and heard her say, ". . . the music of cities. When I was walking around last night, I started wondering what kind of music you were trying to write. It was so obvious when it came to me: the music of cities." She lay back down saying, "You'll find the city's Spiritline." Frida turned away and I noticed the sun coming in through the partially uncovered window. The light trembled a pale, watery green from the reflected brilliance of the surrounding vegetation. There was something new in the center of the light. I couldn't quite get to it, but felt it as a longing in the pit of my stomach, like a dream of birth. It was maddening, just at the edge of touch and smell.

I took off my clothes and lay down next to Frida. She had dropped off to sleep again. I don't know how long I'd been staring into the light. I slept too, leaving the sound loops to play through the speakers in the headphones until they became part of the ambient noise of the room. My dreams alternated between caimans skimming along the surface of a black lake, and a city of light.

10. Limit Point

During many nights alone, and many more with Frida, I would awaken in the dark, panting and sweating, my heart pounding. I could never remember my dreams those nights, couldn't be certain that I'd dreamed at all. But I was always left with a certain sense of *something having passed by*. Like the flood plains of Amazonia, where alien silts move down annually from the north to bury the already drowning trees, the inside of my head was full of an ugly dream residue compounded of hollow dread and mounting paranoia. It wasn't until many months later in Los Angeles, lost among the chattering parrots and jaguars before the vine-festooned hulk of Frederick's of Hollywood, that I would understand what had happened on those sleepless nights.

I've been running all my life.

There is something that's permanently destroyed in anyone who has ever been forcibly institutionalized. For the rest of your life, you're always watching yourself, afraid that some innocent remark or gesture will bring back those looks, those out-of-the-corner-of-the-eye glances that could get you an E ticket on the Thorazine Ride at Bedlam.

When I was at Point Mariposa, I discovered that somebody was selling copies of my weekly psych evaluations to one of the prominent grocery store rags. This annoyed me, not because I craved privacy, but because it was just one more example of how my life was being removed, layer by layer, from my control.

I decided to do something.

Whenever I was alone with any member of the hospital staff, I would confess to having been an abused child. Each staff member got a slightly different, but distinct, story. Sure enough, within the month, the sad tale of my early trauma was smeared in eighteen-point type across the cover of one of the tabloids. The version the paper printed was one I'd told to my physical therapist, a handsome, green-eyed, pre-med boy who gave excellent deep-tissue massages and offered me dope at every opportunity.

One night, I accepted his offer and we smoked in my room. I sat on the bed; he sat on the one chair provided for guests. Around midnight he started getting giddy; around one he started to hallucinate; by one-thirty he was laid out flat, like a prize trout, the DMSO and PCP I'd spread on the arms of the chair having done their trick (anything is for sale in a hospital, you just have to ask the right person; back then, I could always find that person, charting corruption the way some people collect stamps).

I walked the boy to the nurse's dressing room around 2 A.M. and removed his clothes. The next part was the most difficult. I went through all of the open lockers, as quietly as possible, and then slipped whatever I found onto his semicomatose body (topping off the ensemble with a too-small nurse's cap and a stunning black lace push-up bra belonging to a rather zaftig candystriper on the day shift). The next day, I heard that the poor kid had his stomach pumped and then was sent home for an early Easter break. He wasn't expected back.

Some of the staff knew that the kid had been hanging around me, and it didn't take the Big Boys long to come sniffing around with questions. I pleaded ignorance, but they still revoked all my privileges; then they strapped me to my bed and pumped me full of Thorazine. They kept me that way for a week.

It was just a reminder. A note from the teacher,

nailed to my brain, explaining that I'd been bad and that the doctor was God, and that I'd better straighten up and fly right if I ever wanted to get out.

Seeing those straps materialize from under my nice warm bed was quite an education. I learned that while you may think you're Moses, the doctor is always the burning bush. I also learned that a prison with cable TV and clean sheets is still a prison.

Outside, the fog erased the city for days at a time. It rained in the afternoons, a black waterfall from the sky that turned the streets to filthy rivers, micro-Amazons that tugged at the wheels of dead cars, sweeping away strange blossoms and drowned basilisk lizards along with the candy wrappers and lost shoes. Neither of us left the apartment. Frida remained in bed for days after she gave me the sound disks, sprawled under the covers like the guardian of some steel-springed temple. Finally, she ran out of excuses and decided to go back to serving drinks at Cafe Juju. I told her she didn't have to, that I had more money in different banks under different names than I could spend in several lifetimes. I could take care of both of us. She shook her head and confessed that she couldn't bear the idea of losing Frida's job. I didn't tell her then, but I was secretly happy when she decided to go back to work. It was good to see her up and moving around. Also, by then we were living on rice cakes, jam and flat mineral water, the only food left in the apartment.

I was still engrossed in my new sounds and the marvelous lights they produced. From the bed, Frida had taught me how to load and manipulate sounds in the sampler. Using the ODR, I would download the sound of coins dropping into a pay phone or the whooshing of steam from a manhole through the sampler's input. A few seconds later, a jagged visual analog of the waveform would crawl across the screen of the laptop, like an Etch-A-Sketch mountain range. Frida lay on her side with the covers pulled up to her chin saying, "Use the mouse. Pan back a few milliseconds. You need to reset the loop point," or "The input filter is set too low; you're cutting all the highs off that breaking glass." Frida tried her best to teach me properly, but I'd long since grown bored with all the jargon and theory from the technical side of the music biz. I learned to use the sampler the same way I learned to play music—by following the movement of the lights. One of my first discoveries was that when I increased the sampling rate it created shorter and more realistic samples; it also pushed the lights toward the red end of the spectrum. When I chose a slower sample rate for longer sounds, the lights would glide through layers of violet gauze. I learned to pick and choose my sounds this way, too.

But I wasn't ready to record any of it yet. Each morning I set up the ODR, loaded in some samples, and routed them through the signal processors. Then I'd let the light show run.

At the time, it seemed enough simply to play with or alter the ambient feel of the room. I'd set up long sequences in the sampler, creating delays and sound loops in the processor path, and send the sounds out through the speakers. I found a lot of partially disassembled effects boxes lying under snake skulls and piles of macaw feathers around the apartment. I was able to fix a few of the boxes, and to my delight discovered that I could send the sequenced sampler sounds down two different signal paths, using a long digital delay on one to get the sounds out of synch. Then, if I patched them through different sets of processors, I could generate hours of new chaotic sound, a sort of *musique turbulent,* with only the slightest intervention on my part (diddling a switch here, hitting a button there). Every musician's dream. Frida and I made love often in the afternoons to the low pulse of the new music, letting it swell around us, the machines having their fun while we had ours. She would take my hand and guide it to her cunt, easing my middle finger deep inside her. Then her middle finger would slide in beside mine, and she would begin to move, hanging on to my arm as her motion grew wilder, controlling completely the depth of our thrusts, the speed of our breath and the intensity of her own pleasure.

Eventually, I needed clothes. The charm of camping out in someone else's apartment, washing your shirt and socks in the tub, pales quickly. The night Frida went back to the bar, I went back to my place. I'd lost track of the days. How long had it been since I'd last been there? I could to pick up my tapes, too. Maybe, I thought, with what Frida had taught me on the sampler, I could salvage something from those depressing earlier sessions.

There weren't many cabs out in the rain. I stood on the corner with a group of well-dressed sleepwalkers. They ignored the downpour and stared dumbly at ghost newspapers or craned their necks looking for buses that had stopped running. I was soaked by the time I got a cab to stop. I gave him the address and he looked at me for a moment before he started driving. As we pulled away, a bus rolled up to the curb by the sleepwalkers. But it was as unreal to them as they were to it, and they went right on with their reading and waiting.

At the corner, the bus passed us, and I tried to get a look inside. The city kept a few of the electric buses in running condition; they glided past each other almost silently through the streets, like insects engaged in a courting ritual, twin contact poles swept back like feelers from their roofs, taking power—sometimes shaking sparks—from the wires above. Perpetually nervous about being recognized someplace I couldn't easily escape, I hadn't been on any of the local buses. But I

was intrigued by them and the stories I'd heard about
Wire Pirates.

Not that I'd ever actually seen a Pirate. They were
supposed to be a gang of hijackers that worked the out-
lying neighborhoods, hiding in the shadows of apart-
ment-house garages with their motorized boarding rigs.
When a bus rolled by, they'd come out, throwing lines
topped with copper contacts and miniature wheel
housings across the suspended power cables, sucking
up the bus's juice. The wheels of their boarding rigs
(really little more than motorized harnesses) clamped
onto the sides of the suspended cables. They were supposed to be fast, capable of overtaking a bus in a few
seconds. When they did, it was a simple matter of
breaching the emergency exit in the roof or shooting
out the rear window, and they were inside. Then came
the robberies; sometimes shooting; a few deaths, and
they were off—back out the window or over the roof to
their motorized rig, and they'd *bzzzzzzzz* down the
wires, away from the plundered bus. The fact that the
pirates were supposed to be a gang of women (a pack
of renegade National Guardswomen or ex-cops?) made
them even more intriguing. And frightening, too. It
made me suspect that they were nothing more than a
wet dream cooked up by the city fathers to convince
tourists that mugging was the way the locals flirted.

The rain had stopped by the time we reached the
Sunset. I got out of the cab and almost fell, my foot
snagged in a ropy surface root. For a moment, I thought
that the cabby had gotten us lost. Nothing in the street
looked right. Then I understood why the cabby had
looked at me when I gave him the address. We often
don't see, at first, what we aren't expecting.

Golden Gate Park had spilled over its fences and
was engulfing everything around it. Already, a layer of
rotting vegetation covered the sidewalk and much of
the street. Reedy kapok saplings poked up through the

tangled mulch of leaves and lianas, like the forward guard of a slow motion army. Bats skimmed low over the cab, turning circles in the flickering sulfur illumination of the street lights. Ribbons of fog moved through the wavering palms, leaving drops of water on the papery wasp nests until they sparkled like gigantic Fabergé eggs suspended in the tree tops. If it hadn't been for the snakes night-hunting through the carpet of leaves, the street would have been weirdly beautiful, like something I'd dreamed at the clinic. But the soft blue-green sound of snakes around my feet kept me grounded. I paid the driver, then tipped him big to wait for me.

Inside, I took a pull from my hip flask. The building was deserted, and the lights didn't work. The doors to the other apartments all stood open. The surrounding jungle gave a green cast to the orange light from the street. It glowed weakly through the hall windows, describing a web of shadows across the carpets of the empty apartments, creating at each door the profile of jungle canopy from a thousand feet in the air.

Upstairs, I found the door to my apartment open, too, though I knew that I hadn't left it that way. There was splintered wood, shining like clean bones, all around the deadbolt. Someone had put the boot to it. A black birdeating spider stood just inside my door. Bigger than my hand, it reared up on its four hind legs holding its shaggy front legs out before it. It hissed at me. I stamped my heel down on the door frame, but the spider didn't move. So I pulled out the flask and tossed it like a metal Frisbee at the spider's head, knocking it down the hall. "Never forget who's at the top of the food chain, fucker," I told it.

The walls of the apartment were slick with the sweat of water-heavy air and fog that blew in through the broken windows. There were other broken things in the apartment, too. Someone had thoroughly and systematically ransacked the place. Thumb-sized frogs, the color of fire, walked on big padded toes across broken chairs and shattered glass that, in the fog, looked like dry ice. Spiders, smaller than the bird-killer, and fire ants were building nests in the mildewed closets. Young ferns and bromeliads had taken root in the door frames. All my music gear—tapes, recorder, mixer and synthesizer—was gone. A few cords on the floor by the window were all that was left.

Fireflies were turning in some kind of strange formation above the park. I went to the window thinking, No, not fireflies. Planes and helicopters, up north. There was a flash, and a rolling plume of flame. A few seconds later came the muffled boom of the explosion. The government was working in Marin, spraying defoliant and napalm over the jungles in the Headlands. I wondered if Lurie and his Gaia Now friends were somewhere under all that death, burning up with their defiant banners. It would be great footage.

I started back to the rear of the apartment, looking for clothes or any tapes dropped by the thieves. My flask was on the floor by the bathroom, but the big spider was gone, which meant that it was still alive. I've always considered spiders God's second biggest mistake (critics were her first), and wondered for a moment if I wanted to chance going two out of three with a pissed-off eight-legged carnivore back where the streetlight didn't reach. I turned the flask over in my hands. Something snapped, bright and red, in the dark in front of me.

I headed back toward the light, going into the front room near the window. I held my breath and listened, wanting to be sure it had been real and not some fear hallucination. The room stank of mold, a rough blue smell, like steel wool. The sound came again, closer. Then footsteps moving down the hall. I was too far from the door. I turned to the window, and settled into a crouch, waiting.

"You comfortable down there?" The voice came

from somewhere behind me. I continued to hold my breath. "So what's the story? You taking a shit or giving birth or both?" The same voice. No other footsteps. Just one man.

When I felt his hand touch my shoulder, I grabbed the patchcord from the floor and spun, bringing the wire up like a whip, slicing across his eyes. He screamed and backed away. While he was blinded, I lunged at him, digging my knee into his groin. He sank to the floor and I started running, down the three flights of stairs to the street, and outside—just in time to see a young gangly skinhead with acne and an aluminum baseball bat chasing away my cab. He yelled something when he spotted me, but I was already running down the street in the opposite direction. The skin was fast, though, and I'd spent a lot of time on my back in hospital beds. Even with my head start, he was on my heels by the end of the block. In my mind's eye, I could see the metal shaft of the bat cut the air behind my head, a length of spun metal streaked with gold and sea-green light.

I cut hard to my left, plunging into the dense undergrowth of the park. A half-dozen steps inside, most of the light was gone, and I was tearing my hands on the sharp edges of sword grass and brutal palm-tree thorns. I kept running, doubling back on myself, digging further into the blackness. I could hear the skin a few yards behind me, swearing, trying to beat down the jungle with his bat. Another voice called, and he yelled back.

I stumbled into a yielding metallic barrier that bulged out like a fish net. Reaching out my hand, I felt the familiar diamond pattern of the hurricane fence that surrounded the park. I pulled myself over the top as fast as I could, and dropped down onto the other side. Back somewhere in the undergrowth, the skin and man from the apartment were arguing. I caught a flash of light that could have been the bat, and the sharp crack (a smear of silver sparks) of a small-caliber pistol. I moved away from the fence and headed deeper into the park.

It started to rain. At first, it was just a sound, the water gathering in the high, thick branches of the upper canopy. Then the warm drops began to muscle their way down through the vegetation to fall on my head. In a few seconds, I was in a downpour. Between the rain and the dark, I was almost blind, and my lousy-one-eyed-no-depth-perception vision kept me on a collision course with every thorn bush in the area. I finally took shelter under the leaf of a giant elephant-ear plant.

The moment I stopped running, the heat hit me. I couldn't catch my breath, and gulped in mouthfuls of dense, muggy air. I'd never been this deep into the jungle before. In the shafts of streetlight that broke through the upper canopy, I could see steam rising from the spongy mass of the jungle floor. My head was full of wet plaster. I put out my hand to the elephant ear for support.

I don't remember falling, but I must have, because I was on the ground, covered in damp leaves and mud. I couldn't hear the skin or his friend anymore.

The rain came down steadily. I tried to stand, but collapsed onto my knees. While I was out, someone must have mounted the whole park on a turntable, which turned slowly under my feet. I touched my face, unsure in the dark whether my good eye was open or not. When I pressed the lid, showers of phosphenes exploded across my vision. I'd had nights like this when I first arrived in the clinic. Visions. Night sweats. Choking.

I pulled myself up and started walking.

Phosphenes swarmed before me long after I'd taken my hand from my face, the light in my head so bright it lit the jungle like a movie from the surface of the moon, all the colors gone, and everything moving in the timeless and half-asleep manner of things in low gravity. There were animals around me, jaguars and hummingbirds, monkeys and tapirs made of neon and smoke. They hid behind the trees and above the branches, blinking at the light I made. I couldn't see their eyes, but I could feel them through the back of my head, cold and golden as they waited for me to fall. I was meat to the jungle, a snack for a generation of insects and scavengers in the place where nothing mattered except fucking and death. Perhaps, I thought, I should just lie down and wait for them. Give in fully to the situation. Maybe that was the key. The anonymity of meat is what I came to the city for. Meat for the neon jungle, I'd finally yield to the void I'd been looking for all along; then, in some down-the-road lifetime, bring it all back with me, and hand it over to my America— Lazarus back from the dead bringing tabs of God's own acid—taking them with me into fractional space, beyond the bounds of any place we'd been, chasing misery and Cities of Light, an army of blind mutes asleep under leaves in mud and rain.

I stumbled through the jungle that was a city park, falling when vines caught on my legs or when rocks or the cement borders of dead fountains tripped me. Sometimes when I fell, I felt things moving across my legs. Mostly, I ignored them. The one time I did check, all I felt was shredded cloth and my own blood from where the jungle had slashed me.

Through a bamboo grove the park opened up before me. I headed for a building that stood on a slight rise, a circular pavilion with glass walls. The rain beat down harder in the open. Condensation turned the walls of the building opaque white. I found an unlocked door on the far side and went in.

My first thought was that the place was someone's

idea of a joke—the mass of vines, orchids and thick scheflera massed in the center of the room made it look like a perverse hothouse. Then I saw the frozen horses, white and blue and gold, some rearing up, their mouths open, others standing royally waiting for a rider, each impaled where they stood on the wooden carousel platform by a blackened brass pole. I touched the muzzle of the closest horse, brushing away some of the flamingo-pink fungus from around its face. Bolted above my head was the rusted metal sleeve that held the carousel's supply of brass rings. I reached up and pulled one out.

I was standing there unsteadily, holding on to the horse and admiring my find when a child bolted past me, out the door I'd come in. I started after the child, but I lost my footing in a puddle just outside the door, my legs refusing to do what my brain told them. I gave up and went back inside the pavilion, feeling better just being out of the rain.

Sitting with my back to the glass wall, I could just make out the shape of the old carousel structure under its jungle coat. Painted scenes from San Francisco's past, Indian settlements, the cargo ships of the Barbary Coast, the great earthquake and fire, were faded outlines beneath the stranglehold of fat lianas. Deeper in the vegetation, mildew-streaked mirrors set in peeling gold leaf frames reflected shadows of the wind-blown jungle outside, animating the interior of the dead pavilion. The sound of the rain outside was a pale robin's egg blue, while air in the building, a cold gear pressing into my palms.

I stood on the edge of the carousel platform, the rotten wood sagging slightly with my weight. Taking a few cautious steps toward the center, I could just make out the shape of the player piano that had, before Amazonia went mad, supplied the carousel's soundtrack, set between the mirrors in the ride's central spindle, a vertical heart of blistered carnival colors and bromeli-ads.

Pushing through the plants to get nearer to the piano, I was enclosed by scheflera leaves. Young palm fronds cut my hands. Halfway from the edge of the hot-house microjungle and the body of the carousel, I was filled with a sense of suspended motion, as if I were trying to reach the piano through the core of a Menger sponge, a mathematical anomaly that enclosed a kind of negative space (Take the center ninth out of a square, then do the same thing to the eight squares that remain within the first square, then cut the centers out of the next smallest set of squares, ad infinitum, and you get a lattice-work structure that has no surface area, but infi-nite volume).

But I did reach the piano, finally. It lay just on the other side of a steam-smeared barrier of Plexiglas in a bed of Spanish moss or dark fungus. Other instruments surrounded the piano—a ridiculous toy halo of tam-bourines, bells, xylophones, and disembodied violins, all wired to the same mechanism that drove the carousel and the piano.

Not finding a latch on the Plexiglas case, I dropped all my weight onto one leg and sprang forward, kicking it. Next thing I knew, I was on my ass in the grass, without having made a scratch on the case. I felt around through the undergrowth for something heavy, and came up with a club-shaped lump of rusted metal that had once been a monkey wrench. I brought it down three times on the case, and the whole thing split like a plastic Easter egg.

Seeing the piano clearly for the first time, I still couldn't tell where the instrument left off and the jun-gle began. Orchids and wild ginger had invaded the wooden frame, softening it to the point that lianas could push their way through, fusing the piano and jungle into a single organic mass.

I brushed away the leaves and insect droppings from the cracked ivories and pressed middle A. The sound was muffled and out-of-tune, with a fragile green glass sound almost like a muted koto. I laughed and hit a chord, thinking of the effete "prepared piano" experiments of the fifties and sixties, when musicians had attached paperclips and pieces of glass to piano strings to alter and "expand" the instrument's character. Here I was, I thought, without ever looking for it, playing the most prepared goddamned piano ever. John Cage would have creamed his jeans.

I tried a tune then, something lively from the old days, "Mercenary Tango." I heard a sound off to my right—the door opening, then closing. But I didn't care right then. I figured if it was the skin and his pal, they probably deserved their epiphany of blood as much as I deserved mine of music. However, I couldn't let the opportunity pass to turn and say, "Don't shoot me, I'm only the piano player!"

I don't know who was more shocked, me or the child. The woman, whose arm the child clung to, had a face so badly scarred that I had no idea what she thought. She was dark, and her skin had the insubstantial melted-wax look I'd seen in photos of burn wards. Under the taut flesh of her face, I could make out high cheekbones, and a wide forehead, framed by onyx-black hair. She might have been an Indian, Yanomamö or Kayapo; certainly she had some of the blood, but with her hair plastered down with rain, she could just as easily have been a local bag lady with some Mayan ancestors. I didn't know any Portuguese and surprised as I was, couldn't think of any Spanish. I just shrugged and said, "I do requests, but please, no 'Melancholy Baby.' " She didn't smile, but took the boy's hand and turned back to the door. "You should come now," she said in a slurred and heavily accented English. I followed her and the child out into the rain.

We climbed up a hill, and over a rise into an area of black slashed-and-burned ground, turned muddy in the rain. There were dozens of raggedly dressed people working below us. Their camp was thorough and elaborate, with tents, covered cook areas, neat stacks of fuel wood and stolen machine tools. At the center of it all an immense wire and steel tower was being welded together. There'd been street talk about displaced Indians and other homeless clans getting together and blocking off streets in the Tenderloin and the Mission districts, stacking up a dozen mobile shelters into multi-storied tenements, but I'd never seen or heard about anything on this scale. There were at least fifty shelters either on the ground, being hoisted into position, or already secured into the body of the elaborate metal nest. Working under plastic rain sheets, young Indian women, small and quick and unafraid of climbing, were welding shelter frames together in the upper reaches of the mega-shelter. On the ground, short, wiry men used thick ropes woven from lianas to drag truck flatbeds into position nearby. Older women stepped from flatbed to flatbed, securing them together with rusting tow chains. Green acetylene tanks, bearing the stenciled marks of some State construction project, lay neatly stacked to the side.

The woman and child led me to the cooking area where a group of young men sat on their haunches around the fire, smoking and talking quietly. Using a rusted metal scoop, the woman filled a paper cup with the coffee or tea that bubbled in a pot on the fire. I took a polite sip, and fought to suppress the urge to vomit. It wasn't coffee, but some hot native liquor that, from the taste, could have been made from lizard brains and vulture shit. The young men laughed at my obvious pain. A couple of them had scars like the woman's; one boy held a cigarette between the palms of both hands; all that remained of his fingers were bony pink stumps.

"We're *Los Quemados,* the Burned Ones," the woman said. She unbuttoned the top of her quetzal shirt to show me that the scars covered her whole body. "In the south, when the forest gets too big, the soldiers come to burn it. Sometimes our homes burn, too. Sometimes we tell them we don't want to leave, so the soldiers burn us instead." The boy with no fingers caught me looking at him and gave me a big, toothy smile. I looked away.

"You can't stay here," the woman told me. "This is our place. Go to your home."

"I want to go," I told her. "But I'm lost."

She shook her head, squinting. "No, you must go now. Don't come back. We have much work to do."

"I know, but I—" I started to say something, but my head was full of poisoned ice. The woman took the cup from my hand and poured the contents onto the grass. A couple of the young men left the fire and came and stood beside me.

The woman put her face very close to mine. "It's no good for you here," she said. "This place is not yours."

The heat of the fire had become the steady buzzing of a million wasps; the smell of sweating bodies and cooksmoke was curled copper shavings. They scratched my throat every time I drew a breath.

The woman's face was gone, and I was walking in the rain, being led or supported (a little of both, really) by a couple of her young helpers. We moved through what seemed like virgin jungle, but the young men never missed a step, and never let me fall. They took me to the panhandle of the park, and left me where the jungle had been cleared at the base of a statue.

When my legs stopped shaking, I began walking downtown. The woman's homebrew had left my head spinning and my senses stuttering, like falling dominos, one sensation tumbling another into another.

I didn't notice the overhead bus cables humming until their shimmering silver light overwhelmed me. Because I was almost blind by the light in my head, I could never swear to it, but I'm sure that an enormous sling skimmed past me, suspended beneath the power cables. And women in uniform. As they passed, they screamed and blew me kisses, laughing as they rode away.

ii. Feedback/Feedforward

There were soldiers playing basketball in a schoolyard, under floodlights. A crowd of refugees and gang kids stood just outside the hurricane fence watching the men play. They weren't the National Guard troops we were used to seeing, weekend warriors in pressed fatigues, packing nothing more dangerous than rubber bullets and John Wayne wet-dreams. These men were different. You could see it in their play. They jammed hard for the basket, blocked each other with knees and elbows, laughing when they sent one of their own down onto the damp cement. It was the first time Army troops had been stationed in any great number in San Francisco. No one knew if it was a general pull-back, a surrender to the advancing jungle, or something more awful. A prelude to martial law, perhaps.

For weeks the papers had been hinting at problems with the occupation forces. Desertions and atrocities among the troops in the deep jungle; the rape and massacre of Indians allegedly running dope farms in the Central Valley; the burning and looting of Santa Barbara and Palm Springs.

The breakdown had apparently become obvious during the month-long siege of a drug compound in Fresno. The operation had been a disaster, a bloody homebound Dien Bien Phu. Many soldiers simply couldn't see the point of playing cop or defending land that, for all intents and purposes, was no longer America—no America they knew or understood. Some of the deserters were joining the dope collectives; a few were disappearing into the bush with the Indians. Many of those who remained were experimenting with the jungle plants, field testing the hallucinogenic properties of roots and flowers, snorting up lines of ground *hisioma* seeds, sometimes blowing out their hearts and lungs with an Amazon Speedball: a combination of *yagé* and curare, snorted and shot simultaneously.

The soldiers that had stayed with the Army were experienced jungle fighters, as lean and mean as any troops returning from Iraq or Khe Sahn. Clean and loaded M-16s stood in a row against the back wall of the basketball court, decorated with iridescent macaw feathers and animals bones, gleaming under the court's floodlights like the obsidian totems of some hunting clan. If war was good business, I thought, somebody was about to make a goddamn fortune.

Inside Cafe Juju, the damp heat came down like a fat lady sitting on your chest. Even with the doors open, the club was an airless oven. Places like the cafe had been built for air conditioning and electric ventilation. But electricity had gone on the ration list when the Army moved in.

Virilio had a table against the far wall near the back, under the bar's only window. He was wearing a faded black tank top. The name of some band was barely readable where the silk-screened letters were peeling off. It was the first time I'd seen him without his coat. The snakeskin tattoos on his arms extended all the way to his shoulders, curving inward to cover his pectorals, Japanese-style. The sweat on his upper body made his ersatz snakeskin shine like the real thing. I started over to his table before I realized he wasn't alone.

Half a dozen cameras were scattered among the Dos Equis bottles. Virilio was absentmindedly examining a small videocam, while across the table Eric Lurie, documentarian and Gaia Now groupie, talked nonstop. Lurie's hand gestures were weirdly exaggerated. It was like watching Bruce Lee from the waist up, the way he chopped the air. Lurie had to be stoned, I thought. I went to the bar and ordered iced vodka. In the cracked mirror that lined the wall behind the bottles, I could just make out Virilio's table.

In *Passion,* an English-language magazine I picked up while we were touring France, I read that the behavior of people who aren't used to heat can change dramatically at ninety-three degrees. Below that temperature, most people can cope; above ninety-three, they're too fried to move. The temperature in Cafe Juju must have hit the magic number that night. There were fights, and knives pulled when knives weren't called for. The local fashion victims took the heat as their cue to go frantically native; most of them were dressed in Japanese-imported imitations of Brazilian Indian gear. It was like some grotesque acid trip combining the worst of Dante with a Club Med brochure for Rio: young white kids, the girls bare-breasted or wearing the simple Lacandon *hipils* they had seen in some high school slide show; the boys in loin cloths, strutting in their Indian-style bowl haircuts. The patrons of the club moved together in the ritual and eternal dance of scene-makers, coming together and splitting apart (like cellular automata on a video screen or some faintly intelligent bacterium), smoking French cigarettes, gossiping, and arguing about rock and roll.

Frida was dealing with a table of fashion photographers and their long-legged chattel, so there was nobody I wanted to talk to. Somewhere around my third or fourth vodka, I noticed that Lurie was no longer at Virilio's table. I took my drink and made my way over, a little less steadily than when I'd come in. Virilio didn't look up as I approached. Both the cameras and bottles had been cleared away. There were cards on the table, and Virilio was dealing out cards into some kind of odd solitaire spread. Each card held a picture printed in bright Mexican pastels: a heart, a scorpion, a soldier. In the street outside, I'd seen old men deal similar cards for a game that seemed to work something like bingo. I was told that the cards were a bastardized version of a Mexican tarot system that had been wiped out or driven underground by the Church when the Spaniards rode through and introduced new games like Burn the Pagans and Rape the Soulless Indian Women.

Virilio glanced at me over the tops of his shades. "I knew you were coming," he said. He picked up a card depicting a shabby man holding a bottle. "See? 'El Boracho.' The Drunk."

"Very cute. But this is only my third drink of the evening."

"It's your fourth. I've been counting."

"You knew I was here?" I asked.

"I saw you scoot out of harm's way when you spotted Lurie."

I sat and leaned my elbows on the table, scattering Virilio's card spread. "Who is that guy, anyway? He gave me some story about shooting a documentary, but I didn't buy it."

Virilio scooped up the cards from his ruined spread. Call me a drunk, I thought, I'll act like one. "Don't worry about him. He really is a filmmaker," Virilio said. He set the cards aside and passed me a manila envelope. "He gave me these," Virilio said. Inside were several eight-by-tens of the jungle canopy. Outlines of San Francisco in the background. Coit Tower. Refugee compounds in the old Fisherman's Wharf. A shot from behind Alcatraz toward Oakland. "They're very pretty. Does he have his own helicopter or something?" I asked.

Virilio shook his head. "That's what I thought at first, too. Look again."

I took a sip of vodka and spread the photos out before me on the table. Now that I was looking for it, there was something slightly odd about them. Some angles weren't quite right. And there was a subtle strangeness in scale. But I couldn't tell if the problem was the photos or the vodka.

"They're fake," Virilio said.

"All of them?"

"Every last one. Told me he spent fifty K setting up a miniature of the Bay in some sound stage off Mission. He's even got computer animation facilities. The whole enchilada."

"That's nuts," I said. "If he can drop that kind of money on studio toys, he can get a boat or a plane and get all the shots he wants."

"He has. But the guy's kind of a nut case; a perfectionist. Didn't like the shots he got," Virilio said. "They didn't talk to him. That's what he told me, word for word. The film didn't talk to him." Virilio fingered one of the counterfeit photos. "I guess if he splices this stuff in with the real footage and cuts back and forth fast enough, no one will know the difference. Tonight, though, is the capper. I'd love to be there."

"What happens tonight?"

"He burns Marin," said Virilio. "Just like the Army." He smiled. "Little tiny animated barrels of napalm turning over and over, falling on a wee matchstick jungle."

"What did he ask you for?"

Virilio moved back from the table, his face taking on mock severity. "I don't really like to talk about clients. Especially to other clients—" then his lips split open into a grin—"but this guy's a trip. Seems he doesn't have the right import permits for his Japanese film stock. Right now it's all locked up in a Customs warehouse in China Basin. He wants to know if there's anybody that has old stock left behind in L.A., and if I can get him some."

"Can you?"

"Does a stone lion shit bricks?"

My vodka was turning warm, so I downed the rest of it. "He took my picture," I told Virilio.

"When?"

"Frida and I ran into him up at the Headlands and he took my fucking picture."

Virilio shook his head. "I wouldn't worry about it. The guy's a flake. You probably pissed him off the way you piss everyone off, and he was just playing with your head." He leaned forward. "Besides, who among us could resist the face that launched a thousand wet-dreams? And speaking of your face, what happened to it? You look like the poster child for safety scissors."

He was right. My face and hands were swollen and criss-crossed with fresh cuts, like I'd tried to shave with a lawnmower. The scabs on my hands kept breaking, and the salt in my sweat stung. "A couple of goons came after me the other night. I don't know if it was a kidnapping or a robbery or what, but I had to take off through Golden Gate Park to lose them. Got cut up in the underbrush."

"Did you get a good look at them?"

"No," I said. "I thought maybe you could help me there."

"Meaning what?"

"Meaning I think you sent those birds after me." I slipped a hand into my jacket pocket. "I've been fol-lowed on and off for weeks. I've never seen by who exactly, but I know they're there," I said. "I turned down your music offer, so you had those two assholes trash my apartment and come after me."

"They trashed your apartment, too?" Virilio asked.

"Don't fuck with me," I said. Virilio smiled. "I

have Frida's gun." Virilio's smile faded, but never died completely. I held onto the pistol in my pocket. Virilio shrugged.

"So shoot me," he said. "In front of all these people. That'll do a lot for anonymity. Go ahead. Blow me away. But after you do, and there's still someone dogging you, don't forget whose decision it was to put a hole in the one person who could help you."

"I don't believe you," I said. I kept running my sweaty fingers along the edge of the pistol grip, like a kid rubbing a rabbit's foot.

"Ask yourself this—," Virilio said. He leaned forward and I started to pull the gun. Virilio held up his hands and leaned back, the small smile creeping back around his mouth. "Ask yourself this," he began again, "Why should I have you followed or snatched when it's you that keeps coming to me?"

"Because you think I'm unstable, you keep telling me that. I could skip town. Go back to New York. I left an album unfinished back there. I could tour again."

Virilio signaled to a waitress for another beer. "Right, tour," he said. "They'd have to wipe you up with a blotter."

"I might surprise you. Fear of kidnapping; desire to be back on top. Those are pretty good motivations for getting back to work."

Virilio looked at me. By the bar, a half-dozen refugee screenwriters were shoving their way through the crowd, swaying and singing in broken Spanish. Their faces were smeared with candle wax and makeup; over their heads they held crossed *urubu* feathers, in a drunken parody of a *Santeria* ceremony.

"No way," said Virilio. "If you wanted to work you could work here, and you told me you weren't writing. As for touring, you wouldn't be so jittery about staying anonymous if you wanted to see your face back on TV." Virilio picked up his tarot cards and shuffled them.

Keeping the hand in my pocket, I pulled back the hammer on Frida's gun. If Virilio had any idea what I was thinking, he didn't show it. He dealt out a few cards face-up on the table, the sweat from his right thumb leaving a small oval on each cardface. A soldier. A spider. A parrot. A skull. I remembered a hot night outside a warehouse in the San Fernando Valley a couple of years earlier. A bald man walking to his car. The air was like the air in Cafe Juju, dead and thick. I'd been tipped to the record bootlegging operation by the stoned girlfriend of some television producer. I waited until the bald man was in his car before I stepped out of the shadows. I made sure he saw me before I started shooting. I'd made off with the television producer's 9 mm when I made off with his girlfriend.

I blew out all the windows of the bald bootlegger's Mercedes, pumped a couple of rounds into the tires, then emptied the rest of the clip into the engine. The gun made a sound like vermilion wave, a wall of fire that passed right through me; the breaking glass was a storm of burning magnesium. As I moved back into the shadows, baldie, bejeweled in broken glass and urine, crawled out of the trashed auto as his boys came pouring out of the warehouse to see what the trouble was.

I looked at Virilio again. He removed his shades, then tossed them on the table, and lit a cigarette. I eased back the hammer on Frida's gun. I hadn't shot the bald man that night, and I could have. Perhaps the old thief deserved it. With Virilio, however, I still had my doubts. Why would he grab me when he knew I'd always be back asking for something?

"Did you ever get the lithium I wanted?" I asked.

He looked at me for a few seconds as if trying to figure out the shift in my tone. Then he picked up his coat from the chair next to his and pulled out a couple of bottles of pills. He handed me one and kept the other.

"I did some asking around concerning this stuff.

It's not exactly like copping a couple of Mom's Valium.
You can fuck yourself up good; burn out your liver and
kidneys real fast." He set the second pill vial on the
table between us. "You ever try Inderal?"

"No, but I've heard of it," I said, picking up the
bottle.

"It's a beta-andrenergic block. Very fashionable
with your showbiz types. Doctors prescribe it for hyper-
tension, some heart conditions. Supposed to make you
feel ten feet tall and hung like a walrus, with minimum
side effects. I suggest, if you start feeling like you're
wigging out or something, that you try this," Virilio laid
a finger on top of the Inderal bottle, "before touching
this." He pointed to the lithium. I put both bottles in
my pocket with Frida's gun.

"By the way, are you taking your Fansidar?"

"When I think of it," I said. "How much do I owe
you?"

"Well, that depends," Virilio said. "I've had an
inspiration, sitting here listening to your sad story
about those boys that were so hot for your young bod."
The waitress brought Virilio his beer. "Pills aren't the
answer to your problems, Clem. What you need is a
partner. A business manager. Someone to walk you
across the street, keep you out of the underbrush and
away from sharp objects. I happen to know the perfect
person for the job."

"I'm not interested."

"I'm not exactly asking. If somebody does manage
to bag you, how does that make me look? Like a
schmuck. They might even come after me and that
would really piss me off."

"Frida, if you want to think of it that way, is my
partner."

"Frida's your burden. I'm your Tonto, your Robin.
And speaking of business opportunities," he said, "I've
heard from my music friends again."

"Not interested."

Virilio picked up his beer. "Okay, just asking," he said. "The partner thing, however, that's a lock."

On the cafe floor, where the linoleum met the wall, a small green shoot was growing. Some jungle parasite, I thought. The pink bud of a young passion flower was sprouting neatly at the conjunction of the back wall and a booth. I nodded and stood up. "All right, it's a deal on one condition," I said. "You want to be my partner? Find out who the fuck is following me."

12. Escape-Time Algorithm

One hot evening in Tokyo, during a particularly lively show at the Budokan, a young woman in biker leathers jumped on stage and calmly slit both of her wrists with a razor-edged *tanto* knife. She then leaped from the stage—and floated bleeding in the air—held aloft under the lights on the upstretched hands of the crowd down front. A boy with a pompadour followed her a few seconds later, diving from the stage, gripping her knife, streaming red. Soon the front of the stage was awash in the blood of fresh-faced young office workers and students. It was a gesture of love, an attempt at a deeper communion than the barren stadium had been built for. We reciprocated, never losing our nerve, continuing to play as spotlights picked out our leaping, screaming, bloodied fans.

The police finally stopped the show, dragging the possessed children to teams of frantic-looking medics and stretcher-bearers. Someone pushed me offstage and I stood in the dark watching the police and doctors hopping around under the spotlights like wounded birds. A young man in jacket and tie, the very essence of corporate Tokyo respectability, appeared silently from around the mountain of our P.A. speakers. The youth's pupils were wildly dilated. He took my arm and spoke quietly, "You understand, don't you, that Japanese people and Americans hear differently?" he asked. "Japanese people do not judge sounds. They do not say 'This is a good sound and this is bad.' So a cricket and a gun exist in the same continuum. Japanese people interpret sounds with the right brain," he explained, slurring his words slightly. "Americans, however, categorize, differentiate, create sets of things. You hear with your left brains."

He smiled and thanked me, clearly pleased that he had delivered his speech so well, and pleased that I'd listened. With a small bow, the young man walked away, leaving bloody handprints on my shirt as a white-helmeted policeman steered him like meat on a hook to the medicos down front.

There were signs. Portents. Messages spelled out in litter. Codes winked from the brake lights of slow-moving cabs. High weirdness. Confusion. Period doubling. San Francisco was on the verge of some discrete internal shift, accompanied by subtle deviations in gravity, cellular tremors—like a city-sized snake getting ready to shed its skin. I went back to Marin with Frida a few days after the helicopters flew away. In theory, the Army should have been guarding the bridge, but they seemed utterly confused as to their role in the city. We would see them tearing down Market Street in their jeeps or whispering grimly into their walkie-talkies. But the soldiers didn't actually seem to *do* anything. When we started north, Frida skated ahead as lookout, but soon gave it up as we realized there was nothing to look out for.

We needn't have made the trip. All the sounds Frida had gathered were gone. Landscape shapes the sounds that it encloses, and the Marin headlands were no longer part of the jungle. The napalm and defoliants had blasted the vegetation to brittle knife-edged scrub. The inland valley was the dry floor of some vanished prehistoric sea, a dead bowl of volcanic ash and trees like black coral. In the absence of the jungle, the lights of the hill sounds were feeble and colorless. I thought of the young corporate man in Tokyo then. Would I hear all this differently if I weren't American? If I could go beyond the need to differentiate, categorize, and judge? I started to tell Frida about the kid, but took her hand instead and we walked down the hill, away from Lurie's playpen.

After the trip to Marin I became aware that sounds in the city had changed, too. Frequencies were clipped at the top end, shifting their light from whirling pastels to liquid amber and rust. The speed of sound had slowed perceptibly, laden with the freight of all that humid air; voices, traffic, the street markets deals, were like the voices of animals from the bottom of the ocean. Frida and her gun went with me as I recorded sound samples in the evening. I was trying to ride with the city's shifts, to go with the flow, but I always had the feeling that I wasn't quite keeping up. Frida went back to work at Cafe Juju. I continued my recording rounds alone.

I returned late one evening in a light rainfall to find the front door of Frida's building open, the rotten wood around the lock splintered. Upstairs, I found the apartment door open. I set the ODR on the floor, and keeping both feet in the hall, ready to run at the first sound, leaned over the threshold just far enough to feel along the wall for the light switch. When the light came on, I had a deep feeling of déjà vu.

Perhaps there's some specific technique or procedure used by vandals and thieves that, once learned, will tell you who ransacked a place and what they were looking for. "Ah yes," you might say, examining the smashed napkin rings and pried-up wainscoting. "The Briggs brothers, using the old 'Ludovico Two-Step.' No doubt looking for industrial diamonds or counterfeit aircraft components." I didn't have that modus operandi data, however. What I could say with some certainty was that the person or persons who had turned over Frida's place were the same ones who'd done mine. Prominent in the general wreckage of the place was the fact that all her music gear was gone.

In my jacket pocket, I found the vials of pills I'd purchased from Virilio. I popped a lithium, then another, and followed that by an Inderal, washing the pills down with a couple of quick hits from my flask. There were a few crushed diskettes scattered by the bed. "Tapir feeding, dawn." "Ocelot chasing rabbit." I set the disks on the table where Frida's gear now wasn't.

Footfall on the stairs.

I ran behind the eviscerated Rhodes piano, doing a kind of Houdini-in-a-strait-jacket wiggle trying to get the Smith and Wesson out of my pocket. "Bang, you're dead," she said from the doorway. "You're too slow, boy. Could of killed, dressed you out and had you in the oven by now. Good thing it was only me." Frida crossed her arms, not entering the apartment. She was soaking wet, and there was a brightness in her eyes, something of the prairie wife contemplating the remains of a trailer park just after a tornado has blown through. She crouched, leaning on the door frame. "Quite a sight," Frida said.

"These weren't ordinary crooks; these were hard workers. Ex-Boy Scouts or Junior Achievement types." I went and stood where Frida squatted, rocking on her heels. "Why don't you come in?" I asked.

She shook her head. "Not yet." With the sleeve of her jacket, she wiped rain from her face. "Is there anything left?" Frida asked.

"A few disks and tapes. Probably broken. The rest is gone."

She nodded, frowning. "This is all my fault," Frida said.

"I doubt that."

"I dreamed about something like this after the last

trip to Marin." She looked at me. "You don't get it, do you? Amazonia's in retreat."

"That's not true. If anything, it's getting closer and stronger. In a few months, this city will be a swamp."

She shrugged. I sat down next to her. "This is a pay-as-you-go world, babe, and I shortchanged it. I never got the songs right. I was getting close. There were times when I was right up against it. I needed more time, but I misunderstood that, too. Amazonia seemed so big, I thought the time would come right along with it. I blew it. It's a 'Mommy, I need another quarter for the ride' situation. I just never got the songs right. Amazonia took back its sounds because I can't pay for them. They're not mine. They never were. Those Army bastards are going to burn and beat the forest back, and it's my fault."

I pushed Frida's wet hair back from her forehead. She refused to look at me. "Frida, listen," I said. "The people that broke in here tonight, I know them. They stole the recording equipment from my place in the Sunset. They must have found out I was here and they took your gear, thinking it was mine. They were just thieves looking for something to sell, not some kind of guilt monsters from the bush."

Abruptly, Frida stood and entered the apartment, kicking a stuffed toucan out of her way. "Fuck you. For you it's all simple. You get in a car—you get in a plane—you go away. You want a new life, you buy one." She said, "I'm light, Ryder; I can't pay my debts. I took something from the land and I didn't give anything back. Get it? There's a need for compensation." She shivered, throwing her jacket onto a chair. "I'm dirty. I'm going to clean up."

"I'll clear off the bed, so you can lie down," I told her.

"Whatever." She closed the bathroom door and I heard the sound of water running in the tub.

I pulled the top blanket off the bed, scattering

feathers, diskettes, and tape-tangled cassettes onto the floor. I flattened the sheets and fluffed the pillows, smoothing the blanket carefully back into place. There was nothing else I could think of to do. Having been taken care of like some invalid railroad tycoon for the last decade or so, I was lost and somewhat bewildered at finding myself playing Florence Nightingale in someone else's movie. Frida scared me again, the way she had back in Chinatown. Ego-driven animal that I am, I'd thought my fascinating presence might even smooth her out, give her something to focus her energy on besides jungle fantasies. My patience with quaint spiritual beliefs had been worn thin by baby-Satanist record producers and crystal-healing promoters who would read your aura while trying to feel you up and pick your pocket. The lithium and Inderal I'd taken were doing backflips in my stomach. I went into the kitchen, found some lukewarm tea with nothing growing in it, and drank it.

The water was still running in the bathroom when I came back. I tapped at the bathroom door with the top of the vodka bottle. "Frida, you want a drink?" When she didn't answer, I pushed, but the door was locked. I yelled her name, but she didn't answer and the water kept running. I yelled *"Frida!"* once more and started kicking.

Water was just seeping over the edges of the tub. Her clothes were piled in the small sink, skates tucked underneath. The razor she'd used to cut her wrists had washed onto the floor with the first overflow of pink water. Frida's fingers were curled back toward her palms in such a manner that, coupled with the utterly placid expression on her face, she could have been taken for someone in meditation.

I grabbed her by the elbows and pulled her out of the tub, dragging her to the bed. Frida moaned, like someone half asleep, and tried to push me away. Blood streaked her arms, pooled between her breasts and ran down her stomach. "Leave me alone," she blurted as I pulled her onto the bed. I ran back to the bathroom, turned off the tub and found some gauze and antibiotic creme.

The cuts were vertical, I noted as I tried to rub creme into Frida's wounds. I'd hoped that the cuts would be horizontal. That would mean that she was more sad than serious, but even as I thought it I realized, no, Frida was utterly serious. Cutting oneself to get attention was more something *I* would do.

"How dramatic," Frida said quietly. "Where were you when I was six? I always wanted to be rescued when I was six, but the other kids wouldn't play right."

"Shut up," I said. "I'm working with goo up here. You move when you talk; it makes me miss the cuts." Frida lay on her back, limply. I pulled the blanket up over her breasts, afraid she might be cold or go into shock, reeling with the nausea of some unspecified dread.

Frida made to pull her arm away. "Leave me alone, asshole. You don't own me."

I held her tighter, mopping the blood off her arms with wadded gauze. "Here's a flash," I told her. "You cut the right way, but it looks like you just nicked the artery. The bleeding is slowing."

"Christ. I should have used the gun." She leaned into my face, yelling, "Where's my fucking gun?"

"I have it, and you're not getting it back."

"Goddamn it, Ryder. Who asked for your help? Go back to being a veg, I liked you better that way."

I wrapped gauze in overlapping X's over the ugly slashes, testing for tightness, checking the color of her fingers, alert for any blue tinges. "Sorry, but you've got my maternal side all in an uproar," I said.

"This isn't a joke, Ryder. I took something without paying for it. There's got to be a payment, some kind of balance."

"There, you're bandaged."

"It's all going," she said. Frida looked at her bandaged wrists, pressing them to her eyes. "Everything is going. I've got to make it stop. Please help me make it stop."

"Listen, after you rest, I'm going to take you to a doctor."

"No," said Frida. She grabbed my hand. "I hate doctors, and the only ones left are Army quacks. They'll throw me in a psych ward or jail."

Frida's eyes were red and tearing. "All right," I said. "But I at least want to tell Virilio. He wants to work for me. Maybe, he can get a line on who did this."

Frida nodded, still holding onto my hand, satisfied that I wasn't going to tender her to the harsh bureaucracies of military medicine. I stayed on the bed with her, trying to keep absolutely still. I watched her breathe, counted each rise and fall of her breasts to ten, then started over, attempting to synch my breathing with hers, an externalized exercise in Zen. When I thought Frida was asleep, she said, "What's that thing on W.C. Fields' headstone?—'All in all, I'd rather be in Philadelphia.' " She smiled fractionally. I watched her for a few more minutes, satisfied, finally, that she wasn't going to slip into a coma.

"Can I trust you not to hurt yourself for a few minutes?" I asked.

Eyes closed, she nodded. "I promise not to cut anything important."

I ran back to Cafe Juju, splashing through the flooded streets under the thin, steady rain. Virilio was still at his table. He insisted on accompanying me back to Frida's place. A group of homeless had massed their modified mobile shelters around a bonfire near Market Street. The wet metal frames of the multi-story shelters turned a flickering crimson. When we got back to Frida's apartment, both she and her skates were gone.

13. Period Doubling

When the monsoons hit, the rain didn't fall from the sky, but seemed to coalesce directly from the humid air. The monsoons were ponderous, slow-motion storms, fat drops falling through the swollen air like a flickering curtain of glycerin. The monsoons' light was unlike that of ordinary rain; the color of rain hovered between a fishy tapioca and dusty gray, while monsoons were a ghostly neon dragon tail, a free-floating segment of a Sierpinski gasket.

I found an umbrella in Frida's apartment and waited outside, relieved by the breeze that swept in behind the storm. Virilio appeared with the car just after midnight. The vehicle was a stretch limo, a ludicrous hulk of mirror-black body work and chrome, spiny with television, radio, and phone antennae. The limo bore expired consul plates; there were matching cigarette-tip holes on each side of the hood where miniature flags should have flown. The passenger door popped open as the car slowed, and when I realized that it wasn't going to stop, I dropped the umbrella, jogging beside the open door for half a block before I could hop in.

"Subtle," I said. "Tastefully understated."

Virilio smiled, jerking the wheel abruptly, steering us through the deepest puddles. "Zil," he said. "The ultimate in Russian driving luxury. Friend of mine bought it for a couple of grand from a mechanic at the Russian Consulate just before they pulled out."

"We're driving to Brazil in the Battleship Potemkin? There isn't enough gas in the whole state."

"Relax," Virilio said. "This baby's been in the U.S. for a while. Pre-Glasnost tech, you know? Custom-made for diplomats. It could get hit dead-on by a bazooka and you wouldn't even spill your Stoli. Plus it has a special suspension system for those rough post-nuke roads, and a monster gas tank, with two reserves."

I tapped a knuckle against the window. At first I thought the glass was tinted, then I realized that the window was bulletproof. The umbrella I'd abandoned back at Frida's place tumbled by, splashing into the intersection just ahead of us, where it spiralled into the air, twirling above the street lights like some demented albatross caught in the competing convection currents that buffeted the old deserted buildings. A few wasted-looking men waded into the street from loading docks and doorways, and threw bottles at the umbrella, stopping long enough to lob a couple at us. Virilio swerved in their direction, kicking up a wall of water, soaking them.

"Check this out," Virilio said. He thumbed the controls of a Blaupunkt radio, searching for a station. "My buddy had to install this himself. They don't put radios in the front of limos, only in the back for the passengers."

"Thanks for sharing. I've been in a limousine before."

"Right. My mistake. Sorry I can't offer you a blow job or anything, but it'd be hard to steer."

"Your loss," I said.

Virilio steered us through the Tenderloin, toward the lights of Van Ness. Even with the wipers beating away with correct socialist vigor, I could make out very little ahead of us. Virilio was either unimpressed with the storm to the point of derangement, or was so certain of the Zil that he ran us steadily through the dark streets with Le Mans intensity. We slowed only once—when a half-dozen Army security vehicles and troop carriers swung in front of us from the parking lot of a derelict Safeway. They were moving fast, heading south toward Market Street. Virilio ran a red light on Van Ness and kept going.

"You were seen again," he said. "With some survivalists up in Oregon."

"What was I doing up there?"

"Preparing for the apocalypse."

"Kind of late for that."

"We're not going to Brazil," Virilio said, turning the wheel hard. The Zil fishtailed, then caught the road.

My stomach felt full of feathers; I looked at the kid. "We're going after Frida. That was the deal."

"I know what the fucking deal was, but we're still not going all the way to Brazil," he replied. "Listen, the Army's in control of everything south of San Jose. The border is closed. We're in a car, she's on foot. . . ."

"Skates," I said.

"Whatever. Frida's not getting any further south than L.A."

"All right," I said. "You've made the trip. I haven't. You're certain she can't get through?"

Virilio laughed. "Shit, we'll be lucky if *we* make it."

The rain stopped as quickly as it had begun, and the pavement oozed ribbons of steam that twined around themselves like pale liana. Fires crackled off near the street market. We were stuck in something the city hadn't experienced in more than a year—a traffic jam. Buses, gypsy cabs, Army transports and a few of the private autos still working were bunched up near Market, neatly cutting off our way south. Some of the drivers had left their vehicles and were walking toward the financial district. Virilio and I got out and followed.

A riot was going full tilt at the intersection of Van Ness and Market. At first, I couldn't tell who was fighting whom. It was nearly silent, the shouts and hollow popping of tear gas cannisters distorted and carried away by the district's vicious convection currents. There was the flaky chalk smell of burning gasoline. The Army boys were decked in full riot gear, clubbing Indians and groups of local homeless bloody, pushing them out of the street. *Urubus,* black and huge, fluttered around the edges of the fight, picking up scraps of food from the wrecked merchant stalls. A dozen sleepwalkers waited on the corner, impatiently checking their watches and reading phantom newspapers, oblivious to the conflict around them.

The troops seemed more interested in clearing the street than in restoring order. It was a futile effort. No sooner would they move one ragged group of homeless onto the sidewalk when another would take their place. Dark-skinned mothers with naked children tossed bottles; gang kids threw coordinated waves of paint-filled balloons, blinding the troops, before following up with Molotov cocktails.

And underneath it all was an almost subliminal rumbling that blinded me with its light. The sound seemed to come from the buildings themselves, a deep industrial churning that built rather than passed, gaining weight like a metallic tsunami. The riot broke for a moment, and all the fighters looked north. In the lull, a jaguar sprinted into the intersection; its ears were back, and the fur stood up straight and tense along its back. The cat hissed over its shoulder and loped off between the Sleepers' legs. The crowd hung back for a moment, then surged forward, drawn by something I still couldn't see. My gaze followed them toward the intersection—and then I saw it.

It was a mad parade, a public torture, a mass delusion. Something bright and reflective filled Van Ness

Avenue. The metal hive. Screaming people. I recognized *Los Quemados*—the Burned Ones, and the woman I'd spoken to at their camp in Golden Gate Park. She was sweating, her face contorted with effort. Across her chest and shoulders something like a horse's yoke was strapped, and she was tethered by long cargo lines to the base of the enormous hive. So were a hundred other people. They were towing the bright sculpture through the city. Their mobile shelters, hundreds of them, welded together to form a mass burden, a skeletal haven that couldn't be hidden or ignored or forgotten by anyone.

The sound of the hive's movement was huge, drowned out only by shouts of the crowd as they massed forward to lay their hands on the metal base, to become part of the inverse exodus to the heart of the city. Kids were setting fire to the hotels and skyscrapers down the length of Market Street, framing the crowd in a pale, liquid light. The Army fell back in the wake of the rolling shelters, unhurried and unstoppable as any ice breaker.

"It's over for the city," I told Virilio. "Those are the new Indians out there. The new Indians of the new Amazonia."

Virilio put his hand on my shoulder and led me back to the limousine. "They can fucking have it, man." He gunned the Zil's engine and nosed the limo onto the sidewalk, scattering piles of discarded furniture, running pedestrians into the street. When we hit a clear patch on Market, we turned abruptly, doubling back on ourselves—then turned again so that we were paralleling Market. "This is it, boyo. We're not going to get a distraction this good again."

Virilio steered the limo fast down a couple of narrow alleys, and pointed us south. We were bumping down pitted side streets in the old industrial zone, the ancient brick roadbed jutting up through generations of peeling asphalt. Howler monkeys brayed at us from the tops of rusting cranes as we burst out of the darkness onto Fifth Street. Two lone, bored soldiers were smoking and drinking coffee by the guard post at the freeway entrance. As he noticed us, one guard raised his hand for us to stop. "Keep your head down," Virilio said as he floored the Zil.

We had already smashed through the wooden liftgate and were tooling south when the soldiers started shooting. Virilio was still yelling, "Get some! Get some, motherfuckers!" If the soldiers hit us, the limo didn't show it.

Just past the ruins of Candlestick Park, the rains began again. In our headlights, I caught a flash of a body on the road—an anaconda, at least twenty feet long, its head and body crushed under the treads of one of the Army's transports. I began to wonder what I'd gotten myself into.

14. Dissipative Structures

A year or two before, I'd performed my first big solo rock climb on a small island called Koh Samet, three hours outside of Bangkok. I'd gone at the wall like John Wayne with a hard-on, but it had been hot and I got tired. Halfway up the cliff I was done in. The climb was no longer pleasant. I looked around—*I actually looked around*—for whoever was running the ride to tell them that I wanted to get off. All I saw was jagged cliff in front of me and rocks below like broken teeth. I knew I was in deep, deep shit, and that death was a genuine possibility. I couldn't walk away from the situation just because I didn't like it. I'd gone too far. I couldn't take a cab or call my lawyer or get a note from my doctor. I thought, "I could die. Right now. No one can fix this. These are your hands, and they are getting tired."

Somehow, I made it up the rock. This part I don't remember, but I must have climbed because I reached the top and I didn't have angel wings. When I got over my own wonderfulness at having conquered the cliff, I fell on the ground and puked up everything I'd ever eaten.

Later, at the hotel, I told my favorite old bartender about my adventure on the rockface. I really played it up, with exaggerated gestures and funny voices and everything. The bartender, an ex-mercenary who had fought the Americans in Vietnam and the Khmer Rouge in Kampuchea just smiled, showing his gold front tooth, and said, "Sometimes shit can't help but get real."

We headed south on 101, past the airport—full of the hulking white ghosts of jumbo jets tethered to runways by wrist-thick lianas dripping with sap and fungi—through Redwood City and Palo Alto. Lizards darted across the road, their backs jeweled in the Zil's headlights. The sun was just coming up as we passed through San Jose, bathing everything in a neon-green light that felt like cotton batting and smelled like raw earth. On the walkway beneath an illuminated road sign, a jaguar was feeding on the body of a young tapir.

"How you doing over there?" asked Virilio.

"Just fine," I said.

"You asleep? You've been awfully quiet."

"Just thinking."

"About Frida?"

"Yes," I said. Virilio nodded.

"Don't worry about her. She knows all about living in this kind of shit," he said, glancing at the jungle. "It's the real world she can't cope with."

"I think I know how she feels."

With the sun up, the temperature in the car began to rise, even with the air conditioning on full blast. Man-size ferns, elephant ears and palms formed a fleshy wall down both sides of the freeway, isolating us on the road. We were enclosed in a green corridor that could have come from any time in the last hundred million years. We were moving, I finally understood, in time as well as space, sailing in a refrigerated box down a concrete tributary of the Amazon itself. I wondered if there were underground rivers that we didn't know about, but had somehow sensed in our dreams, linking us to the Brazilian jungle. Over time, these subterranean channels could have shaped the course of all the roads and freeways in California, forming an externalized dream river in concrete.

"Hey." I jumped when I felt Virilio nudge my arm. "You were asleep again," he said.

"Guess so." The sun was higher in the sky. Mist bled from the roadbed, making the trees seem unreal, like the abandoned set from some action B-movie.

"Hand me some of that speed in there," Virilio said, nodding toward the glove compartment. Somehow, the image of Virilio jacked up on speed didn't thrill me. "I could take over for a while," I told him.

He snorted. *You* could drive us to Never-Neverland, or maybe over an embankment. Just feed me."

There was an official-looking Russian seal emblazoned on the door of the glove compartment. I opened it to find three or four dozen orange prescription bottles lined up in neat rows, like cartridges in a belt feed. "Jesus. Are you afraid they're going to stop making drugs while you're gone?" I asked.

"Unlike certain people in this car, I believe in being prepared. We've ups, downs, antibiotics, an amusing assortment of antivenins—which reminds me. Have you been taking that Fansidar?"

"When the mood strikes me."

"That's what I expected. Take a couple now, and hope that if you get bit it's by a snake and not a mosquito." He looked at me and smiled. "Snakes we got covered."

I looked through the bottles until I found some Desoxyn, and handed Virilio two of the little pink tablets. He reached down on the far side of the driver's seat and pulled out a full bottle of Stolichnaya. "Grab the wheel a minute," he said. I reached over and steered us through the mist while Virilio broke the paper seal on the Stoli, unscrewed the cap and took a long pull, before gobbling his speed. "Breakfast of champions," he said, and handed me the bottle. I found the Fansidar and filled my mouth with vodka before swallowing a couple. Even through the liquor, the bitter taste of the pills was awful, like cold nails in the soles of your feet.

Without thinking about it, I held onto the Stoli, taking small pulls at the bottle to pass the time. While playing with the radio dial, I got a quick look at myself in the rear-view mirror. My eyes were red and sunk deep in my face from lack of sleep; my beard was streaked pearl white. I was thirty-four, but the face in the mirror could have been any fifty-year-old insurance salesman, weighed down by a mortgage and payments on the kid's braces. It wasn't an MTV face. I wondered where he had gone, the person with that other face. I was so tired. I'd never liked heat. Why had I come to this place? Why was I on this road, in this car with this speed freak street hustler?

I tried to imagine where Frida was at that moment, but all the images I conjured were flat and out of focus. I seemed unable to hold her in my mind for more than a few seconds at a time.

"You got writer's cramp?" asked Virilio.

"No."

"Then loosen up on that bottle and hand it over." I gave him the Stoli and he took a long hit. It felt hotter in the car, but I couldn't tell if it was the lame Russian air conditioning or the liquor. "Ryder?"

"Yes?"

"I used to be in a band. We had good management before we broke up. Played the Whiskey A Go Go, and had interest from the majors in our demo tape."

I closed my eyes and leaned my head back on the seat. "You're not going to sing for me, are you?"

"Sorry," he said, petulantly. "I thought you might find it interesting."

"Nothing personal, but every delivery boy and car mechanic I know had a band. And they all had a demo tape. And every one of them had interest from the majors."

We drove in silence for a while, passing the bottle back and forth. The tension in the car grew with the temperature. Finally, I opened the window, just to feel the breeze on my face.

"Ryder?"

"Still here."

"I got into music in an interesting way," Virilio said. "I killed someone."

I turned and looked at him. The sun was up. He had a pair of Wayfarers on, so I couldn't see his eyes, but his face had arranged itself in an odd shit-eating grin that left me inclined to believe what he'd said. I felt a coolness in my face and stomach, and took a drink. "You don't have to say that to impress me," I ventured.

He might have laughed a little at that; I wasn't sure. "I'm not saying it to impress you. I'm saying it 'cause it's true."

"You don't have to talk about it."

"You don't believe me, do you?"

"It's not a question of belief."

Virilio shook his head. "You're a great disappointment to me, Ryder. I thought you were a man of the world. Are you telling me that with all the dealers and gangster-types hanging around the music biz, you never met a killer before?"

"Not one that wanted to chat about it."

"I did it in Beverly Hills."

"I never liked Beverly Hills."

"Who does? But I was a thief at the time, and that's where business took me."

"I would think that those houses would have pretty tight security systems."

"I wasn't going for houses. I went for cars," he said. "Car assaults, man. Picture this: I'm nineteen and fast. I run up with a hammer—Boom!—smash the driver's window, grab his watch, grab his wallet, gold chains from his turkey neck, his wife's purse, whatever, and I'm out of there, clean and fast."

"They would just stop and wait for you rip them off?"

"I had a partner, this chick I was living with back then—Eva was her name. I was in an old Ford pickup and Eva was in an El Camino, one of those early seventies land barges, you know the type. We'd cruise Hollywood, Westwood, Bel Air, looking for likely assholes. We kept in contact over cellular phone. We'd scope someone out, and then one would call the other.

"You never hit them out in the open. Always somewhere residential. People get all goofy when they're close to home. They start feeling soft and warm. Let their guard down.

"The way it worked was this: Let's say Eva spotted a mark—a BMW or a Mercedes; maybe the guy's driving a little drunk. We'd follow him until he left the main road; if he didn't, we'd cut him loose and look for someone else. If he headed for a residential street, though, I'd maneuver in front of him, and Eva would come up from behind. We'd block him at a stop sign, a traffic light; sometimes we'd just slam on the brakes, and catch him in the street.

"One night, though, it's a Saturday. A big Coppola picture's opening in Hollywood; the Stones are playing in town. School's just started, so all these UCLA kids are hot-rodding around with purses full of coke and Daddy's credit cards. We're on Hollywood Boulevard. Eva spots a guy in a Jag heading into Beverly Hills. He's going fast; he's going slow; he can't get the damned thing in gear. You can tell just by looking the guy's hammered. So we follow."

Virilio shook his head, remembering.

"He turns up Mulholland, and I'm thinking, 'Perfect. A lot of curves. Dark. Who could ask for more?' "

"We hit this dark area, no street lights, no illumination—it's up near where Jack Nicholson lived. I was there at a party once. Anyway, Eva and I are on the phone, I give the signal, and we do our number. I slam on my brakes, and Eva taps her accelerator, and we pin the fucker between us. I'm out of the truck with my hammer, and I'm on the Jag. Only, once I'm out of the truck, it's darker than I'd thought.

"I grab the guy's Rolex, and wallet from out of his jacket. Then I'm starting back to the truck. The whole things taken ten, maybe twenty seconds, which is usual. But like I said, it's dark, and I step off the pavement, almost go sliding down the fucking hill. I'm off balance now, turned around, but I get my footing and I'm heading back for the truck, when Eva starts yelling. The drunken asshole's out of his car, waving a gun in my face. Can you believe that shit? So I hit him.

"With the hammer?" I asked.

"Of course. One shot, across the temple, and he goes down. I remember it clearly. Now Eva's really screaming. I push the guy's body down the embankment, into the weeds, and take his car keys. Then Eva and I peel out, down the hill. We stole another car in Hollywood, and I finally talked her into driving back up Mulholland. I didn't like the idea of that Jag sitting up there all lonesome. One, it would attract attention, if it hadn't already, and two, it was cherry, and worth some serious cash.

"When we got back, the scene was just like we'd left it. Eva dropped me, and headed back to Hollywood. I followed her in the Jag. We used the cellulars again, scouting for cops, but they all must have been at the concert or the premier or Winchell's having bear claws.

"We run both cars down to a warehouse area in Culver City. I pop the Jag's trunk, and what do you think I find?"

"Jimmy Hoffa?"

"Fuck no, I find a Stratocaster and an amp. Here's

this guy, I think his ID said he was a real estate sales-men or something, driving a forty thousand dollar car, house up on Mulholland, and what's he doing? Playing rock star with his buddies on weekends. It was an amazing moment. Part of me thought it was really pathetic, and part of me understood—even with all this guy's money and his car and his movie star friends, he couldn't let go. Somewhere under the flab and the gold pinky ring, he was still dreaming he was Jimi Hendrix. I knew right then that between the guy pulling the gun, me whacking him, and finding all this gear, that it was a sign—time for me to move on and up. We left the Jag, but I took the guitar and amp, and started putting up leaflets for people who wanted to put together a band."

We drove into a valley where we were swallowed up by mist. I could hear birds calling to one another. We silently passed the bottle back and forth.

"And here we are," I said. "A long way from god, Hollywood, and show biz now."

Virilio glanced at me. "You're a lot further than I'll ever be."

"Amen to that."

15. Far From Equilibrium

The world had been transformed into some vast green engine, spewing steam and stinging insects, sucking up everything that got in its way. It was like a Victorian-era steam engine, but with the furnace door on the outside, right at the front. The engine's feeding moved it forward, and its forward motion brought it food. Unlike the train, however, the jungle didn't destroy its fuel—it *subsumed* it, remaking each thing it devoured into itself, wasting nothing. Order out of chaos. The green engine was soft and fleshy, lubed with some thick juice like blood and diesel oil, and it pulsed to the rhythm of our tires on the road, the beating of my heart.

Just north of San Lucas, we slowed to little more than crawling speed. Heat, humidity, and the roots of giant plants had burst the road, turning it into a series of petrified waves. Virilio seemed used to this kind of driving, and steered us over the deformed road for hours, until the sun began to go down and the temperature began to drop. Occasionally we would spot a military helicopter headed north over the jungle canopy, but we didn't see another car all day. When the sun was low and swollen behind the clouds Virilio said, "We'll stop up ahead for the night."

Up ahead was Los Robles, an old lumber town that had been used by the Army as a way station in the early days of the Amazonian invasion, but had now been abandoned even by them. We turned off the freeway and drove through the deserted center of town, parking behind a derelict Highway Patrol office. The building's boxy institutional architecture had mutated into something unearthly beneath terraces of wildflowers and vines.

"You hungry?" Virilio asked.

I realized that we'd been drinking on and off, but hadn't eaten all day. "Yes, very," I said.

Virilio went around to the back of the Zil. When he didn't return after several minutes, I got out of the car. I found him leaning into the trunk, cursing and stacking up wet cartons of half-defrosted TV dinners. When he saw me he held up a wilting box in each hand and said, "They killed 'em. The dumb fucks killed all our food." From what I could see, it looked as if the guards back in San Francisco hadn't been such bad shots after all. There were a dozen or so holes in the trunk lid and a few in a leaking plastic cooler inside the trunk.

"You brought frozen food out into the middle of the rainforest?" I asked.

He thrust a carton of beef Stroganoff at me. "There's a microwave in the back seat, man. It's gonna take a couple of days to get down the coast. You're such a goddamn flake I didn't want you freaking out over camp food or something."

"Is any of this edible?"

"Only if food poisoning's your idea of a good time." He sniffed the Stroganoff and threw it into the bushes, gathered up the rest of the offending boxes and tossed them, too. I laughed and in one lightning movement Virilio had me by the throat and was shoving me down against the fender of the Zil, choking me. "You stupid fuck. Don't you *ever* laugh at me!" I couldn't breathe. The heat of the tail pipe hummed a bright high E very close to my face. I had Frida's gun in my pocket, but when I thought of reaching for it, the world seemed to lurch a very long way away—

Virilio let me go suddenly, and my feet slid sideways, dropping me onto the damp pavement. I could hear Virilio cursing, but his voice was different— embarrassed, contrite. He tried to help me up, but I pushed him hard and sat down on the bumper taking deep breaths, trying to clear my head.

After a moment he said, "You want a drink or something?"

I shook my head.

"This baby's got a full bar in the back—TV, VCR and rack full of Jap porn tapes. If we can't eat, at least we can get drunk. It's not like a cop's going to pull us over or anything."

"I'd like some lithium," I said. "And some kind of speed."

Virilio climbed into the front seat and came back with a couple of pills and a glass of Stoli. I swallowed the pills, coughing when the vodka stung my throat. Virilio stood over me guiltily. "You always mix your dope like that?" he asked. I considered tossing the rest of the Stoli in his eyes, but lobbed the glass at the high- way patrol building instead. It smashed somewhere out of sight, setting off blue sparks behind my eyes. "I'm going to take a walk," I said, voice raspy. "Alone." I stood and Virilio nodded.

"Okay, man, but don't go far, and take this," he said, retrieving something from the back of the Zil. It was a small walkie-talkie, about the size of a credit card. "You get lost, give me a holler. Just push the Talk button; the frequency's already set."

I nodded and walked away from him. He said, "Sorry again, man. About the food—and stuff. We'll have a drink when you get back." I coughed loud enough for him to hear it. I left him there talking to himself.

Los Robles lay within a zone that bisected an area of newly emerged flood plain. The streets were shallow lagoons, each flowing into the next, forming a seamless opalescent grid that quivered with water striders and feeding birds. A snake glided along the pavement just ahead of me, disappearing under the cover of giant ferns, only to re-emerge a moment later through the cracked linoleum of a McDonald's. The setting sun was swollen and huge as it dipped toward the ocean, a sluggish gas giant sinking into the primordial goop. I half expected to see the silhouette of a pterodactyl against the horizon. A cooling rain began to fall. My throat ached where Virilio's thumbs had dug into it, and I was lightheaded from the alcohol. The stillness of the streets and the absence of people made me uneasy. Even with the rain coming down, the air felt dead. I was still in the Horse Latitudes, I knew. Time to toss some cargo overboard, and see if we could catch some wind—but what to leave behind?

Black *urubus* chattered and hopped like arthritic old men around the body of a dead poodle, pulling at its insides with their hooked beaks. The *pivetes* considered the birds to be the embodiment of bad luck. I crossed the street, giving the scavengers a wide berth, and heard something from one of the nearby buildings. The sound was like a chorus of sighing voices. I thought for a moment that it might be some new military vehicle patrolling the town, but the structure of the sound was all wrong. It had thin tendrils that itched like fiberglass. And it was too irregular and subdued. It was as if the street had drawn a breath.

I followed the sound until I was standing in front of an old movie theater, one of those places they threw up in the fifties that looked bad even back then. The display cases in front, which should have held posters for Bruce Lee festivals, were sodden terrariums, bloated with fungus, and squirming with termite colonies. A gust of wind blew in from the highway and the building sang—a dense cluster of tones like women's voices and metal scraping piano strings.

The doors were open, knocked off their hinges. The lobby had been gutted. Even the lighting fixtures were gone. I'd heard about the Army looting some of the abandoned towns, but up till then had never seen their handiwork. Bullet holes peppered the cash register at the concession stand. It looked as if someone had used bigger ordnance in the manager's office. There was a hole behind the desk where a floor safe had been blown free. Lizards skittered along the walls feasting on fat black beetles. The jungle rustled and the building sang.

I went into the theater itself, slipping on waterlogged carpet, feeling myself swallowed up by the blackness of the room. The roof had collapsed midway between the entrance and the blank movie screen, leaving the theater open to the sky. Rain misted down on an enormous canary palm that had rooted itself in the center of the theater. The tree was surrounded by a thicket of displaced jungle—glistening ferns and razor grass and wild brasiletto—growing there, green and lush, between the rotting velvet seats.

I went to the patch of solitary jungle and stood in the wet grass, letting the rain come down on my face, washing some of the gummy sweat from around my glass eye. The building sang and a meteor flashed across the open patch of darkening sky. Watching the meteor fall, my cheek brushed against something almost invisible, the source of the building's voice. A matrix of slender wires had been strung from the palm tree and nearby seats to the reinforcement rods protruding from the edges of the damaged roof. Flattened metal discs, remnants of the gutted concession stand, vibrated in sympathy with the wires, amplifying their extraordinary sound.

I sang a note in harmony with the windharp, but my throat spasmed and I doubled over, coughing at first, and then laughing. I imagined what Frida would have said about the gesture, my singing to the empty theater. "Addressing the multitudes again," or something (and so I was).

That I'd begun to love Frida, and had grown dependent on her, both of these things were true. But that was only the surface of things, the tidy press-release version of life. When I played back our time together, I understood that I'd always remained at a slight, but definite, distance from Frida, always held back some portion of myself.

I was on guard in her presence, playing Daddy, mentor, stumble-bum sophisticate. Envy didn't describe my feelings for her. Suspicion came closer. The suspicion that she was what I wanted to be. I never allowed myself to think about this when I was with her, and after our meeting in Chinatown, I convinced myself that I'd opened myself up to her. The truth, of course, was that I'd used her, forced her into the role of Muse and then hated her guts for it. I'd known that the men who had stolen my tapes would come to her apartment the same way they'd come to mine. And they'd take her music, assuming that I'd composed it. I wanted that. I needed her music destroyed. I needed her innocence obliterated or her madness to overwhelm her because those, I knew, were the roots of her talent, and I couldn't bear it.

I sat down in the razor grass, suddenly tired, and hooked a finger around a strand of vibrating windharp wire. My head swam and there was a strange metallic taste in the back of my mouth. There was something else, too, fluttering over my head. It was recording tape, yards and yards of it. How had I missed it earlier? The tape snapped and glittered in the tree, wrapping like a strangler fig around its trunk; the tape dripped rain from exposed ventilation ducts in the wrecked ceiling and looped around the theater seats. Tape twitched like snakes up the drafty aisles and lay in great drifts by the exit doors.

Meeting Frida had been a bifurcation point in the scheme of my life; losing her, betraying her, had been another. Objects and events were swirling around me, the reluctant Strange Attractor. I looked up at the tree full of recording tape and thought, for the first time, of how betrayal shakes up the universe. We had entered a state of period doubling. Time could stop here, or run backwards; light could drown you; sound might peel your skin. There were visions here, snapshots of convulsive beauty and your own death; they were in your head and in the sour sweat of your clothes.

The wind gusted and the rain blew down and the building's song grew louder, until the sound shook the floor and split the theater's eggshell walls. I fell, spinning down a shaft comprised of sound, toward a city of light. My senses buzzed with a cold fire that echoed the light through which I passed, and then I realized that I was the light and the city and the sound which held it all together. And I kept falling, not slowing even when I entered the great black beetle-shaped fractal heart of the place. . . .

I was wet, and my whole body shook, but not with the building's song. Something sliced my cheek. I rolled away from the palm tree, but the ground kept moving. It was an earthquake.

Overhead, the windharp wires snapped, cutting the air like a whip. I crawled beneath the seats, pulling myself into a ball. Chunks of ceiling and lengths of rebar thudded into the aisles. And then it was over.

The building gradually grew still, but I was still shaking. I crawled from beneath the seats and tried to stand, but my legs wouldn't support me. I was dizzy and soaked with cold sweat. A mosquito settled lightly on my arm and began to drink. I crushed the insect, my hands shaking and wet, an early symptom of malaria.

I stumbled out of the theater and into the street, trying to get away in case of aftershocks. Outside, the cooler air revived me, and within a few minutes I could walk again. The streets looked the same, except now I could see what I'd missed before. There was recording tape everywhere, tangled around lampposts and traffic signs and spilling from broken store windows. I splashed through the streets back to the Russian limo and threw open the back door. Virilio, intent on the television screen and what one young Japanese beauty was doing between the thighs of a second, jumped back in his seat, spilling Stoli all over his lap. "You asked me before if I was sure we were going the right way to find Frida. We are, and I have proof," I said, holding out a mass of the tape that filled the streets. Of course, the hand that should have been holding the tape was empty.

16. Twin Dragon

Before coming to Amazonia I'd always imagined the jungle to be mostly silent, an exploded version of the museum dioramas I'd seen as a child. I was wrong. At every second of every hour of the day and night the jungle talks to itself in the voices of birds, tree frogs, monkeys, insects, predatory cats, lizards, and a thousand other unnamed eardrum rattlers. From the moment we'd hit the highway, this underbelly of Amazonia had lit up in my head with a neon migraine. I was getting used to it, but that only made me wonder whether I was changing to suit the jungle or it was changing to suit me.

The Russian air conditioner finally gave out, but the monsoon rains returned with the morning, so we were forced to leave the limo's windows closed. The Zil was a rolling steam bath, already beginning to take on the musty odor of mildew and our bodies.

"You were really howling last night," said Virilio, steering the car around the blackened skeleton of a small twin-engine Cessna, a victim of the local drug wars.

"What did I say?" I asked.

"It was pretty squirrely, let me tell you. I couldn't understand a lot of it. Mostly you sang."

"Really. Any old favorites?"

"No. You weren't singing words, just melodies. Then you'd stop and shout something like, 'There it is!'

or 'I can see it!' " Virilio's smile was both hungry and indulgent. "You high or something? What did you see out there?"

"Sirens," I told him. "Bands of angels. Groupies from the id. They asked about you, but I told them you were in management now and no longer indulged in such base behavior."

"You've one-upped me there, man. I've never had any angel pussy."

"No need to get crude just because you feel left out."

"Fuck you. Don't get superior with me. How do you have the balls, after you've banged all those little girls and boys, to tell anyone else about being crude?" He was glaring at me, ignoring the road. "I don't want or need any of your crazy-ass fantasies."

"They always speak highly of you," I said. I was buoyantly drunk. My throat still ached slightly from our go-round the previous night. I took the bottle of vodka that lay on the seat between us and refilled my glass, which was already half-filled with quinine from the bar. I was engaged in the fine art of self-medication. My malaria symptoms had faded in the night and not reappeared; however, I was still weak and slightly feverish. I was popping Fansidar and Inderal cocktails, washing them down with quinine, hoping to hold off a full-bore malarial seizure until we got to L.A.

From time to time I'd still catch glimpses of tape-covered forest out of the corner of my eye. I didn't turn to look anymore. The tape would always been gone when I looked at it directly, so I let the vision go. It didn't matter anymore if what I was seeing was real or not, whether the tape was a manifestation of Frida's Spiritline or the side effect of a malaria fever. The wind harp had been real enough. I'd made Virilio stop by the wrecked theater on our way out of town to confirm it. The mangled wires were still there. The few intact strands buzzed like startled locusts right where Frida had left them for me. She'd wanted me to see the Spiritline, but knew I wasn't capable of it on my own. I knew now that I was on the right path and that Frida wanted me to follow her. But I wasn't sure why.

We passed through swampy ghost towns and the overgrown remains of derelict Army checkpoints—rusting Quonset huts, empty jerry cans and collapsing hurricane fences, the last transformed into a primitive Christo running wall by tightly interlaced strands of liana and rope-moss. We drove higher into the hills and the Zil was buffeted by the cool and constant breeze that blew in off the ocean. Gorging themselves on the moisture in the perpetually foggy air at the top of the pass, the flora had grown to enormous sizes, elephants ears as wide as a man is tall, car-size ferns, and orchids like the henna-stained hands of Arab women. The smell was like the popping of champagne bubbles all over my skin.

"Action up ahead," said Virilio. I sat up suddenly, startled to find I'd fallen asleep. Virilio was pointing to the ridge of hills in the distance. It was nearly dark, but through the gloom the headlights of the approaching truck convoy were clearly visible.

"Army?" I asked.

"No one else would advertise themselves like that."

"What should we do?"

Virilio gunned the engine and wheeled us onto an off ramp and down a secondary road almost completely obscured by the jungle. The big Zil took the corner like a dyslexic whale, bottoming out with a hollow thud and a fringe of sparks from the undercarriage. This other road was in much worse shape than the highway. The jungle had closed in from both sides, leaving only a gray slit of pitted asphalt clear in the middle. Virilio didn't let up on the gas. In the flat, metallic gleam from the headlights, palm fronds and liana slapped the windshield; the hidden trunks of oaks and coconut palms tore gashes in the Zil's paint. Finally Virilio killed the lights and slammed the car to a stop, looking up at the sky through the windshield. Two helicopters passed by overhead, high enough that we could barely hear them over the ticking of the overheated engine.

"We got lucky," Virilio said. "Those were Apaches. Either they weren't looking for us or they didn't care. Either way, we aren't moving anymore tonight. We can't move with the lights off, and the next chopper's sure to spot us if we have them on. And that one might not be so indulgent." He turned and crawled into the back seat, laughing. "Hey cuz, it's a campout!" He cracked the seal on another bottle of Stoli and took a long pull, lying back on the wide seat. "You don't mind if I take the bottom bunk, seeing as how I've done all the driving?"

"No, it's fine," I said.

"Good." He drank some more vodka and turned on the porn video I'd interrupted the night before. "Back to nature, I love it!" he yelled. "You know any ghost stories, cuz? No wait—you are a ghost story." Virilio laughed and pointed at me.

We each retired to our bottles and didn't speak for some time. I listened to the tree frogs and night hunters in the distance, and to the grunting and toneless dialogue coming from Virilio's video. "Virilio," I said, leaning over the seat to look in the back, "I know why I'm going to L.A., but why exactly are you going there?"

"What?" Virilio asked, not looking up. "I'm here to keep your loony ass in one piece. Leave me alone."

"Who's paying you to keep my loony ass in one piece?"

"Shut up. I'm trying to watch this."

"Who are you delivering me to in Los Angeles?"

Virilio frowned in my direction and said slowly, "As if you didn't know. As if you didn't fucking know."

I nodded. "Nikki?" I asked.

"Of course it's Nikki. Who else?"

"Then you lied to me before," I said. "It was you who stole Frida's gear. You knew her weak spots. You manipulated her into running south knowing that I'd follow. You're just here to gloat and protect your investment."

He was shaking his head before I'd finished. "Wrong, man. Wrong-o. I had nothing to do with that. Why would I take a chance bringing third parties into a deal like this? You're a pricey item, Ryder. Why would I let them rough you up, maybe get a chance to bootleg your tapes? No. But you're right about the last part; I am here to gloat. And you are my investment." He smiled and wagged a finger at me. "Tell you the truth, I thought that maybe you were the one who set the wheels in motion."

"What, I stole my own gear? And Frida's? Why would I do that?"

"Well, for one thing you're mentally unstable. You could have danced naked on the Bay Bridge and not remembered it," he said. "I figure you manipulated Frida for an excuse to head for L.A. I figure you want to get the *juice* back."

"You're wrong."

Virilio smiled at me. "No. You want it. Your face in the paper. The best table. Jets. Dope. Money. A hundred thousand Girl Scouts, all wet and ready for you."

I took a sip of the vodka and quinine. "That's what I came here to avoid."

Virilio shook his head. "Don't kid a kidder, okay? I grew up in L.A. I've been around guys like you all my life. Players. You're all the same, man. You're like a junkie who knows that the next shot's going to be the last one. Boom—flatline. The Big Sleep. But it doesn't matter, cause when you've got a taste for the needle and when the hunger hits, death is a lot less scary than not feeding the dog. You're an addict, Ryder, and Nikki's your fix."

"Yours, too, from the sound of it," I said. "What did she promise you? More than money, I bet."

"She's not doing me any favors. I played her my demo tape and she made up her own mind. Ours is a manager/client relationship; strictly legitimate."

Virilio turned the video up loud and settled back against the seat. Another Apache went by overhead, moving lights on its belly turning the upper canopy of the jungle into an acid white sculpture. "I didn't know it was Nikki," I said finally.

Virilio gave me a look of utter contempt. "If you didn't, then you're even dumber and more out of it than I gave you credit for."

I downed the rest of my drink and poured another. The rain started up again and just over the tops of the trees I could see a silent lightning storm somewhere out over the Pacific, great dendral bursts of electricity arcing across the darkened sky. My head and heart pounded, and not entirely from apprehension. Nikki. I took another Inderal.

17. Flux and Force

When I awoke it looked as if someone had packed cotton batting over the Zil's windows. I stared half-awake, my gaze caught up in all that blank acid whiteness, until a flash of green caught my eye and I realized that what I was looking at was the morning mist. In a few minutes the temperature inside the car began to rise. By the time Virilio stirred a half-hour later, the sun had arced higher in the sky and what had been a solid membrane of whiteness had been cooked to sluggish streamers, the burning ends of a thousand cigarettes in some overlit Trader Vic's.

Red-eyed and grim, Virilio climbed into the front seat, gunned the Zil's engine and jammed the car in gear without a word. He drove with grave determination, speeding through the jungle half-blind from vodka damage and the thick undergrowth, struggling to keep the limo moving forward over the eviscerated road. I started to comment on this, but stopped myself; not because I was concerned about Virilio's reaction, but because I knew it would do no good. If I'd learned nothing else, it was that it wasn't in Virilio's nature to slow down.

We drove through the morning in crystalline silence. I didn't bother to ask if he knew where we were going because I knew he wouldn't answer me. Around noon Virilio switched to one of the reserve gas tanks. I drank quinine and vodka. My fever ebbed and flowed, timed to some mysterious bacterial clock. When the hallucinations came, and they came frequently, they were fluid and hot. I was in my bed at Point Mariposa, unable to move, a pretty Japanese nurse cleaning the inside of my mouth with a sterile cotton swab. I was back on stage at the Garden playing one of the old songs, the band wailing behind me, all of us locked together in one of those synchronous moments of pure *essence,* with the light in my head just right, knowing that for that moment the music wasn't forced, but the ecstatic conjunction of guitars, drums, and audience. Underneath the dreams I felt the pull of Frida's Spirit-line, even when I watched myself wiping her blood off the bathroom floor.

And suddenly, we were at the edge of the ocean.

We had come around a corner, as dark and saturated with dense lower canopy smells and crushing heat as any other, and unexpectedly found ourselves moving over an open paved road, awash in light and air. The sense of relief was overwhelming; even Virilio muttered a relaxed, "Oh yeah." We were still surrounded by jungle, with vegetation spilling from the edges of our mountain road down to the beach on our right, but everything was suddenly different. For the first time in what felt like days we could breath air not ripe with jungle rot and the buzz of carnivorous insects; it was as if we had suddenly awakened from a long and brutal hibernation. When the morning rains came lashing in off the ocean, we were still high from our discovery and driving became an act of ritual bathing, a cleansing of the body and the spirit.

And then we were skidding. The rear of the Zil fishtailed wildly, cutting up the asphalt between the jungle and the drop-off to the beach. Virilio twisted the wheel and shouted something I couldn't hear, but might have been a warning. We were moving sideways, hydroplaning toward a jagged gray mass that filled the road.

———

I have no memory of the impact; the crash was locked into my memory like a clumsy film splice, an instant of white noise between reels. When I was aware of myself again I was outside of the car in the rain, admiring how cleverly the rear of the Zil had twisted itself into a metallic knot of guard rail and axle, filigreed with sandstone from the rockslide that blocked the road. Virilio came around to survey that damage and I said, "She's pulled up lame, Marshal. Best to just put her out of her misery." Virilio didn't reply to that, but walked slowly back to the car (a slight limp on his right side, I noted), got in and started the engine. To my amazement, after a few minutes of judicious rocking and grinding of gears, Virilio managed to coax the Zil free of the twisted mess. He left the engine running and came back to where I waited.

"Let's go," he said. There was a fine line of blood running from under his hairline and pooling over one eyebrow.

I took a step away from him. "You're facing the wrong way. L.A. is that way," I said, nodding toward the rockslide.

Virilio shook his head. "Even if we could get around that, there's no way this car's going to make it to L.A. I can maybe nurse it back to one-oh-one. There've been choppers overhead all morning. We can get a ride with one of the Army columns, tell 'em we were escaped conscripts from a dope farm or something. Come on," he said, reaching for me.

I shook off his hands. "I thought you wanted to be Buddy Holly. Fame and fortune are waiting down south."

"We can't make it. Listen, we'll go back to San Francisco and get Nikki to come up north."

I shrugged and started away from him. "No thanks. You take the car and go fuck yourself and tell Nikki to fuck herself, too. I'm out of here."

Virilio lunged at me, which I'd expected. Slow and

clumsy on his bad leg, he looked genuinely shocked when I pulled out Frida's Smith and Wesson and pointed it at him. Something interesting must have happened on my face because he backed off without a word. I went back to the car and slid bottles of vodka and quinine into the side pockets of my coat, then dropped the Fansidar and Inderal on top, all the time keeping the gun on Virilio. Then I went back across the wet highway and stepped over the rusted guardrail, sliding through the fine sand, ice plant, and razor grass to the beach.

"What the fuck are you doing, man?" yelled Virilio.

"How far is L.A. from here?" I shouted back.

"I don't know where we are."

"I don't believe you, but that's all right. Thanks for the lift. Have a nice career."

"You can't walk there from here," he shouted.

"Watch me," I yelled back, but the wind swallowed it up. I put the gun back in my pocket, but kept my hand around the grip.

I walked away from Virilio and the Russian limo. Within a hundred yards, I already regretted it. The combined adrenaline rushes from the crash and my John Wayne Moment faded quickly behind waves of malarial shivers and dizziness. But I was committed to forward motion and my small gesture of will. The truth was that coming as far as we had, I was afraid to stop. Not afraid for Frida or afraid of Nikki, but afraid that I was repeating myself, that everything since Point Mariposa had been nothing more than just another pop-star indulgence. A grasp of the crotch, a sneer on MTV. If I stopped now I would die, I was certain of that. And to leave this world as foolish and blind as I felt then would be a high crime. I had come too far to run away; there were real and secret costs to mucking around in other people's lives, and I needed to discover them and to try, as best as I could, to make restitution.

The wet sand stuck to my shoes and legs, weighing me down. It was like walking through half-set cement. After walking just a few yards, I was sweating and I could feel my fever surfacing like the bloated sac of a Man-o-War. I counted my steps, placing one foot in front of the other, without regard to a goal, merely accepting the accumulation of single steps. In this type of concentration exercise, numbers quickly lose their meaning, becoming a backbrain hum, a measured mantra. Rock climbing was sometimes like that. Not a movement up a rockface, but one handhold leading to another and so on. Up the beach a frigate bird and a gull were having a squawking argument over the remains of a blue crab.

One step, and then another.

Sweat rolled into my eyes, but when I touched my forehead, it felt weirdly cool. My feet had trouble finding the beach. The sand was doing the mambo beneath me, but I kept a steady pace. Virilio was to my rear, a few dozen yards back, trailing me like a whipped dog. The gull and frigate bird got into a tug-of-war over the blue crab, which wasn't quite dead, and when each managed to pull off a leg, the remaining body twitched and tossed on the sand like the hand of some prisoner being tortured.

I've come a long way to get nowhere at all, I thought. And I've spent everything I have to get here.

A sudden wind surge drove a wave up around my knees. I retreated to the upper part of the beach where the sand was softer and it was harder to walk.

Some of the hardier jungle grasses had taken root in the sand and islands of green, micro-Amazons formed a living archipelago along the beach in front of me. Basilisk lizards scrambled from the jade patches to the jungle, running upright, on their hind legs (the same trick that allowed them to sprint safely across the surface of a lake), so that they looked like a team of absurd cocktail waiters.

The flora and fauna of the region were adapting quickly to the rules of the the new Amazon. I wondered if we as a species had it within us to keep up with the changes, or if these lizards would be among the new rulers of California.

One step, and then another.

I wasn't aware of Virilio coming up beside me. He insinuated himself slowly, over the course of minutes or hours, I wasn't sure. He kept up a steady line of chatter, asking me if I was crazy, telling me to turn back. I heard him and understood, in some dim way, what he was saying, but my awareness had been battered by my sickness, so that everything was flying straight through the storm of my fractured senses. The light in my head registered the beach as a kind of music, a chaotic Coltrane free-jazz riff with the surf and rain pounding a schizo beat, and the birds and wind playing intersecting melody lines. Was this sensation a side effect of following the Spiritline or just another fever dream? The screeching of the gulls sometimes sounded artificial, like the beeping of a heart monitor. I shivered and swore I felt tubes in my arms.

The monsoons returned suddenly and brutally. Each drop of rain was a watery punch, and they didn't stop. After a couple of hours of relative mental clarity, my fever came back, and this time it brought friends who filled my head with clay and turned up the heat, baking bricks inside my skull. The beach was a turntable and I, a skipping needle. A moment later, I was spitting sand and Virilio was pulling me up and hauling me down the beach; my legs were pumping, but doing little for our forward motion. It was obvious even to me that we couldn't go on.

We were near what could have been the remains of an upscale beach town. A long pier snaked across the sand almost to the water, collapsing a few yards short of the surf in a pile of charred and splintered planks (yielding the black and spongy smell of burned wood). There was more wreckage beyond the burned pier. The prow of a Coast Guard cutter pointed almost straight up beyond the breakers where the boat had hung itself up on a submerged rock outcropping. Nearby, an oversized power boat—painted in the flat black of a smuggling ship—had been washed ashore, its belly torn open by the rocks or gunfire. Virilio pulled me across the beach, and we both tumbled into the boat.

Madonna was giving glamorous birth to Elizabeth Taylor. David Bowie's mouth was open as if in midsong, but his features were softly distorted, his high cheeks stretched and melded with the cheeks of Ronald Reagan, like a pair of natty amoebae splitting. Humphrey Bogart lay locked in a carnal death-grip with Michael Jackson. Worst of all, I spotted myself among the celebrity trash—face down, a disembodied head lying at the feet of a sequin-robed Liberace.

A slap of cold wind and rain convinced me that I hadn't died and gone to some Disneyland version of Hell. I scraped my nails along Liz Taylor's ankle and came back with curls of flesh-colored wax. Brochures and posters from the Hollywood Celebrity Wax Museum fluttered around the charred hold of the gutted boat like soggy pigeons. I sat up slowly. Virilio was smoking and watching from a perch just inside the gaping hole in the boat's belly. He smiled and leaned over to stroke Marilyn Monroe's breasts.

"Do you believe this shit?" he said. "Dope I can understand, but this . . . ?"

"Don't be too hard on them," I told him. "They were just rescuing their gods. The Mayans hid their codices from the Catholic missionaries for five hundred years rather than have them burned. Whoever ran off with this bunch believed in something. You should feel humble. You're in the presence of faith."

Virilio laughed and mock chanted "Aum Mane Padme Aum." Then he put out his cigarette in Marilyn's eye.

"What time is it?" I asked.

"I don't know, but it's almost dark." Virilio nodded

outside. "There's a fogbank hanging just offshore. In a little while this place is going to be socked in. We can spend the night here and go back to the car at first light. Then we'll head back to San Francisco like we should have done in the first place. Right?"

I didn't answer, but Virilio nodded as if I'd given him a Yes which, in a sense, I had, because I hadn't said No. At that moment, though, I didn't want to think about it. I didn't want to think about anything. I closed my eyes and relaxed against the bulkhead of the smuggler's boat, waiting for my fever to return, hoping in some childish way that I could will it back into being. But I remained maddeningly aware of the boat, the wax dummies, Virilio and the wind, locked into one of those interfever periods of crystalline lucidity. In the end, even disease had failed me.

Virilio gathered wood from the unburned timbers of the pier. I drank vodka and quinine, emphasis on the vodka, and popped a lithium. As Virilio was trying to get a fire started, the first tentative curls of fog drifted across the beach, settling over us like a frozen blanket. It was going to be a miserable night. Nikki would love it, I thought. "Too cold is almost cool enough," she used to say. She would turn on the air conditioner, even in New York's January blizzards, and stand by the radiator freezing and heating herself simultaneously. I never quite believed this personality quirk. There was something cultivated about it, like perpetually wearing a single color or affecting a mother-of-pearl cigarette holder. It was the kind of quirk that got you talked about.

And it bothered me that Nikki's contrivances always worked. I held a clear image of her in my memory, a sexy postcard pose she'd struck at our release party for *Lust and Neurology.* She'd perched on the edge of a banquet table piled high with champagne and tiger prawns (carefully juxtaposing herself against an ice sculpture depicting an eroticized CAT scan), poured into a backless black leather minidress, her engineer boots polished to mirrors. All my memories of Nikki were tinged with smells and colors, like the recollection of some natural disaster, a tidal wave or a volcanic eruption.

Virilio cursed, holding a fistful of uncooperative kindling to the business end of a plastic disposable lighter. I splashed a little vodka in his direction, trying to up the flammability of his wood with a little alcohol. Virilio didn't see this as a help, however, and screamed at me to sit back and go crazy quietly. I laughed at him, letting the chemical magic of the vodka and lithium erase all trace of me from the inside out, until there was nothing left but a black singularity.

The wind picked up as Virilio got his fire going. Shadows of dead celebrities scrambled over the walls like packs of fighting dogs. The fog felt the way cinnamon and raw sewage smell. A triangle of white hovered in the darkness above the ocean. A sail.

I was up and stumbling across the beach before I had any awareness of moving. I screamed and waved my hands. The schooner was very far out, however. From the fire Virilio said, "They'll never hear you." I brought out Frida's pistol and Virilio hunkered down in the sand as I fired three shots into the air. Nothing happened. But as I was preparing to fire again a light from the boat flashed at the shore three times. I whooped when I saw it, but Virilio just sulked by the fire and asked me to put the gun away.

About ten minutes later, a black Zodiac buzzed through the breakers, and we waded, waist-deep, into the surf to climb aboard. I started to thank whoever was piloting us back to the schooner when he turned and I could see the filmmaker's smiling face. Before I could say anything Lurie cut me off with, "You boys are lucky I decided to take the scenic route home. If I didn't need footage, you'd have drowned when the tide came in."

18. Autopoiesis

Ever since my glimpse of the city of light in the Los Robles movie theater, I'd been contemplating the nature of what I'd been looking for. The light was a color of infinite depth, and the color bound within it a city whose substance was an infinitely complex light. The name for the light and the color was "fractal," but I hadn't always known that. I learned the word from an article in some pop-science magazine I picked up in a shop during a stopover at Heathrow. Once I had a name for the light, I was left with the light itself, and the same questions I'd always had, only now I could ask them more easily, like, why were the light, the color, and the city bound together in a thing called a fractal?

A fractal, as I understood it, was an object of infinite depth, just as a city is, in its own way. You can never know a city completely. Beneath the pavement lie electric lines, phone lines, sewage lines, ventilation ducts, tunnels, subways, insects, bedrock, plants, microscopic organisms, all the way down to the atoms and the quarks that spin within them; the process is endless. Peel away one layer and there is always another layer underneath, other structures, other lives, other desires.

The music of cities that was the key to the light, was also a fractal dance, a pattern that never quite repeated itself, but described the intimate angles where skyscrapers met the street, the convective turbulence of steam escaping from manhole covers, the million wavelengths of light that came at you from neon signs, the headlights of delivery trucks, the flash of curiosity in women's eyes.

A city is something that can never be fully described because it is a dynamic system, always changing, always inventing. You can come close to describing it, and when you look again, in the time it has taken you to gather your thoughts, the city has shifted and you must redescribe it from the beginning. We reinvent our cities in our minds even as the cities endlessly reconstitute themselves.

Does a city have its own Spiritline and its own song? I wondered. I'd moved so far outside of everything I'd ever known I could no longer say no.

The steady white-noise hum and snap of the sails, combined with the slow rolling gait of the schooner, dropped me down inside myself like a caiman sinking beneath the night-colored waters of the Rio Negro. My muscles turned watery, chest coming closer to, and finally touching the handrail at the bow of the boat. My eyelids, unsupported by even the smallest muscles, drooped shut. That last lithium and vodka tranquilizer was singing me a lullaby through my blood. There were voices in the distance, occasionaly bursts of radio communications, dispatches from a faraway world. My legs would barely hold me and I had to keep a tight grip on the handrail to stay upright. The fog held everything suspended, like nature frozen between two thoughts.

"You look like you could use a pick-me-up," came Lurie's voice. I turned, and he was standing there just as big and bearded as I remembered him from our meeting in Marin. He held out a finger-size vial of white powder. "Eat up," he said. "We've got plenty." Which didn't surprise me. His schooner was over-manned and the extra bodies all looked like they'd come straight off some dope collective; each had a Kalashnikov slung over his or her shoulder (I wasn't surprised to see Virilio in earnest conversation with a couple of the less aloof smugglers).

"What about her?" I asked, pointing to a woman who'd been filming me ever since Virilio and I'd come on board. The woman's parka and camera pack bore NHK logos. Lurie waved her off, and the woman wandered away to film the shore and the night sky, careful to keep the lens pointed at the deck whenever she approached any of the smugglers.

"Sorry, but we're shooting a documentary, you know. You're part of the story now. She's doing her job," he said, and handed me the tube of powder. I took a quick hit in each nostril, and felt a lovely wave of hot static move across my brain, from the frontal lobes, all the way down my spine. I thought for a moment that I'd found a cure for malaria, as my chills and fever seemed to lift from me. "Bless you, doctor," I said, and tried to hand Lurie back the vial, but he gestured for me to keep it. He smiled and I felt my feet hovering a few inches off the deck. "Is this what you're moving with these thumb-breakers?" I asked.

Lurie was untroubled by the question. He leaned on the rail beside me and lit up a cigar. "That's right. Of course, we're running empty now. The market's all up north these days. There aren't enough people left down south to interest this bunch."

"These are dangerous people, Lurie. When they catch on that you're just slumming they're going to hit you on the head extremely hard and throw your ass over the side."

"No," he said, puffing on the cigar so that the tip glowed like a small star. "We've got a good situation here. With me they have ready-made cover as part of my crew."

"And what do you get out of it, besides kicks?"

"Security. The local authorities don't like us filming in their region, so I can't get any protection for myself or my people. These folks," he said, gesturing to the smugglers, "are my guard dogs, my Rottweilers. They keep other dopers away, and put some money in my pocket along the way." He leaned close to my ear and spoke softly. "At first, I didn't want their money, just their presence. However, if I'd refused, they'd be sure I was the heat and would have shot me on general principles. It's a tragedy of sorts. I'm being forced to show a profit against my will." He laughed at that.

I pulled my coat up around my neck as the cold night air seeped through to my bones. "I still say you're slumming. Virilio told me that you had a miniature set up so that you could get footage of Marin without going there. You could have done the same thing for the coast and slept in a nice hotel every night."

"Not so," replied Lurie. "Marin is a small, known area, the coast is changing too fast to duplicate convincingly. Every day, some new species of flower or animal winds up in front of my cameras. No, you can't capture a world in flux in a studio." He stopped and looked at me. "I hear a tone of disapproval in your voice. Are you that much of a purist that you'd deny me a little art along the way?"

"Are you interested in the jungle at all, really? When we first met you came on like a hardcore Green, now you're Cocteau with artillery."

Lurie puffed his cigar and peered out into the darkness toward shore. "I hate this fucking place," he said finally. "The jungle's a sewer on wheels. It eats civilization and spits out shit. There are more organisms out there that can kill you or give you some gruesome disease than anywhere else on the planet. On one level, of course, that kind of coarse vitalism is interesting, but no more than, say, a head-on collision or an autopsy."

I shivered. "I don't like swamps either, but even *I* find parts of the jungle beautiful."

"You're wrong. My films are beautiful. Amazonia is a corruption, like infected flesh. A virus, an invading organism." Lurie lowered his voice as the Japanese camera woman moved past us to film a school of silvery flying fish that were just visible through the lower layers of fog.

"Why do we build?" Lurie went on. "Why do we create art, books, and films, and appreciate the beauty of our creations? We create beauty to remove ourselves from that dung heap out there. Beauty is our weapon against nature. It is our escape from the murky formlessness of bacteria and the jungle."

"Whatever happened to 'Truth is beauty, beauty truth'?"

"A school boy's wet-dream and an academic's comforting lie, that's all that is. Truth, literal truth, is the last refuge of those with nothing to say. I create my own truth because what I create is beautiful. Beauty justifies itself; it exists on its own. I can illuminate the situation in, say, Marin through my miniatures faster and better that I could with a thousand camera crews on the ground for a year."

"And you don't have get your feet wet," I said.

Lurie gave me a look of sadness or contempt. "How can you stand there sweating and shaking, obviously sick, and come up with such shit?" he asked. "Are you stupid or just a fool?"

I hadn't realized that I was shaking, but Lurie's question threw me back inside my body, where things weren't going well. I was, in fact, shaking considerably, partly as a response to the frigid dampness of the fog, but on a deeper level I was shivering in time with subtle chemical changes inside me. All the drugs I'd been taking, coupled with the bouts of malaria, the lack of food and sleep, were recombining in my gut, changing, I speculated, my basic cell structure. Perhaps I was on the verge of a mutation of my own. That would put me on the brink, in Lurie's eyes, of genuine beauty, since I'd been administering all the medications myself. Perhaps I'd found a shortcut to the city of light. That was a comforting idea. For Lurie, even an OD could be considered an act of creation, just as the *thugees* in India considered murder an act of sacrament directed toward Kali. I was going to mention this to Lurie when a barrage of gun fire startled me.

I spun around in time to see six or seven of Lurie's smugglers laughing and firing their Kalashnikovs at the flying fish, who were still pacing the boat. "You're right, man," I said. "Civilization's got it all over the jungle."

19. Logistic Evolution

The sun was up and blazing and the fog had lifted by the time we docked at Santa Monica. During the last few hours of our transit down the coast I'd begun to wonder about old Francisco Pizzaro, navigating down the Amazon River for the first time. Did he feel complete displacement and doubt, as I did? He was a Spaniard, a Conquistador, bred to drag fistfuls of the world's goodies home for the King and the Church. Doubt was probably beyond him, but I was certain that we must have had at least a moment in common, a sense of utter *weirdness* at the sight of a hundred scarlet ibises lifting, like a pink cloud, into the air, or a white usistus alligator masticating the carcass of a careless coyote.

I was caught off guard by the sight of the Southern California coast. Even the drive through the central valley jungle hadn't prepared for me for the unrestrained wildness, the Pre-Cambrian clutter of the region. There were no signs of human life or habitation, though we must have passed Santa Barbara and Malibu during the day. In San Francisco, I'd found the juxtaposition of the old with the new fascinating and amusing—a Cadillac swallowed up by blossoms or a government office building transformed into a haven for bats—but the south was ripe with a kind of succulent desolation. I began to wonder if Lurie wasn't right, that the jungle was fine in the abstract, but unbearable in reality. It made one thing clear, though. The south had been wholly abandoned by the government, who weren't even making a token effort to keep the jungle back.

During the night, I'd fallen asleep and dreamed through a wicked bout of fever that left me rubber-legged and weak. In my dream, Nikki and I were in Mexico, on the Yucatan coast. We lay on the beach, relaxed, warming ourselves in the sun. With the practiced casualness of someone accustomed to being photographed, Nikki removed a long filet knife from her beach bag and cut me open, with a single neat line from crotch to throat. She threw my insides to the gulls, who gathered to feast on the sticky red streamers. I was drowsy with the sun. There was no pain, just the feeling of Nikki's busy fingers inside me. I didn't fight her, but remained passive, motionless within the center of my breath.

Docked at the slip next to ours was a pirated sailing ship, an enormous three-masted monster right out of *Mutiny on the Bounty*. Lurie told me that they were taking on a cargo of bones. Sure enough, one of the crates fell off the forklift that was raising it to deck level and it exploded a yellowish jumble of ribs, horns, femurs, and jaguar skulls like monstrous dice across the dock. Lurie said that the recent deaths of the last few elephants and walrus in the wild had sent the underground ivory market into a feeding frenzy, grabbing up all the bone they could get a hold of. Most of what was being loaded in Santa Monica was destined for Japan, Singapore and Saudi Arabia, countries where desire was still defined by economies that could afford it.

Lurie went on, perhaps for my benefit, about how legitimate ivory importers were making contributions to some wildlife preservation fund or other, but by then I'd stopped listening. I spotted Virilio and his new smuggler pals on the dock looking over the spilled cargo. Suddenly I wanted to sit down very badly, but my body wouldn't move and when I tried to say something my mouth just opened and closed a few times, like that of a suffocating fish. Then my vision went black.

When my senses kicked back in, the first thing I was aware of was extreme heat, a new and intense round of fever, which my brain transformed into the sound of out-of-tune trumpets and the feeling of fiberglass and hot wax trying to burst through my skin from the inside. The air was thick and moist; the daily monsoon fell down heavily around us, so I knew it was probably afternoon. I lay stretched out in the back of some vehicle, a van or a panel truck. We were bouncing over a rough road. Through the windows I could see things in the trees, animals like baboons, but not quite, some New Amazonian freaks; they screamed at me, burning in a state of such genetically programmed fury that their teeth and eyes nearly glowed. They kept watch, and when one would see me in the van, it would call out to another animal up the road. Sometimes one would launch itself from the top of a coconut palm and land on the roof of the van with a hollow *bang* that would shake the whole vehicle. I could hear the baboons digging their claws under the edges of the metal roof, gnawing the rivets with their bright sharp teeth. Under other circumstances, I might have tried to run away, but I couldn't move (my body was locked into some kind of soft-shell paralysis), and I didn't want to move because I saw the recording tape again, hanging from the trees, billowing and streaming rain like the lianas. The angry creatures tore at the tapes, ripping to pieces those they could reach. I might have said something to that effect because Virilio's face swung into view. He looked stricken, as sick in his own way as I. He was watching his investment sweat himself to death. For some reason that struck me as very funny, and I managed a feeble, "Fuck you," before blanking out again.

I drifted through the same semiconscious state for

days. From time to time, I was able to pick out bits and pieces of my surroundings, but often found out later something that I'd taken for fact was nothing more than another hallucination. For at least one day, I thought I was back at Point Mariposa, or on a ship made of animal bones, sailing for Brazil. The truth didn't turn out to be much more comforting. Lurie had stashed Virilio and me at a site he had commandeered, an abandoned biological research station anchored high in the trees literally atop the upper jungle canopy. The station was essentially a huge inflated wagon wheel, with tough nylon netting between the spokes. Virilio and I were set up in a large geodesic mountain tent used to store camera equipment and cases of freeze-dried food.

It was days before there was any real break in the fever. It had been days since I'd taken out my glass eye, and the socket ached. When I was lucid, Virilio fed me freeze-dried Salisbury steak and mashed potatoes, which I promptly threw up. After that, we stuck to canned milk and miso soup. Invariably, after eating I felt stronger and would try to get up. Sometimes I made it; mostly, I didn't. I slept and dreamed through the endless rounds of fever and, the new addition, chills. Lurie came to check on me every day, dogged by the omnipresent camerawoman from NHK and her whirring Arriflex rig.

Sometimes I would swim up from a bad bout of fever and listen to Virilio hustling one of Lurie's film editors or lighting techs, offering them dope or travel permits or hard-to-come-by replacement parts for their equipment. More than once, the fever swept back over me in a black wave while I was listening. The network of nerves forming the imperfect matrix within which my brain took in sensory data would go off like a roman candle behind my eyes. The sound of voices became a roiling flow of viridian lava. My mouth would curdle at the sour tension of the Army cot against my back; I'd hear the musk of jungle rot, and feel undissolved knots of dried milk melting in the back of my throat like opals sinking through glycerin. The bifurcated edges of the city of light flickered in and out of time to the relentless chirrup of birds and insects in the trees. Then it would abruptly stop, like film running out of a projector, and I would sleep.

And then one morning I awoke and the fever was gone. My arms and legs were weak, and the inside of my head felt too big for the outside to contain, but the fever had lifted and I could think. I sat up on the cot. Virilio wasn't around, which only later did I realize was a lucky break. I got up and went to the tent entrance, remaining just inside, careful that none of Lurie's crew saw me. There I got my first good look at both the station and the jungle canopy.

Everything was different from above. The light and air were clean and boundless. I hadn't realized until then how the densely packed body of the jungle crushed everything below into a kind of claustrophobic stoop. From above, though, New Amazonia was a pleasant flood plain of treetops—dark greens, blacks and dusty browns, broken up by bursts of colors where flowers and quetzal birds had found their way up to the undiluted light. These were the winners, Darwin's championship team, and they looked it. Far off, I could just see the hard Euclidean silhouettes of buildings, evolution's losers, dim old ghosts stained as green as the jungle in the bright morning light.

There was little activity on the research station. A couple of tanned, shirtless techs were rewiring the small portable floodlights they used for night shoots. Some Indian refugees worked as laborers, pulling cable and humping food and supplies through the stifling heat of the jungle; wisely a number of them were asleep amidst the coils of cable and crates, as the hour reached midday.

I was wondering how they got up to the station

when a couple of young *mestizos* appeared over the far lip of the wagon wheel on a jury-rigged platform. There was a large winch anchored over their heads. The winch, which was fed by a small gas-powered generator, functioned as a sort of dumbwaiter, lifting both people and supplies from the ground, and bringing them down again. I watched the station through the afternoon. Electricians, camera operators, and Indian laborers came and went as they pleased. There didn't appear to be any security on the station or down below.

Later, when Virilio appeared on the dumbwaiter, I went back to the cot, lay down, and closed my eyes. He entered the tent a moment or two later, and stood over me until someone followed him in. When I heard the whirring of the movie camera, I knew it was Lurie and his shadow. The filmmaker asked how I was and Virilio grunted, saying, "Stick a fork in him and turn him over, he's done. I don't know if this boy's ever getting up again." Then it was Lurie's turn to grunt. He and Virilio started talking business. Apparently, Virilio had been renegotiating Lurie's deal with the smugglers, trying to get a better price for transporting their dope up north. The filmmaker and the kid tossed numbers back and forth, their low voices forming small, familiar, and oddly comforting spirals of color in my head. Lurie cut off the discussion abruptly with, "I have to get back to the shoot, but I'm going out this evening to check some locations." He asked if Virilio wanted to go with him. The kid said he would, and they went out, still batting percentages around, leaving me alone.

I found some crackers and a can of bland corned beef, and ate them while waiting for nightfall. At evening the sun appeared flattened against the western horizon, its light a buttery smear across the lower half of the sky. I found a box of T-shirts with NHK logos on them and put one on, throwing the sweat-stained rag I'd been wearing behind the cases of food. The sun was sunk in the treeline as if tangled in the densely packed branches. Looking east, the jungle canopy flared suddenly orange, and then sank into deep shadow. With the change of light, the sounds from below changed. The birdsongs stopped for a moment and, as if on cue, the tree frogs took up the call. Then the night birds started up, the shifting patterns of sound reforming the light in my head even as the light in the sky shifted.

The station buzzed with workers as the day's shooting wound down. I threw my jacket over my shoulder and stepped outside, picking up a coil of cable as I went. The cable I slipped over my shoulder, covering the jacket, and I made my way around the hub of the wagon wheel to the dumbwaiter. I had to walk slowly. Even after eating solid food, the floor seemed to shift under me with every step. The cable became very heavy very quickly.

I stood among a group of Indians who were waiting silently for the platform to return from the ground. None of the Indian laborers looked directly at me, and I wondered if I was committing some gross social faux pas, but none of them seemed visibly angry. And I wanted to ride with them. I figured that they, of all the people working at the set, would care the least about some ragged *estrangeiro* they'd never seen before.

The dumbwaiter creaked up and we all piled on, too many of us probably, because the platform swayed a bit and dropped more quickly than I'd expected. I grew dizzy as we were lowered, and I had to set the cable down, jostling several men's legs. I apologized and a few of them nodded, but none spoke to me. When we were on the ground, I hoisted the coil back onto my shoulder and tried to blend with the men as they made their way to a flatbed truck. I dropped the cable behind a mobile editing van (crimson and sapphire light bleeding from around the doors) and climbed onto the back of one of the flatbeds. In San Francisco these trucks were known as Indian Cadillacs, a particularly nasty reference to their role as transportation for a lot of the poorer refugees headed north. There had been some attempts to make the trucks comfortable—padded benches along the sides of the truck bed, an awning that could be hoisted during monsoons or to keep off the sun—but these feeble amenities didn't make the truck anything more than what it was, a way to ship cargo quickly and cheaply. I took a seat on the floor, up near the cab, keeping my head down and my face covered, feigning sleep until the truck's engine turned over and we headed for the highway.

The flatbed was overflowing with men, most of whom sat shoulder to shoulder, legs jammed against their neighbors' legs. No one touched me, however. The Indians gave me a wide berth, crowding themselves rather than risk coming into physical contact with me. Again, I felt no hostility or threat from the men, just a blank spot where I should be occupying space. I imagined that they regarded me in much the same way that we would regard someone on a bus carrying home live lobsters for dinner. We might note the presence of the lobsters, even sneak a look at them and marvel at their ugliness and to see if their claws were taped shut. Most of us, however, wouldn't feel any need to strike up a conversation with the lobster simply because it was on the bus and alive. I knew, as we headed inland, that *I* was the lobster on this bus.

The highway was a clear ribbon of gray at the bottom of a sea-green valley. I was surprised and happy to see that every third or fourth lightpole along the median seemed to be working. Amazonia had overgrown whatever structures paralleled the road, and spilled down the embankments. Even with the light, there were no landmarks that I could recognize. Someone, presumably the Army, had removed all the highway markers and overhead signs.

The air grew heavy and stagnant as we drove away from the ocean. Within an hour I spotted the first of the lagoons; a dull metal grating in the roadbed gave it away. I stood to get a better look, but the driver sped over it without slowing. No matter; we soon saw other gratings, each covering an ocean-filled fissure where Southern California's endless earthquake mambo had torn the land open. Anacondas and fishing birds, having grown accustomed to untraveled roads, slithered away or launched themselves into the air in surprise as our truck rumbled past the grating where they were waiting for their dinner.

We were travelling along a vaguely familar section of highway when the truck lurched suddenly to the right, nosing toward one of the unmarked exits. The ramp off the highway rose at a steep angle and intersected with a vine-choked overpass. The driver ground the truck's gears, downshifting so that we could take the grade. I rose from my little island of space and waded through the crowd of men to the back of the flatbed. As the truck came level with the overpass it almost stalled, its momentum barely keeping the wheels rolling. I waited until the truck had come almost to a stop, and then I jumped.

I landed hard, trying to roll away from the truck, almost jarring my glass eye right out of my head. When I looked back, the truck was just rounding the corner, picking up speed as the driver ground the gears into second. The Indians on the flatbed were looking at me with mild interest, but nothing more. As they drove away, I could just see their dark eyes glittering back at me in the darkness; they seemed to say, Who can account for the behavior of a lobster?

I got up slowly, put on my coat and started walking, favoring a sore ankle. I headed across the overpass, in the opposite direction of the truck. In the distance were lights whose colors persuaded me that I wasn't headed for an Army base. I assumed that I was somewhere in Los Angeles. I took a lithium out of my pocket and swallowed it dry. No more drinking, I thought. Besides, I'd lost my flask long ago, and the bottles were no longer in my pocket. Neither, I realized, was Frida's gun. I went back the ramp and poked through the undergrowth, just long enough to disturb a nesting tarantula. So much for armaments. . . .

I'd walked perhaps half a mile when I found a street sign beneath some loose lianas. I was standing near an Exxon station, half sunk into a swamp of ocean water and leaking petroleum products. The street sign read "Hollywood Blvd."

20. Elementary Catastrophes

Los Angeles had always seemed to me to be the ideal city, one whose borders were more a feature of mental geography than of physical limit. The Los Angeles of my memory could encompass anything. It was America, wallowing in the holy excesses that the entire country covertly wished for itself. It was an orchard in the middle of a desert, an entertainment skycity whose chief product was demographically constructed dog shit. A whorehouse that came on with all the tricks, and a fortress that locked you out. Yet, through all its idiocy, Los Angeles drew us to its secret heart.

How could it not?

By the end of the twentieth century, no one really believed that any good girl or boy could grow up to become president. But anyone might sell a screenplay. Or star in a movie. Or write a hit single. You heard the stories everywhere you went—the earnest waitress who signed a million-dollar contract for her first film. The ex-grease monkey whose band was opening for Springsteen at Wembley Stadium. The one-eyed synesthete whose first four albums went double platinum. Los Angeles had mythology the way the rest of the world had history.

If you played the game right in L.A., you didn't just get a Gold Card future, but you erased your past. The land and its inhabitants were one in this, tabula rasa. Plastic surgery was its sacrament, and you could change your life as easily as your face if you were talented enough, persistent enough, or lucky enough.

But the Hollywood I saw after jumping from the truck was something new and unknown to me. Hints of the old city were still there, jasmine and silk trees blooming in a knot of ferns, the cat piss smell of eucalyptus drifting down from Griffith Park. Tramping through the undergrowth I saw broken car phones and moldy publicity stills, a stringless Stratocaster, a strapless Gaultier gown, vials of melting Prozac and a twisted pair of Porsche mirrorshades; a pair of purple fishnet stockings were tangled in the razor wire topping a fence enclosing a vacant lot full of undelivered copies of the Hollywood Reporter and Daily Variety (now, slowly composting themselves into the asphalt).

The new Los Angeles seemed remarkably smaller, and somber; the most extroverted of cities had turned introspective. This was the sleeping face of L.A.—its dream face. Under its jungle coat, all the fantasies that the city had birthed, appropriated, conceived or destroyed moved raw and wild beneath the luminescent green canopy of the kapoks and palm trees. When it gave itself over to Amazonia, Los Angeles had found itself—a hermetic fusion of city and rainforest, half construct and half dream—as solid as the omnipresent HOLLYWOOD sign still visible in the hills, and as fragile as a dragonfly's wing.

Assuming that the highway I'd just left was 101, and that the lights in the distance were in central Hollywood, I turned left and walked along the edge of the swamp toward what was probably Sunset Boulevard. I needed time to think.

Clouds of mosquitoes and biting flies rose from the black water and attacked my face and hands. The sound of their wings enveloped me in burning light, and their assault was so painful and unrelenting that I ran down Sunset, tripping over plants and debris in the street, straight into a dense patch of jungle, black as oblivion. Any predators nearby must have cleared out, because I tore straight through the undergrowth, only stopping when I couldn't hear the mosquitoes' whine any more.

I hid in the dark until I'd caught my breath, and then headed toward Melrose, trying to put some distance between myself and the lights. The more I thought about them, the more they unnerved me. I wasn't ready to stroll into Hollywood, explain myself to anyone yet. I had no plan at all. And no real idea how to track Frida down, assuming that she was, in fact, here and that I hadn't hallucinated everything—the Spiritline and the city of light—on the trip from San Francisco.

I passed the old Hollywood cemetery, completely overgrown, a relic of a more naive age; a single white cherub extending into the air above the tangle of plants to mark the spot for future archaeologists. Ahead was the old Paramount lot. The studio's formidable white walls were stained with a Rorschach pattern of lichen and mildew. A few malfunctioning street lights flickered along the length of Melrose. I hung back in the shadows of the old buildings and the jungle, wondered where the power was coming from. It had become a game now, avoiding the light, something a kid might do. If I'd been six, I would have flapped my arms like bat wings and pretended that I was Bela Lugosi.

I wasn't headed anywhere in particular, I just had to keep moving, to get a feel for the city, and not let the enormity of coming here get to me. I wondered if I'd made a terrible mistake, chasing a mad woman to a dead city. How did I come to this John Wayne decision? I was sick, uncertain of where I was, and had no way to get back north with Frida—even if I could find her.

My head spun and my hands began to shake, more from anger than anything else. I kept moving along Melrose, digging through my coat pockets until I found the prescription bottles. My throat was dry and the lithium and Inderal went down hard. I couldn't stop shaking. At the corner of Melrose and Vine the ground opened up before me. Blood red lava light flooded the street. Frida, on the opposite side of the open pit, took one look and jumped. The ground squeezed shut around me like a mouth closing. The ground opened again. The light. Once more Frida jumped. And again.

I turned and walked away from the hallucination, into the darker streets of Hollywood, telling myself that I wasn't insane, that what I had seen was a side effect of the fever. All around me, I could feel the hungry eyes of the baboons. From the windows of empty buildings and the trees they were waiting for me to stumble, or for the fever to overtake me. I wouldn't let them have me. I'd come too far. No matter what happened, I wasn't going back to Point Mariposa, that much was certain. The sanitarium seemed like a million years ago, and the only reason I had thought of it was that I knew it wasn't suicidal to come to Los Angeles, it was merely foolish. There was an enormous difference. I reminded myself of that repeatedly as I walked. I might have even said the words out loud to the baboons. If I did, however, I received no reply.

I awoke with a start, my legs cramped, neck stiff. The sun was up and the morning mist was lifting from the city. I felt an oddly familiar sensation, like waking from a dream to find yourself in the place you'd just dreamed about. After a moment, though, it came to me. New-city anxiety. It was a condition that happened a lot on the road. You wake up, drugged and jet-lagged, and look out the hotel window. Nothing. No recognition at all. You could be looking at London or Bangkok or Jersey City. Then new-city anxiety kicks in and any excitement about being someplace new dissolves as you anticipate the tedium of negotiating breakfast, taxis, and laundry in a language you can't speak, with currency you can't count. I thought I'd escaped all this nonsense when I'd died. Yet, here I was, feeling exactly the same combination of boredom and tension that had dogged the band around the world. Just when I thought I'd left everything behind, there's all this baggage I see I've been dragging around with me. No wonder I was so tired.

Both of my feet were asleep, shoved at odd angles under the pedals of the old Mustang convertible in which I'd fallen asleep. So much for paranoia keeping you alert. At least by surviving in the open I'd proven that the animals in the trees weren't real, and that the city wasn't nearly as malevolent as it had seemed through the fog of fever that had addled me when I entered the place. Knowing that might help when the animals reappeared or when the ground decided to open up again.

Stepping clumsily from the Mustang, I stamped my feet, trying to get some circulation going, and massaged a knot of twisted muscles at the base of my neck. I must have wandered after the unsettling apparition of Frida the night before. I dug through a mass of vines and found a street sign. I was still on Melrose, though a good mile from my last memory.

I took a right at the next corner, Fairfax, and headed back to Sunset. I had to admit that I couldn't find Frida on my own. And anonymity was a luxury I could no longer afford. Still, I didn't relish the idea of walking up to strangers and introducing myself, "Hi, I'm Elvis, back from the dead. Have you seen a friend of mine, about five seven, dyed-black hair, a nose ring, insane?" I needed help from the right kind of people, the kind that would understand without a lot of silly questions. The doorman at the Whiskey A Go Go, what was his name? He seemed to know everybody and everything happening in town. And one of the bartenders at the Roxy. I couldn't remember his name either. Someone had to be around, though, I'd seen Hollywood lit up from the freeway.

I was surprised by the number of people I saw in the streets. Indians, mostly, although I had to duck behind parked cars a couple of times to avoid Army patrols. Some of the tribes had set up camps in parking lots and jewelry stores, cooking wild pig over fires fed with twigs and Presto logs, and fishing with their oversized bows and arrows in the fissures that cut through the streets at irregular intervals.

The tribes in L.A. looked hardcore. They hadn't returned to the old ways; they were deep forest types who had eluded the U.N., the social workers and the trucks full of soldiers. Probably, they'd come north following the animals as the freak jungle squeezed them out of their hunting grounds. They were nomads now, but they seemed to be coping. Some of the younger children laughed when they saw me. The men nodded or said a few words when they realized that I was just passing through. Many of the adults sported thorns more or less permanently affixed around their nose and upper lips, marking them as one of the cat-worshipping tribes. A group of women were singing a rhythmic work song as they dug manioc from the floor of a video arcade. I watched them for a moment, wishing that I could understand the words, and perhaps speak their language. I might be able to ask them if it was the animals or the Spiritline they were following, and if there was some way that I could see it, too. Mostly, though, I seemed to be a source of amusement whenever I stopped, so I kept moving.

There are many different ways of being wrong, I'd learned. The two most common are to Fuck Up (as in, to make an honest mistake); the other is to be Clueless. Walking down Sunset Boulevard, it was clear that I had entered a state of sublime cluelessness.

The clubs, both the Whiskey A Go Go and the Roxy, were about where I remembered them—situated within a block of each other on the Strip. But the Strip itself was hardly there, sunk beneath a deep green wall of vegetation. Even in the middle of Sunset, the undergrowth made the road almost impassable. The Strip must have been one of the parts of the city allowed to go native. Of course, the local authorities would want to close down the clubs first. It was perfect L.A. cop siege mentality. Cut the riffraff off from their places to drink and congregate. It also occurred to me that the Strip might have simply collapsed under its own weight. How many people are going to be willing to stand in line for a Def Lepard reunion during an Army evacuation?

Still, I couldn't just walk away. Tearing my coat on thorn-covered palm trees, and my hands on razor grass, I dug through the undergrowth to the doors of the Whiskey. They were chained and padlocked shut, crusted over with lichen and grime. It might have been a century or more since the place had last opened. I dug my way back out feeling angry and foolish, as if someone had played a joke on me.

I found two undamaged cans of minestrone soup in a little grocery at the edge of a strip mall further down Sunset. There wasn't much left inside the store. Food wrappers; broken bottles; the muddy hump of a termite mound. Like the theater in Paso Robles, even the lights and the cash register had been torn out. I had to open the soup by beating the cans against a jagged spur of concrete over one of the fissures that scarred Sunset.

There were more of the ocean-filled cracks than I'd first imagined. Some seemed to go on for miles, snaking their way in from the Pacific or down from Laurel Canyon, cutting the city into an urban archipelago, each concrete island connected to the others by the streets that so far had remained tectonically sound. Decades before, some local developer had dug canals out by the beach and called the area Venice; now the city was slowly transforming itself into a real Venice, only it got the setting wrong by a million years or so. If it hadn't been for the vicious clouds of mosquitoes and black flies, the place might have been beautiful.

The strangest features of the landscape by far were the coral islands. The man-made corals were a byproduct of an early Army plan to handle the "refugee question." When the first waves of dazed refugees had arrived in L.A., the Army began a massive building campaign. The presence of the jungle, however, made it difficult and expensive to truck in building supplies from elsewhere, and there weren't enough locally. Some Army engineer then hit on the idea of "growing" temporary housing in the ocean. It had been done before on a small scale; here was a chance to try it big. Using banks of solar panels, they passed a small electrical charge through heavy wire mesh and lowered it into sea water. Free-floating microorganisms attracted to the charged wire accumulated there and died, forming a compact, rock-like structure. At first the engineers just made floors and walls with the sea water method, cementing the final shelters together. But when they got the hang of the process, they found that they could accrete entire buildings straight out of the ocean. As parts of L.A. started sinking, someone had the bright idea to accrete islands in the levelled areas, and use those newly cleared sites for inland shelters. Like most of the military and civil plans, however, the building project had been abandoned when the pull-out orders came. The accreted shelters, though, remained.

They looked like brutal collaborations between Gaudi and Max Ernst at his most biomorphically primitive. Coral towers caught the light like some of Yves Tanguy's organic beach scenes. The most interesting shelters were the ones that had been forgotten, rather than abandoned. Near Cahuenga stood a coral island whose builder must have neglected to pull the plug. A relatively normal cubicle shelter rested atop a slow motion explosion of accreted coral five or six stories tall. The base had engulfed not only the buildings on either side, but the nearby jungle as well. The coral was the first thing I'd seen that could keep Amazonia at bay, and if this shelter was still getting power (which was entirely possible) the coral tumor would still be growing, and would continue to grow until the power died or the whole thing sank into the Pacific. The other possibility was that it might continue to grow until it covered all of L.A. with the bones of a billion billion microscopic animals. There was something appealing about that. Los Angeles might rewrite its own history, passing from a desert era to concrete to jungle, and finally, to end its days as a cemetery for desiccated marine organisms. Virilio would probably like the idea—it had the apocalyptic tone of the little speech he had given me about the *Santeros* back at Cafe Juju.

Finding myself back near Vine, I turned north and walked to the Capitol Records building, which, even surrounded by jungle, still looked like an oversized stack of plastic motel ashtrays. Inside, it was dead as the Strip. I wasn't going to find any old acquaintances here. The place, though, had a kind of magnetic attraction for me that I couldn't deny. I was like some junkies I'd known; once they kicked, they never used again, but they still hung around dope and other users. The people, the scene—it just felt right. I'd spent years of my life in buildings like this. Pretending that I could just walk away with no regrets had been my first mistake, I realized.

Industrious looters had used a dead potted plant to prop open a fire door on the far side of the lobby. I started up the stairs quietly, listening. When I was satisfied that there was no one above me, I went up at a normal pace. The first few floors were like the lobby—dead, stripped bare. Some of the corridors leading to individual offices were blocked by rolls of carpet that someone had begun pulling up and then discarded. The middle floors contained recording studios and most of them, too, had been cleaned out. On the sixth floor, though, I found some offices that were relatively intact. Above that was a floor with three recording studios that had been dismantled in only the most perfunctory manner. A quick tour of the area told me that by cannibalising all the studios, it would be possible to put together one very tasty recording situation.

I was thinking this over in the control room of the last, and most intact, studio when something on my blind side brushed my hand. I spun around. There was an eviscerated couch against the far wall, facing the mixing console. Two black eyes regarded me steadily from the back of the couch, while smaller things squirmed in padding torn from the cushions. Another step, and a little light from the corridor brightened the room.

On the back of the sofa sat a reddish-brown tamarin, a Brazilian primate, about the size of a well-fed squirrel. The tamarin looked at me steadily, showing its teeth and making annoyed chirping noises. It must have been a female, and a mother, too, because the squirming things in the sofa cushions looked like a couple of nearly naked tamarin babies. I backed out of the control room and into the hall, letting my gaze play over the blank spots where acoustical tiles had fallen or been pulled from the ceiling. From each black spot, dark eyes watched me. I held up my hand towards one set of eyes and saw a cautious tamarin face emerge from the shadows to sniff my fingertips, then quickly disappear. My ears, attuned to the mother tamarin's chirp, now picked up other similar sounds from the ceiling and the other studios. The light from the chirping was like a rotating chain of cobalt-blue doedecahedrons. I went back to the stairs, trying to imagine what I'd do with the tamarins if I decided to get one of the studios working. If I had a working recorder, I could sample them for Frida. I imagined myself setting up rabbit traps all over L.A., baiting each one with a few feet of recording tape or sampler disks. That would bring her to me. . . .

One more floor up, I found a chain of executive offices. Letterhead, Fed Ex envelopes, and royalty statements lay scattered through the offices and corridors. In some of the offices, humidity had buckled the wood paneling away from the wall. I looked out of a sealed and thermally tinted window over Vine Street, back toward Hollywood. The jungle canopy obscured most of the city, fanning out in all directions, some of the trees reaching and even growing past the window. Still, I had a decent view of the street directly below, and spotted a half-dozen tribesmen lugging home a dead capibara, tethered to a pole resting on their shoulders. A second or two after they'd passed, a woman skated into the street, turned a lazy circle, and rolled into a record shop on the corner.

Three floors down and sprinting, I lost my footing and slammed into a wall, cursing my clumsiness, until I realized that the whole building was shaking. Dust sifted down from the ceiling. The earthquake had the staircase rattling and wheezing like a slow metallic squeeze box. Abruptly, the shaking stopped. The building rocked for a second or two more and grew still. I got back on my feet and ran the rest of the way to the lobby, out the double doors and into the street.

I didn't see anyone inside the record store. Not surprisingly, the sales bins were mostly empty. Coming down Fairfax earlier, I'd noticed a few of the senior Indian men had CDs shining atop their formal lip plugs. Near the dirty cut-out bins in the back of the place I noticed a familiar silhouette. Approaching it, I saw that it was my own. It was a life-sized holographic cutout, a promotional item from my last album. I had my arms crossed, shades perched on the end of my nose, over which you could just see my eyes. I had to laugh at the thing, hardly recognizing myself, feeling only the faintest connection with the mildewed clown in the Armani jacket. Touching my own face, I was surprised, though, at how thin I'd become, how wild my beard had grown. I didn't even have the same name anymore. This was a common situation, I recalled. In nonlinear systems, turbulent flows collided with other flows created by earlier generations of its own movement. Neither state was superior, and neither, ultimately, stable. They often met at the point of a phase change in one or the other. The unsettling aspect to a phase change was that it was practically impossible to tell what was going to change, or how. Some previous state might reassert itself, or something new might develop, wiping away all traces of previous states. It was like betting on a horse race, knowing that your horse not only might not finish the race, but might be an albatross by the time it crossed the finish line.

While I was still contemplating my die-cut twin, the skater darted past the store window, blowing down Vine. I took off after her, but she was very fast. I couldn't get close enough to see if it really was Frida. It had to be, I thought. But then why was she running from me?

The woman cut to the right at the next intersection and I followed, a bit too fast, it turned out. The street narrowed to a sliver just past the corner. The rest was an open fissure of warm water, alive with mosquito larvae and snakes. I barely made it out without becoming a notch on some water moccasin's gun.

I staggered back to Vine, sick, out of breath, and disgusted with myself. Even that little effort left my hands and legs shaking. I took a lithium and shook the bottle. Only a few left. I couldn't go on like this. I could chase Frida or phantom Fridas forever, like some demented butterfly hunter. I rose shakily to my feet and found my reflection in the record store window. Wet, starving, and filthy. My alter ego was leaning cockeyed back against the empty racks. I had run out of options, but I knew what to do.

In a phone booth, I tore a rotting page from the Yellow Pages, and walked to an address on Sunset. As I suspected, the looters and the soldiers had only performed a cursory hit-and-run on the tuxedo shop. I dug through the racks until I found a silk tux (a decent Armani knockoff, in fact) that didn't stink badly of mildew; then a shirt, tie, and some shoes. I washed myself off in a sink in the back, combing my hair for the first time in weeks, and shearing back my beard with a pair of millinery scissors. When I checked myself in a mirror, I was starting to look and feel like a human again. I stacked up bolts of wool and crushed velvet, and made a cot in the back. Before I settled down for a nap, I carefully laid out the tux beside me, so that I could dress in the dark. Then, stretching out on my makeshift bed, I slept until nightfall. It was time to look up Nikki.

21. Irrational Numbers

Los Angeles, at least around central Hollywood, was a very different place at night. Bars and shops that had appeared dead in the morning were doing steady business after the sun went down and the temperature dropped. Hollywood Boulevard held a mixed crowd of soldiers and prostitutes, street vendors and show business hangers-on. Walking west, I noticed a subtle hierarchy developing. Most of the Army personnel, exhausted prostitutes in too-tight dresses, old men selling fruit and *milagros,* were packed around a few bars between Vine and Cahuenga, while the carefully coiffed and more prosperous-looking types were headed for the brighter lights down by La Brea. I fell in with this latter crowd. I knew that Nikki, if she were here, wouldn't be seen anywhere but the best club in town. It didn't occur to me, however, that she'd be running it.

The club was situated on one of the coral islands, in a converted multistory shelter that must have been some engineer's pride and joy. The approach to the club was long and dramatic. The walkway cut through a bamboo grove (no doubt transplanted just for the effect; I should have seen Nikki's hand in that). When the wind came down from the hills the trunks of the bamboos thumped out a hollow gamelan above us, while their leaves hissed like static on a phone line. The effect was genuinely beautiful, giving off a soft amber light in my head. On the island, the walkway ended abruptly in a false beach made of crushed shells and bleached animal bones. I was all admiration for the work involved. It was like some demented piece of folk art. When I looked up and saw the neon flashing above the club's entrance, however, my knees felt so cold and watery that I had to lean against one of the large bamboos to hold myself up.

I swallowed a lithium and an Inderal. All evening, and during my dreams in the afternoon, I had wondered how Nikki would react when she saw me. Now I knew. The gracefully curved neon above the club said it all: KAMIKAZE L'AMOUR.

How long ago was it? A year ago? When I abandoned my last album, it was supposed to be called *Kamikaze L'Amour.* It had been dedicated to Nikki. The name was a joke, really. A millennial version of André Breton's ideal, *L'Amour Fou.* Mad Love. Total love. Nikki was going to produce the band's world tour, plus a full-scale stage show around the album. But it never happened. I couldn't finish it. I dreamed I was a machine and that my room was full of animals. The baboons had been hovering in the shadows, even then.

Nikki had always been way ahead of me. As much as I wanted to turn around and walk away, I couldn't. Nikki had known that when she built the place. The only way I would ever see the sign was when I had no defenses left, and couldn't walk away. Virilio would be sorry that he'd missed his chance to walk me through the bamboo to Nikki's sign. He'd be laughing at me now; instead he was probably out slogging through the swamps in Santa Monica. That, at least, was some consolation.

There was a bouncer stationed at the door. I blew right past him, affecting the look and walk of the Heavily Connected. Inside the bar the air felt strangely brittle and weirdly cool. I'd grown unaccustomed to air conditioning in the last few weeks. The club was crowded, surprisingly so. I hadn't imagined L.A. capable of sustaining such a high-priced mob. The air reeked of expensive tobaccos and marijuana, perfumes and colognes I hadn't smelled in months. They seemed terribly exotic after all this time. I recognized a German film director and a record producer's concubine from the old days. There was a definite Alice-Through-the-Looking-Glass feel to the place, as if I'd stepped through some time/space anomaly and been transported back to some early-nineties scene-makers' party in Soho. I was under siege by acres of Italian suits, perfect teeth, and store-bought breasts.

Around the walls of the club was a kind of pop-star shrine. Bright trinkets behind high-impact plastic. A Maoist suit worn by Bowie when he'd headlined the first Saigon Pop Festival. One of Slash's top hats, with a hole in the brim—the result of an unsuccessful assassination attempt. Henry Rollins's weight bench, and one of Kim Gordon's basses. Near Iggy Pop's horse-tail belt was an oversized shot of me, and the leather jacket I'd worn when I played a drug dealer in my one tiny movie role. I hadn't exactly been a success in the cinema. Having spent so long learning to play different versions of myself, I simply couldn't summon up the skills or courage to be someone else.

Leaving the little museum behind, I pressed my way to the bar. On the way, I noticed that the place was turning over a lot of drinks and food. I wondered if Nikki had cut some kind of importation deal with the Army, or if she was in bed with the smugglers, like Lurie. Either way it was a good sign. It meant that she'd already carved herself a piece of local power, which is exactly what I was counting on.

Nikki had done nothing to disguise the origins of the club. The walls were bare coral, and where refugees had left animal drawings or gangs had tagged the place, nothing had been touched. The bar itself was disturbingly familiar. She must have pulled it out of the old Maya Club or some other pre-Amazon chic spot and installed it here. I ordered a vodka tonic. My palms had turned clammy, but I couldn't tell if it was fever or just nerves. When the bartender returned with the drink I said, "I need to speak to Ms. Price."

The bartender nodded solemnly, but didn't make any move to call her. He was a big guy, almost as wide as he was tall. Samoan, perhaps. His shiny black hair combed tight across his scalp. "Who are you?" he asked.

"Just tell her Elvis is back from the dead, and he'd like to buy her a corndog."

The bartender's face changed over the next few seconds. I couldn't tell if he was going to hammer me or make the call. Suddenly, he brightened, looking about six years old. "Hey, I know you," he said, and extended his hand over the bar. We shook. "On TV they said you'd gone Muslim. Ran off to Iran or Iraq like that fucking folksinger, what's his name?"

"Cat Stevens?"

"Yeah. Asshole."

I gave him my best talk-show smile. "The Mullah thing didn't work out. The hours are too long and I've got this trick knee. Nasty for praying."

The bartender nodded. "Cool." He picked up a phone by the cash register, punched in a few numbers, and started talking. I sipped my vodka, letting it burn the cracks in my lips. A moment later, the bartender came back and said, "You're supposed to wait here. Someone'll be down for you in a minute." Thankfully, before he could re-engage me in conversation, he was called away to make flaming something-or-others for a group of young-looking Japanese girls in matching school uniforms. Hookers, I thought, turning to look for familiar faces in the crowd.

There were some television writers and a comic I'd

known vaguely through Nikki's lawyer. They were whooping it up in the corner, drunk and looking like they'd just closed a big deal. Still, there was something wrong with them. In fact, the whole room was off, dizzy with something far more corrupt than drugs. There was a shrillness in the voices. The laughter seemed to explode and die too quickly, and the sound had a hard, hysterical edge. For all their high-gloss beauty, beneath the smoke and body oils, the club mob smelled bad. Their breath, their skin, and their sweat carried the barbed metal reek of disease. The evidence was on their faces. Some covered it with makeup or a veil, but you couldn't miss the spray of scarlet rash across a cheek, the yellow, jaundiced eyes. They were dying, their immune systems succumbing to any and all of the millions of infections Amazonia offered.

"Excuse me, sir," said a small woman at my elbow. I hadn't seen her approach but knew by the coal-colored Yohji Yamamoto dress that she had to work for Nikki. "Would you come with me, please?" I followed the woman through the crowd. She was dark-skinned, and deeply beautiful, with obsidian-black hair pulled back from her face in a long French braid. I wondered if she might be at least part Indian. It would be a perfect Nikki gesture to have an Indian secretary out here. The woman led me to the far wall where a couple of men, large and imposing enough to be first cousins of the bartender, flanked a metal door. Nikki's secretary pressed a coded card into a slot in the wall, and the door slid open. It was a small, private elevator. The woman motioned for me to come inside, and pressed the Up button (there were only two buttons on the panel, the other being Down). The door closed, but there was no sensation of movement whatsoever. We stood there, and when the doors opened to reveal a tidy business office, I had the sensation that I'd just taken part in someone else's magic trick.

"Please wait here for a moment," said the secretary as she disappeared down a short hall.

Alone, the utter weirdness of this clean and perfect room in the middle of the jungle overwhelmed me. My gold and platinum records were hung at intervals along the walls. In the corner, a built-in Trinitron video-wall silently played CNN. On an antique table nearby were joysticks, goggles, and gloves for total-immersion video games. A fax machine in the corner purred out sales figures from a Dutch music distributor. I couldn't read the copy, but I did find my name. The secretary's chair felt like leather, and the cigarettes on her desk were Mirs (a gold-embossed rendering of a Russian space station on the box), a pricey Eurotrash import. Across the room, beneath a spray of hanging orchids, was an expensive Korean negative-ion generator. No bad vibes around here.

I couldn't help thinking that the room was like what Noah's Ark would have held, had Nikki been in charge of gathering a cross-section of the best and brightest. Being this close to the objects, big-ticket connections to my past, affected me more than I was prepared for. My hands drifted instinctively to the video game gear, my gaze to the stock market numbers gliding along the bottom edge of the satellite news. Above, a handsome middle-aged reporter was doing a standup on Broadway and Forty-Second Street. My desire was boundless, curling itself into a knot of pain in the center of my chest. I craved all of it, the objects and the place, and the radiant, frictionless life at which they hinted.

The secretary reappeared from around the corner. "Ms. Price will see you now," she said, and sat back behind her desk. I carefully set the video game gloves back where I had found them, and walked down the corridor from which Nikki's secretary had emerged. There was a single door at the far end. Touching the door's surface, I could feel coolness radiating through the wood, and Nikki's office—The Abattoir—high above Manhattan. "Come in," she said, as though reading my mind. I opened the door.

I just stood there looking at her, my heart racing and my head full of every kind of shit: anger, lust, fear, love. . . . Her skin was paler than I remembered, like milk whitewashing the supple bones of her face. Her jacket, a short sea-green Gaultier number, had oversized lapels and a collar that framed her face. It made her look like a heroic piece of Bauhaus sculpture, something to be worshipped or overthrown. As I closed the door and went to where she sat—collapsing the immense gulf between us into a few simple steps— she stood up from her swivel chair and kissed me on the cheek. She smelled of the floral shampoo she'd always used, and Japanese sandalwood soap.

"It's the boy himself," she said softly. "You don't look so bad, all things considered. What do we call you these days?"

I shrugged. "Ryder's fine. Or whatever Virilio calls me when he reports in."

"He calls you a variety of things," said Nikki. She led me to a dark Shaker chair, then perched on the corner of her desk. "It depends on what you've said to him recently, whether you've hurt his feelings."

"Virilio's a machine, a wind-up hustling toy. I piss him off because his schtick is so old, I can spot where he's going before he makes a move."

Nikki shook her head. "You've got him all wrong. He worships you. I'm not even paying him to be your babysitter."

"Oh, Nikki, what did you promise him?"

"I'm his manager, didn't he tell you?"

Of course. "Does he have any talent at all?"

"Not in music," she said flatly. "But I'll get him a contract anyway, let him open for some other bands I'm working with back East. He'll make a wonderful dog act." I hadn't heard *dog act* in a long time. It was what promoters called the second-rate local bands they booked to make headliners look better.

"And in a year, the record company will drop his contract," I said. "Then he'll be back on the street. I wouldn't want him to know where *I* worked when that happens."

Nikki laughed and picked up a joss stick that was burning in an ashtray on her desk, waved it in the air between us. "God, you don't know anything about people." She set the stick down again. "Virilio is a cursed figure. He's cursed with hope. I'll let him keep working for me. And as long as he's close to the business, gets to see it and touch it, as long as he can hold out some shred of hope of becoming you some day, he'll be a good boy. You watch him." She was right of course. Nikki was always right about these things. I'd seen her induce grown men to fall for her or pee in their pants with just her voice or the movement of her head. It was her greatest gift.

"It's good to see you, boy-o," she said, and ran one of her Donna Karan pumps up the inside of my leg, close to my crotch. Her skin was the stuff of Celtic wet-dreams. My head was full of fever, and shit still swirled behind my eyes. Anger. Lust. She was wearing a short, beaded Ralph Lauren skirt. My body bent without my willing it to, and I kissed her calf. Love. Fear.

I kept my head forward, directly in a stream of frigid air from a wall vent. Nikki's smell and the objects in her office were all from our place in Manhattan, heavy with history—souvenirs of another life lived in other places, far, far away. A *thanka* framed in glass. One of my old Stratocasters. A photo of me as a teenager standing next to Roy Orbison. The walls vibrated with the past, with objects carefully constructed to form a kind of time machine, a neural trap intended to lead me back to what and where I was before I tried to snuff myself. I leaned back in the hard chair looking for neutral ground. "It looks like you're out here more or less permanently now."

She withdrew her foot. "More or less permanently. It depends on how some things work out."

"What kind of things?"

"Things. Business. Opportunities. Did you know that you have number-one records in both France and Russia?"

I shook my head, letting her comment pass. "Back in San Francisco, did you have anyone besides Virilio tailing me?"

"Why would I do that?" She slid off the desk and took a bottle of Pelligrino water from a small refrigerator behind her desk.

"I'm thinking of a tag team. A skinhead and a cowboy. Sound familiar?"

"No. Could they be friends of Virilio's?"

"I doubt it. They stole some tapes from my apartment and a friend's. The two of them had this very terminal air about them. Like maybe they wouldn't have minded breaking some of my bones."

Nikki poured water into two cut crystal glasses she retrieved from a desk drawer. I'd given them to her on a trip to Switzerland. Subtle torture. "Then you know it wasn't me," she said. "Whatever problems we've had, you know I could never hurt you."

That wasn't strictly true. There had been several stoned nights toward the end when we'd laid into each other with fists and feet. Nikki's blood didn't clot well, so afterwards we'd have to drive to the emergency room in her Jag, and pay off ER staffers, security guards, interns—anybody with a hand out—to keep such a low-rent scandal out of the tabloids. The next day, the seats of Nikki's car would be sticky with blood. She finally got so tired of replacing seat covers that she sold the Jag, with the remains of our last bout still in place.

The volume of the music in the club jumped a notch. Even though the room was soundproofed, the bass still made the floor vibrate. "Where do you get your power for all this?" I asked, gesturing to take in both the club and her office.

"Long Beach," she said. "They have a cluster of decommissioned nuclear subs parked in the harbor. The Army ran powerlines all the way into town. It's their contribution to keeping the city open."

"I got the impression that the government had pretty much given up on sunny California."

"Power never gives up power. Or territory. Los Angeles will always be on the menu." Nikki went back behind the desk and sat down. "You're sweating, dear. Are you sick? A little bird told me that you've become quite the hypochondriac."

"I'm fine, mostly. A little worn out. Might have a touch of malaria, too," I said. It was a cheap ploy. Nikki had always been a sucker for sick animals. "It's kind of glamorous, if you think about it. Very literary. Very Joseph Conrad."

Nikki picked up a sky-blue pack of Sherman Slims. "But Mr. Conrad retired from the sea. He knew when it was time to come in out of the rain." Nikki fumbled with the top of the cigarette pack and finally pulled one out, with uncharacteristic clumsiness. I was about to say something smart when I got a good look at the bandages on her hands. Both thumbs and many of her fingers were mummified beneath flesh-colored elastic wrappings. Her jacket hid most of the bandages, but I could see that they extended further up her arms. A moment later, Nikki noticed me noticing.

She popped the long, thin Sherman in the corner of her mouth and held up her hands. "You know me. Malaria's just so de rigueur these days," she said lightly. Her hands had jolted me out of the orbit of my own need for the moment. That Nikki could really be sick, could perhaps die, had been unimaginable to me.

In my memory, she lived at too large a scale to be trapped by something as prosaic as germs or death. Beneath her makeup, however, I could see just how tired she was, how the kohl she used around her eyes was partly to hide dark patches of exhaustion. She lit the cigarette and took a deep drag. "It's called filariasis. Like yours, my little problem comes from a damned mosquito bite. Only my mosquito had a tiny worm in her system, and when she bit me, she passed it on. The worm had lots of baby worms in my bloodstream. They've moved into my lymph nodes now. Clogged them up good." She set the cigarette in an ashtray and looked at the backs of her hands. "I had such beautiful hands. Remember? Now my circulation is like some third-world sewer system." She flexed her fingers, regarding her hands like some alien growth. "The swelling gets so bad sometimes my arms start looking comical. The Pillsbury Dough Girl."

"Jesus, Nikki, why aren't you in a hospital?"

"Been there. Done that. Now I get drugs from the local Army quacks. They want me to go back to New York for surgery, but I know their games. It's their way of getting rid of me."

"I don't understand."

"What's that old saying, 'To a hammer, everything looks like a nail'? To the Army, the world is just a lot of coordinates for a potential combat zone," she said. "They resent the handful of us who want to see Los Angeles back in the world again." Nikki dropped her cigarette in the ashtray, came around the desk and kissed me hard, biting my lower lip as she pulled away. She leaned back against the desk. "Listen, Washington is giving what amounts to unlimited salvage rights to anyone who can reclaim and maintain urban area lost to the rainforest. Do you know what that means? When the big media houses, the record companies, the movie and cable outfits pulled out, they left a lot of facilities behind. Soundstages, broadcast studios, film labs, satellite uplinks. It's all free for the taking. It would be like digging old Hollywood—like Angkor Wat—from out of the jungle. And we could do it together. Own it all. Run it all." Nikki was off now, the exhaustion fading from her face, into one of her Deep Money riffs. She was inspired at these moments, evangelical almost, and the adrenaline glow that lit her made her look more like the old Nikki that I remembered. "And that's just the beginning. L.A. is—was—the entertainment center of the world, right? In a bigger sense, though, entertainment wasn't just the product produced here, it was the place itself. Do you know where you are? The Seven Cities of Cibola. El Dorado.

"Everyone wants to see Amazonia. Europe, Australia, even New York, whenever I talk to them they want to hear about life on the wild frontier. We can bring it to them."

I shifted on my chair, trying to get a bit of comfort where there wasn't any. "Picture this," Nikki continued. "Los Angeles as the greatest amusement-park ride of all time. We can give people all the exotica of the Amazon from the safety of the city. We have the hotels, the roads, all the basic infrastructure we need to carve a grown-up Disneyland from this disaster area. It can be our baby. I already have investment offers lined up from both Japan and Singapore."

"Nikki, this is fascinating. What does it have to do with me?"

She leaned forward, bracing herself on my legs. "It's all about you and your comeback." It was the old Nikki, all right. Fear. Anger. Shit.

"No . . . ," I said.

"Don't 'No' me, boy-o. I know the inside of your head better than anybody, certainly better than you. You needed a little vacation. An adventure. Fine. Now it's time to sit at the big table with the grown-ups and get back to work."

"No way, Nikki."

"Your whole catalog is back on the charts. Brazil wants you. Asia and Australia are desperate for you. You always wanted to play Eastern Europe—Prague, Moscow, Saint Petersburg—now's the time. I can have you on stage in Wembley Stadium or even Beijing in six weeks." I didn't say anything. I couldn't. Nikki got up and went back behind the desk, straightening her suit. She looked focused, but a little unsteady. The sales rant had taken a toll on her.

"You're a musician, Ryder. A star. You think you're going to be happy playing Tarzan games forever? We have our roles in this life. You make music. I arrange for people to hear it, and for you get enough of a return so that you can eat, have somewhere to sleep, and play dead when you want to. Is that such a bad life?"

"Virilio said something like that to me. Only he called me a junkie. Said that I needed all this." I waved at her office.

Nikki nodded. "Virilio's right sometimes."

I held the cool glass of Pelligrino water to my forehead. "It's not like that, though. Too much has happened. I'm not the same person I was when I left Point Mariposa."

"Okay, we can work with that," Nikki said. She took some pills from her desk and downed them with water, following them up with two quick snorts of white powder. She offered me some. "Smack," she said. "Almost pure. It'll help your fever." I declined and she put the heroin away. "We can come up with a whole new look and approach for you. Prince changed his name and made it work."

I shook my head. "Not interested."

Nikki looked at me hard, at the same time starting to nod into the smack. She grimaced a little. It occurred to me that she might have been going through the whole meeting while in great pain. "You're such a fucking child. Why did you come here? What do you want from me?"

"I need your help."

"You always do." She picked up her cigarette and puffed. "Tell Mommy how she can make it all better."

"I need to find a friend. She might be sick or in trouble."

Nikki smiled vaguely at that. "Right, your little girl from San Francisco. First you lose me, then your career, and now her. You can't keep hold of anything, can you?"

"I need your contacts, Nikki. I don't know anyone here anymore."

"Virilio told me about her. You don't need that bitch," Nikki said. "What you need is a gig. You need to finish *Kamikaze L'Amour.*"

"Fuck you, Nikki."

"Is that all you have to say? How can I make a deal with that?"

"A deal? What kind of terms?"

"I want your soul," Nikki replied in a goofy Bela Lugosi voice. "No, really, you have to finish the album. We'll use your comeback to kick off an international investment campaign." She went on for several minutes, laying out a whole bankroll scheme with interest point-shaving, banks in Liechtenstein and the Bahamas and tricky tax shelter setups to obscure our cash flow. When she finished, she sighed at the thoroughness of her vision.

The junk had a good grip on her now, playing God-knows-what kind of games in her head as it mixed with the other dope I'd seen her take. The junk did something else, too. It relaxed her enough that Nikki's real face emerged from behind the carefully constructed business mask she wore while negotiating. When I looked into her watery gray eyes, there was a hard and genuine hatred there. I knew right then that I'd been utterly deluded in coming to see her. Whatever she said from then on, whatever deal we made, there would be no help from her. Unsure how to play it, I agreed to everything. The album. The tour. Playing point man for her investors. "I'm yours," I said. "You own me."

"Damned right," she said, and leaned back in her chair. When she drew her right arm up from behind the desk, she was holding an automatic pistol in her hand. I froze, my eyes locked on the gun. But Nikki settled back in her chair, her eyes closed, the gun held loosely in her lap.

I stood slowly and went around the desk. Gently, I took the gun from her hand and put it back in the open drawer that also held her pills. I checked the labels on some of the bottles. Dilaudid. Nembutal. MDMA. Desoxyn. Only one of the dozen or so bottles seemed to have been prescribed for the *filariasis*. I took a couple of the bottles not related to her infection.

Nikki was drifting, nodding in the junk interzone between consciousness and sleep. Her lips moved, and as I leaned down to listen, I realized that she was going through her sales pitch again. She must have run through the scene we'd just played dozens of times before. Nikki's cigarette had fallen from the ashtray and burned a small black patch on her desk. I picked up the butt, and crushed it out. I touched her throat, feeling for a pulse. Then, when I was sure she was breathing clearly, I let myself out of the office and told her secretary that Nikki didn't want to be disturbed. Coming out of the elevator downstairs, the big bartender caught my eye and shrugged as if asking a question. I gave him a quick thumbs-up and he smiled, then I got out of the club as fast as I could. Nikki would awaken in a few hours and never be sure (despite what her staff might tell her) if I'd been there or not. Just one more bad dream come and gone.

22. Flow is Shape Plus Change, Motion Plus Form

In a ransacked liquor store off Sunset it was my bad luck to find what had to be one of the last full bottles of *aguardiente* left in Los Angeles. I popped a couple of pills without looking to see what they were, and swallowed them with a mouthful of liquor. It all went down burning and soothing, like a mouthful of warm needles—liquid acupuncture. Slow-motion suicide. I was drunk and lost, back in the wildest streets of Hollywood. Friedrich Nietzsche, sister-fucker, atheist, and syphilitic philosopher, once said something like "That which doesn't kill me only makes me stronger." I couldn't agree. I'd faced the thing I feared the most, the monster under (and in) my bed, and I didn't feel stronger. I felt like hammered shit.

I saw sleepers for the first time since coming to the city. Smugglers were making deals with phantom partners, while hookers negotiated with invisible johns. The most unnerving sleepers, though, were the soldiers reenacting their patrols, glassy-eyed, talking in papery whispers to buddies who weren't there. With their empty hands they mimed guns, slung and unslung them, shooting ghost bullets at things they probably couldn't have seen even when they were awake. I never saw an Indian sleeper and wondered if they possessed some kind of immunity to the syndrome. It wasn't until later that I learned what the Indians did instead of sleepwalking.

Millions of bats flew in tight formation down from

the hills like some black, haunted river, filling the sky with piercing squeaks and the fleshy flapping of wings, the latter a falling rain of neon checkerboards and the former a hot pink icepick jabbing into the back of my skull. I slipped in mud where souvenir hunters had crowbarred up parts of Hollywood Boulevard to steal the sidewalk plaques stamped with movie stars' names. I had received my own star on the Walk of Fame after my third album, a star containing a smaller circle within a circle meant to represent a record. When I asked someone on the committee how it was they had placed hundreds of stars along the boulevard and not run out of room, she told me that the committee repossessed the stars of celebrities no one remembered. I asked for the plaque of the actor I was displacing, and they gave it to me. Joseph Kray. I'd never heard of him and couldn't find any of his movies on video or disk, or in any of the archives I called, but I kept his plaque in my studio, as a sort of talisman to time and memory.

I killed off the last of the *aguardiente* and discovered that I was back on Sunset, near where the street turned to run along the edge of the hills. The vegetation was thick and wild there. I threw away the bottle and picked up a metal pipe from the street. Swinging the pipe like a machete in front of me, I beat back the jungle so I could move toward a familiar structure. It wasn't until I was practically in the lobby that I recognized it as the Chateau Marmont, a high-priced Hollywood relic where movie stars used to come to tryst and, occasionally, OD. I'd stayed there for a few weeks myself when Sony Films hired me to score some bloated sci-fi extravaganza. The picture was a disaster and I couldn't write, so I mostly stayed in my room, getting stoned and watching frenetic foreign game shows off the satellite, cheering when contestants won a case of American whiskey or a tractor.

The hotel was built like some ersatz Swiss chalet. I

made my way around to the back, tripping and laughing in the dark. I swung the pipe like a rapier, thinking of Errol Flynn and Douglas Fairbanks. My room had been around back, facing away from the street, on the upper floor. The door was locked, so I had to smash the lock with my pipe, before lurching in. Inside, it smelled like some greenhouse gone mad—humidity, rot, and the fecund odor of growing things. The breeze from outside, though, was worse. The wind had changed and the air had gone rank with the nauseatingly sweet stink of overripe mangoes. I stuffed sofa cushions in the broken window to keep the mango smell out, found the bedroom, and collapsed.

Everything in Los Angeles reminded me of something else, mostly things I wanted to forget. That, I suddenly understood, was why I hated coming to the city. It was the place I'd always gone to fail. I'd stayed in this room with Nikki when I was pretending to write for Sony. We played with the maids and watched porn on cable and I tried to kill myself soon after. Here I was again, deep in some neurological wet-dream, closing a circle that seemed to be seducing me into the real death I no longer wanted. Every step I took in L.A. submerged me further in my own lousy history.

How could I have created the monstrous and overwhelming Nikki that I'd been carrying with me since Point Mariposa? Had that other Nikki ever existed, or was she just an amalgamation of all the things I hated most about myself? Nikki, things, kept disappearing when I looked at them, although you could turn that around and say that I had trouble seeing things as they were.

Sweat poured down my arms, like insects crawling over me.

Nikki and I had stayed at some producer's house in Malibu. Once, when a storm washed some porpoises ashore, we all went down to drag them back out into the surf. When we got there, though, we saw that the porpoises were monsters. Extra eyes peppered their faces like parasites, and their snouts bulged with long ragged rows of half-formed teeth. They were freaks, mutations from the polluted and radioactive waters that hugged the dead nuclear reactors along the southern California coast. . . .

I shivered. The heat inside me turned to cold, and I rolled up in the moldy blankets on the bed and tried to rest. My body alternated between hot and cold, burning and freezing, my past and personality flaking away like the rotten stucco on the ceiling above the bed. I wiped the shreds of plaster from my eyes and drifted into an unsettled sleep.

When I awoke, my head felt full of broken concrete, and my body was bathed in a sour sweat that cooled on my skin. It took a couple of tries to open my eyes, the lids were so gummed. Which was worse, I wondered, waking up from the fever or waking up hungover? Try as I might, I couldn't fully surface from sleep, and I found it difficult to complete any thought or movement without frequent and irritating narcoleptic lapses. To move my hand, I had to engage my shoulder; this allowed me to locate my hand on the bed. I then had to turn the hand over, and move the fingers slightly, just to reconnect it with the rest of my body. Only then could the hand move and perform simple tasks, like brushing my hair from my face.

The first thing I saw when I could focus was a row of tiny green windsurfers on the mattress near my head. I closed my eyes, battled back from sleep, and refocussed, finally making out a single-file line of leaf-cutter ants moving down the wall, onto the bed, across my legs and onto the floor. Each ant held a neatly trimmed triangle of leaf over its head. The leaves caught the morning light, illuminating the veins inside. I laid my finger over the ants' trail and there was a moment's confusion in the ranks, but once the first ant made it over the obstacle, the others followed quickly behind. I sat up in bed, looking around for the ants' destination. They marched in an endless line across the thick hotel carpet and out the door.

I stood up by subdividing the act into a series of smaller manageable steps, and followed the ants out onto the hotel walkway. I must have fallen asleep a couple of times as I trailed the ants around to the front of the hotel, because the jungle and sky seemed to change in a series of jump cuts. At first there was just the closest vegetation and the thick morning mist. A few steps, and then a new layer of plants, the mist thinning. A few more steps and the sun threw columns of light down from the upper canopy to the floor of the jungle along Sunset.

I dug through the thick vegetation at the hotel lobby trying to follow the ants' trail. My head spun. Nothing would stay in focus. I fell once, twice, my legs only sporadically obeying my brain. I kept flashing on bad dream images, Nikki's swollen arms, horrible animals dying and gasping in the sand, Frida running away from me.

I walked just to feel myself move, to exert some control over the body from which I'd recently become disengaged. I still couldn't focus on objects, and had few clear memories of events before coming to Los Angeles, just glimpses, hints, and frozen images. I was an empty vessel, alone, looking for something with which to fill myself up.

But not really alone, I realized. A half-dozen or so men and women walked past me on Sunset, made their way around one of the fissures, and disappeared into the thick jungle fronting the hills. The group was chanting quietly as they walked, their bodies painted with black geometrics, like living schematic diagrams. They ignored me as they passed, so intent were they on their chanting. When they were out of sight, I followed them through the brush. The Indians moved through the vegetation silently, stepping by instinct and long training on the firmest parts of the trail. I slipped and skidded over sticks, curbs, and parking meters hidden in the undergrowth. Two or three minutes into the bush, I was lost and, now, truly alone. I could just make out the Indians' hushed chanting up ahead. I wasn't worried anymore about where they were going, I just wanted out of the blinding green, green, green in which I felt I was drowning.

When the Indians were both out of sight and hearing, I panicked and tore through the bush blindly, emerging suddenly into a clearing, the Hollywood hills rising behind us. The clearing appeared to be a natural structure, with a vaulted cathedral-like ceiling where palms and the trunks of thick bamboo bent overhead. Sunlight filtered through several layers of canopy and threw jaguar spots on the ground. The Indians were seated on low wooden stools around a fire. In the center was seated an old shaman. I started to back out of the clearing, understanding that I had stumbled into some kind of religious ceremony, when the shaman locked his gaze on mine. I wonder now what I must have looked like to him then. I was still wearing the tuxedo. I don't know how many days I'd lain in the Chateau Marmont. My hands were covered with dirt and fresh scratches from blundering through the brush. I started to back away again when the shaman gestured for me to come closer. I started to say something, but he gestured for silence, and pointed to a spot near the edge of the circle. The shaman's gaze never wavered from mine. I sat between two young men, one of whom wore a football jersey with NIKE in white letters across the chest; the other bore a startling resemblance to Charles Bronson.

The old shaman began chanting again, his lip plug bouncing in counter-rhythm to each syllable. The other Indians picked up the chant. I stayed silent, letting the light from their voices wash over me. Without missing a beat, the shaman took a palm leaf brush that was sitting in a filigreed china tea cup, came to where I was sitting, and began painting geometric figures on my hands. That done, he painted my face and continued the black designs down onto my white dress shirt.

The chanting quickened, rising in both volume and frequency, into a high, loud falsetto. The shaman returned to the center of the circle and dropped a bundle of leaves into the fire. A pungent white smoke filled the clearing. With a fan made of quetzal feathers, the shaman directed streamers of smoke into the face of each man and woman in the circle. The whole setup made me nervous; I wondered what I'd walked in to, but the smoke had a soothing effect on me. I felt light-headed, but relaxed, a neutral observer of my own body.

Returning to the fire, the old man brought out a decorated clay bowl and used a dipper to fill small palm-nut cups with a green watery liquid. He gave each of us a cup, and took a cup for himself. The chanting stopped abruptly, and the old man held his cup up to me pointedly, indicating that it was time to drink. I put the cup to my lips and sniffed. Nothing. Then I gulped the liquid down. It was just like hearing a door close and open somewhere in my mind. Despite my fears, the liquid didn't taste too bad at all, like watery corn. The cups drained, the shaman picked up the chant again, starting from the frenetic falsetto of a few moments earlier.

Almost immediately, I felt a warm and pleasant metallic buzz spread throughout my body, a subtle kind of drunkenness, but with a sensory clarity I hadn't experienced before. From the bushes behind him, the shaman produced a long bamboo tube and a pouch of black powder, like a finely ground pepper. Still chanting, he went from person to person in the circle, inserted one end of the tube into each person's nostril and blew in a pinch of the black powder, like he was using a blow gun. He then blew a pinch in the other nostril, and moved on to the next person. As he went around the circle, the people the shaman dosed began to shake. To my right, Charles Bronson's eyes rolled up, and his lips slid back from his teeth, flecked with foam. Then it was my turn. When I hesitated, the old man laughed and reached out with a strong calloused hand and bent my head back. The tube went in my nostril, and I felt the powder fill me. Same thing in the other nostril. Already I could taste it at the back of my throat. I suppose I could make some excuse that the shaman forced me in some way to take the *yagé,* but it wasn't that way at all. He acted more like a doctor trying to get an uncooperative child to take his medicine.

Until the *yagé* hit my system, the things I'd seen during my breakdown in Point Mariposa had been the most vivid hallucinations I had ever experienced. But they didn't prepare me for what came next. My hands began to shake, and the fever took hold of my body, knotting me with cramps on the floor of the clearing. My nose was running copiously onto the grass. I couldn't see. Chills bubbled up below the fever, beginning in my legs, moving up my body until my head was full of poison, skin stretched tight like the body of a jellyfish. When the pressure was its worst, my head sort of *popped* like a balloon, and the fever was gone. I was drained, empty again, but able to stand, with a weirdly vivid sense of euphoria. The shaman lead me to the other men and women. They didn't look in any better shape than I. Bronson and Nike, both of whom had taken bigger hits of the powder than I, shook and groaned in the thin morning light.

Then the sound started, a low humming at the base of my skull. When I turned my head, the humming altered its tone and frequency, but never stopped. There were halos around all the objects in the clearing, like a Kirlian panorama. The sound grew louder, becoming painful, like feedback, the noise filling my body until my teeth shook. It was the light, I realized; I was hearing the light.

The shaman was coming down the line, handing each person an object—a woman up front received an animal bone, Bronson a carved wooden figure, and Nike a bundle of feathers. Each person on receiving his or her object cradled it out like a compass and moved off into the jungle. We were supposed to go on some sort of spirit walk, I thought. The objects were our guides. My body soon grew into a strange kind of tune with the light-noise in my head. I relaxed into a kind of waking sleep, mobile, moving on automatic pilot.

I was the last in line to receive an object. The shaman placed it in my hand wrapped in a palm leaf. I started way from the old man, pulling the wrapping from the thin rectangle inside. It was white paper, and printed in bold letters on the top was

MAP TO THE STARS' HOMES.

I used to see headbangers from the Valley hawking them on street corners for five bucks, trying to pick up money for dope and records. This map was damp, and had been folded and refolded so many times that it felt like soft suede. I turned around to ask the old man if this was a joke, but he was gone, the clearing deserted. I opened the map. A winding trial that looped through Beverly Hills and Laurel Canyon was marked red with *achiote* juice. I stuffed the leaf in my pocket and wandered back to Sunset, where the trail began.

The humming in my head was settling down into a pattern, a kind of rhythmic hum, like a didgeridoo. It shifted with the irregular pattern of lights as they crossed my field of vision. Moving deeper into the vegetation, I fell steadily into the *yagé's* trance. Time was the first thing to go, but chaos theory tells us that linear time is an illusion anyway, that time in period doubling situations can move in any direction. Quantum mechanics says something similar, but on the quanta level, the infinitesimal level of things like photons. Were individual photons packets of time as well as light? I wondered.

I didn't recognize the streets anymore. I couldn't be sure if I was following the shaman's map; I wasn't even sure if I should. I was following the light, moving toward the places where the light and sound were most consonant. It was like songwriting with my whole body. Spheres and cubes rotated in the air before me, describing the outlines of the five Platonic solids.

I climbed slowly up a hill. The southern California scrub and manzanita were mixed with the more lush plants of Amazonia. It occurred to me that what I was doing, tracing a path based on the shade of lights and sound, might be exactly what Frida had been doing in Marin. I'd thought she was crazy then, and treated her like it. It wasn't in me to believe in things like Spiritlines, but maybe she saw or heard something invisible to me, in the same way the lights in my head were invisible to my father and the doctors who locked me up. I was aware of the baboons in the trees, but they kept well back in the branches.

The wind whipped over the hills and the map fluttered in my hand like a deranged gull. I was near the crest, before the long drop into Laurel Canyon and the walled compounds where the wealthy held out before the onslaught of both Amazonia and the Army. I wasn't sure I wanted to go that far. Bad karma down there. The place vibrated with it.

I fell again, but it didn't hurt because the road was

covered with a mossy layer of jungle detritus. Birds sang and iguanas rustled in the undergrowth, adding to the confusing light in my head.

How perfect, I thought, to come looking for Frida and find Nikki. I'd failed them both and now, apparently, even failed myself, because I couldn't move. I contemplated the air above and around me, the ceaseless movement of clouds above the jungle floor. I could stay in this spot forever, I thought. It wouldn't be hard. Behind the drug, I could imagine (feel, even) tendrils, extending from my back, rooting me to the road.

Green, cellular light.

But the tune just didn't make it. The sound of the green light was meaningless for me. I was trying to be Frida. Make up for her loss by writing the music she would have written. But I couldn't play it, anymore than she could play the music of cities.

From where I lay, I could turn my head and get a perfect Cinemascope view of Los Angeles. It shimmered below me, giving off a dense fractal light that almost, but not quite matched the sound I'd heard during my suicides. My body was a dry husk, an empty locust shell. My head spun, and I was stumbling down a corridor of colored lights. I saw the afterlife light that the Buddhists talk about in the Book of the Dead, the pure and formless light Greek mystics believed to be the body of Nous, God. I heard Gnawan drummers in Marrekesh, beating out patterns that were known as colors, and colors that were rhythms. I wandered through the light in the head of Olivier Messiaen as he played his apocalyptic quartet in a prison-camp theater, bringing Nazi officers to tears. The different lights gave off a heat that burned me from the inside. What little was left of Ryder was searing away. I felt my bones crumble like cigarette ash, my muscles dry to stringy ropes and my skin to a leathery membrane, like the wings of the bats above Hollywood. I would rather have been with them than sweating on this awful road. And I almost heard the music, staring out over the city, but it was beyond my reach, like a radio in a passing car, Dopplering away. It was gone.

Done here, I went back down the hill. When I reached the flatlands I discovered that I was still on the shaman's trail (the thing doubled back on itself). I headed back toward Hollywood, passing Jean Harlow's and Rita Hayworth's overgrown mansions, goddesses and ghosts from the L.A. dreamtime. Somewhere along Santa Monica Boulevard I fell in with Bronson, Nike, and some of the other Indians who had been at the ritual. All the spirit walks seemed to be leading us to the same place. I unfolded my map to see where we were headed, and at the same moment spotted the woman with the recorder. Although I wasn't sure it was a recorder now; it might have been a camera. The fractal city light blurred the edges of things, and baboons growled in the abandoned mansions of Beverly Hills. "Frida?" I said. "Frida?" The apparition of the woman stood in the middle of Santa Monica with her camera or recorder or whatever, the light and sound of the city dazzling around her, another illusion among the parade of illusions that followed me. I waited for the ground to open or the baboons to come, and when they didn't I backhanded the camera, expecting my hand to move through empty air. Instead, I struck something solid. The woman backed away, kicking and cursing at me in Japanese, before she ran away.

23. Solitons as Dissipative Structures

We crossed over to Melrose, a strange crew of urban tribal types and me, dressed in my filthy tuxedo like a maître'd at the Apocalypse. At La Brea, we crossed paths with an Army patrol hiking south toward Santa Monica Boulevard. The soldiers were all young, teeny-boppers mostly, draftees probably, sweating and grimacing as they made another pointless turn through the muggy Hollywood streets. None of them gawked at the spirit-walking Indians, but just stared through them with a sullen kind of contempt. The Indians, for their part, ignored the soldiers as utterly and effortlessly as ignoring your own shadow.

Just when I thought we'd get off scot-free, a couple of the young grunts spotted my strange getup. They nudged their buddies, nodding toward me and laughing, moving their hands over their faces and pointed out my painted features to each other. There was an older-looking grunt near the back of the patrol, a tired-looking sunburned sergeant with almond eyes and high Mongolian cheekbones. He didn't laugh; he stood stock still in the street. As we drew abreast of them, he barked something and started toward me. Befuddled by the light and *yagé,* my mind went blank. I pirouetted away from the soldiers two or three times, singing non-sense syllables at the top of my voice, acting as complete a lunatic as I could manage. That really broke up the young grunts, who always appreciate sophisticated humor. The sergeant remained where he was, seemingly undecided about how to handle the white boy who had gone so weirdly native. In the end, he just shook his head and walked away to rejoin his troops, his face already composing itself into the same mask of passive contempt as the others', before he marched them away.

The mist had burned off and the sky was clear as the jungle heat moved toward its deadening midday apex. Emerald parrots and macaws squawked above us, dropping berries and mango seeds on the street. Past a stripped and rusting police car, I followed the other spirit-walkers into the open gates of the Paramount Studio lot. Inside, a couple of dozen locals were gathered around a fire; the old shaman who had dosed me was leading them all in a chant. I couldn't follow this one. It was loopy and arrhythmic, at least to my ears. Bare-breasted women shook rainsticks, and several men blew notched bamboo flutes, imitating shrill, stuttering bird calls with complex melodies whose light was dazzling and chaotic. The shaman danced in a low crouch, advancing and retreating from the fire, menacing it with the totems he held, a necklace made of bird bones and a remote-control unit from a VCR.

"They're singing the Spiritline of the place," said a familiar voice behind me. "This part of New Amazonia, it's theirs now."

I turned and looked at her, blinked a couple of times. Frida remained in place and in focus. She smiled at me and tugged on my shirt. "I'm no hallucination," she said, "but I know how you feel. I've taken the powder myself." I put my arms around her and felt her reach for me. We stayed like that, Frida a little longer than she wanted, I think, the way she gently, but firmly patted my back. But I wouldn't let her go, afraid that I would open my eyes and find myself in some lockdown ward in Point Mariposa or back on the road to

Laurel Canyon. Finally, we parted. She smiled at me, more warmly than I probably deserved.

"Hello, Ryder."

"Hello, Frida."

She shook her head. "Not Frida anymore. I'm me again. Catherine," she said.

I nodded. "Call me anything you want. I don't think I'm anyone I was before." I looked at myself and then her. "You look wonderful." And so she did. She had on a loose khaki vest, like something a photographer would wear, Army pants and boots, and unlike me she looked clean. I realized how hot I was in my tuxedo, and pulled off the jacket, tossing it away. Along with her clothing, Frida's—Catherine's—face had changed. The contours had shifted, revealing a kind of grace and solidity that had been hidden under the tense musculature of her San Francisco face. Her forehead and cheeks were dyed red with *achiote.* On her biceps she wore shell-bead bracelets, and on her hip she had a leather sheath holding a big-bladed hunting knife. Her ear piercings were accentuated by smooth sticks she wore Indian-style through exaggerated holes in the lower part of each lobe. And she had an ODR recorder slung on a strap over her shoulder.

"So you live with this tribe now?" I said, nodded at the others.

"The Xingara," she said. "They kind of adopted me."

I touched the recorder. "They didn't give you that."

She smiled and shrugged the recorder strap to a more comfortable position. "No, I copped that from one of Lurie's sound boys. Teach him not to leave his gear when he runs off to relieve himself."

We walked away from the fire, over to an alley by one of the sound stages where it was quieter. "I was supposed to be rescuing you, you know," I told her. "You were supposed to be the Wild Woman of Borneo by now. I was going to squint and do Clint Eastwood for you."

"Well, it's the thought that counts," Catherine said. She wiped away some of the sooty black dye from around my eyes. "Yes, that is you under there. I had a feeling you'd end up here sooner or later. If you came down, of course."

"I owed you that, at least."

"You don't owe me anything."

"I cost you your music."

Catherine looked as the shaman dropped bundles of leaves into the fire, sending a pillar of white smoke above the cinderblock walls. "No, I'd reached a dead end in San Francisco. Besides, you didn't take my tapes. Lurie did."

"Lurie?"

"Don't you get it? He and his crew have been filming over at the Troubadour and the Hollywood Bowl. There's even talk that he's going to bring in a crew to dig out the Whiskey. He's shooting all the places you use to play. *You're* the documentary now. Not the rainforest."

"Shit."

"He probably recognized you back in Marin. Remember, he took your picture?"

"I wondered about him turning up so conveniently in time to pick Virilio and me up on the coast. He could have had choppers tailing us all the way down from San Francisco. Look, are you dead sure about this?"

Catherine lifted the recorder. "When I took this, there was a tape dupe of my music inside it."

My head was spinning. It was insane. I was insane. The little that I thought I understood, that I had a handle on, was slipping away. "But why would he care this much?"

"You're out of touch, dear. I get to read the newspapers the soldiers throw away. You have no idea how much bigger you've become since you disappeared.

You're Elvis and Jesus, only without the body, so it's so much sexier. The longer you're gone, the bigger you become."

"Christ, I thought people would get bored and the sightings would fade away in a few months."

"If they did, Lurie blew your cover. He's apparently leaked some footage of you to Japanese TV."

I leaned back against the hot metal skin of a soundstage door. "I guess I'm not entirely surprised," I said. "I think I attacked one of Lurie's video crew on the way over here."

"She probably deserved it."

"I thought she was another hallucination," I said, shrugging. "I'm still sorry about your tapes. It's one thing to throw away work, it's another to have it taken away."

"I don't worry about them anymore. You shouldn't either," she said. "Listen, everything is different here. I was greedy up north. I wanted the whole rainforest for myself. I thought if I could record and catalog all the sounds, I could own them. But I was wrong, and I made Frida miserable trying."

"So what are you playing now?"

"It's not the sound that's so different, it's the approach. And that makes a bigger change than you might think."

I looked back at the Xingara, moving in their ritual around the fire. "And what about the Spiritline? You gave up trying to claim that, too?"

"Looking for it the way I was, that was greed, too. I don't have to own the line to know it's there, to see it and hear it and try to play it."

I shook my head. "Despite appearances, I'm still a basically rational person. I'm never going to be able to buy the idea of the lines."

"You know what they say, 'When it's so hard to

believe in anything, why not believe in the impossible?' "

"You asked me that before. I still don't have an answer." I didn't know what to do with my hands. I wanted to make some gesture of understanding to her. No matter what she said, I still felt that I owed her something. Wanting a drink, I took the lithium and Inderal from my pocket.

"Where'd you get those?"

"Virilio. They're medicine. You want one?" I said, unfairly sarcastic.

She took one of the lithium tablets and examined it. "You know that when Virilio and I were an item, he had a neat little trick he liked to pull on people with too much money. He'd find out what kind of dope they liked and give them psychedelics instead. Acid. Ketamine. Said it really fucks people up when the walls start talking to them for no reason."

"Ah," I said, feeling kind of sick and humiliated. It had never occurred to me to check the drugs out. I poured the remaining pills onto the ground. I couldn't blame him, though. "That's perfect. You know, I begged him for it," I said to Catherine. "I begged him to rip me off."

"It's what he does. He dosed me, too, when he broke up. It's his way of keeping power."

"We're a pair, aren't we?" I said.

"You don't have to go back. Neither of us has to get ripped off any more."

I looked at her. "What happened to you after you left San Francisco?"

She turned away. Her hands tugging uncomfortably at the recorder strap. "I was as crazy as you can be and still walk," she said. She held up her hands, showing me the deep, ragged scars across her wrists. "I don't know how long I was alone, just skating over whatever roads I came to. Hiding from the Army, smugglers, refugees; eating whatever plants were around. After a while it wasn't too bad. Then I kind of got to like it. You know up in San Francisco, I hated my life. I hated the city. I hated everything. After those first few days of wandering down the coast, getting lost in the hills, not seeing the sun for days at a time through the canopy, I realized that as hard as it was, it's where I belonged. In San Francisco, I'd been a coward, running to the rainforest for sustenance and inspiration, then running back to the city when the forest overwhelmed me. I was trying to keep a foot in both worlds, but without committing to either."

"How did you end up with the Xingara?"

"The old shaman found me wandering around the Hollywood Hills while he was spirit-walking. He took me back to their camp. My wrists were infected, my hands were so swollen, I couldn't even bend my fingers. They took care of me. So I stayed." She leaned back against the long white wall. "I've started thinking that maybe I was meant to meet the Xingara. Be with them. Wandering down here from San Francisco was kind of like my own spirit walk. . . ."

"Uh oh, you're fading again. I'm losing you."

She shrugged. "Believe whatever you want. All I know is that down here I've found out where I belong. This is a place I can work and these are people I can be with."

Catherine was looking back at the Indians. I had the urge to tell her about finding her shaman on my own, but I resisted it. My mind was already divided over the idea, part of me wanting to tell her how it was magic that I found the same old man and how he led me here, and my higher mind telling me that it was a coincidence having to do with proximity and the movements of people with common interests. "I ran through a lot of possibilities when I was coming down here," I said. "But it never occurred to me that I'd find you happy."

Catherine pulled a woven *etsemat* from one of the pockets of her vest and used it to tie her hair back from her face. "I am. You could do it, too, if you'd only let yourself."

The sun was well in the sky and the temperature was rising in the parking lot. A sultry heat rippled off the asphalt, so the Indians looked like watery video images on a bad monitor. "I don't know. I think I missed that boat," I told her. I slid down to the pavement, trying to stay out of the sun. Catherine sat down next to me and rested her hand on my leg. "It doesn't really seem an option."

"All right," she said. "Just let it go for now."

We sat there together in silence for a few minutes. I'd run out of logic. A prime fool, wrong about everything from the very beginning. Nikki wasn't a monster, and I couldn't just toss off the fame and mythology I'd worked so hard to manufacture. I wondered if I even had malaria. The entire enterprise—from my escape from Point Mariposa, to my exile in San Francisco, to the music I was writing—had all been built on deluded ideals. I was Dorothy in *The Wizard of Oz,* flying off to some ersatz enchanted kingdom; only in my version, I was both protagonist and tornado, sweeping up those like Lurie and Virilio who were close enough to hitch a ride, and those who got too close to the eye of the storm, like Frida. It was a pitiful thing, I thought, to have been so complicit in such an elaborate practical joke on myself. I was going to say something to Catherine about that, trying to figure the best words to make it into a joke, when the ground turned to jello beneath us.

The first surges were long and rolling, and it felt as if the quake might end at any moment. But it didn't, and the waves shortened into jagged, staccato blows that knocked people off their feet. When I looked back,

I could see rubbery waves rise and fall in the surface of the asphalt, as if humpbacked giants were wrestling underground. The quake roared in my ears, and screaming animals fled through the trees. Above us, the air itself seemed to fracture and come apart like an ice floe, and in the moment of its shattering burn off all its oxygen, leaving us breathless and gasping.

The wall around the lot cracked, sloughing off its cement skin and scattering the red brick at its center like autumn leaves. Catherine and I had to crawl away or be pulverized. Through the gap in the wall, I could already see black smoke rising in the distance.

Still on my belly, I crawled to a set of utility stairs attached to the side of the sound stage and began to climb. I wasn't thinking anymore. The soundstage swayed around me, like a ship caught in a storm, trying to shed the staircase and me with it. I hung onto the railing and crawled up one step at a time until I reached the roof. How long did it take? My whole life, it felt. And when I made the roof the shaking still hadn't stopped.

Above the treeline, Los Angeles was alive with fire. The noise was unbearable. I closed my eyes against it, but that only made it worse. When I opened my eyes again, the city lurched into sudden negative, like a photographic plate, unfolding like the transparent panels of a crystal *shoji* screen. Within each panel were held the sounds of the city, luminous dragonflies. Each beating of the dragonflies' wings set up echoes which the other dragonflies redoubled, birthing new, smaller dragonflies, who, in turn, birthed their own miniature twins, down and down until their radiant wings reached such a state of fine detail that the light shining from them resolved itself into the dragon-tooth bifurcations along the edge of a Mandelbrot Set.

And then the sound came to me, shaking me from the inside out, the music of the city, of my suicides.

The brilliant, unbearable sound thundering from the city and my body enfolded me utterly within itself. The sensation was as electrifying as a sudden fall from a rockface or a gun shot. I was undone, overwhelmed by the force of it all, like someone waking from a coma, and I screamed to crack the crystal lattice of my bones, to destroy myself right then within the bounds of the music.

24. Vacuum Bubble Instanton

I was done in. Emptied of desire, moving my body like a puppeteer—first one foot, and then the other. In this way, I made it down the stairs and back to the ground. Catherine grabbed my arm and pulled me into the open ground in the middle of the parking lot and away from the soundstage, saying, "Jesus, you are crazy." When I looked back over my shoulder, I had a better idea of what she was talking about. The sound stage was a wreck; most of the wall facing the parking lot had caved in, pulling down part of the roof. All of the nearby buildings appeared to be damaged or on fire. Needles of glass fell from shattered windows all around us. The surface of the parking lot had buckled under the strain of the quake, leaving ridges like shallow veins in the asphalt. Several of the Xingara men were stamping out the remains of the fire, which had been scattered across the lot. Mothers and fathers comforted crying children. The whole tribe looked as shell-shocked as I felt.

Catherine went to where the old shaman was talking with a group of older men. Overhead, black, rolling plumes of smoke had begun to block out the sun where it came through the forest canopy. The breeze was heavy with the smell of gas. Of course, lines had probably popped all over the city. I wondered if the Army was equipped to put out the kind of fires that were probably already cooking their way from South Central to North Hollywood.

A familiar face came swaying through the Paramount gates. It took a second for me to conjure up a name because I'd only seen Virilio out of his trench coat once before. The quick, jittery way he was moving through the lot, shoving his way past the Indians, tripping over ripples in the asphalt, put me on guard. I started to angle around to where Catherine was talking to the shaman, trying to keep a blind of Xingara between me and Virilio's line of sight. But he spotted me, and when I started in the opposite direction, he pulled a pistol—Frida's pistol—from the waistband of his jeans and pointed it at me.

"Don't you move," he called. "Don't you fucking move!"

I moved away from the Indians and waited for him. He held the .45 out before him like a third eye, guided by its barrel to me. I kept looking at his arms. He had on a sleeveless T-shirt, revealing the snakeskin tattoos. In the light of day, it seemed such a trite gesture, cartoon badass stuff. But there was the gun. When Virilio was close enough, he snapped his boot up into my stomach. I doubled over and fell to the ground, unable to get up as he kicked me again, halfheartedly. "You sack of shit! We had a deal!" There was something oddly pleading in his voice, as if my disappearance had wounded him in some deeply personal way. He kept walking away and dropping the gun to his side as if thinking, then he would spin around, and put the boot in a couple of times, only to walk away again, shaking his head. "It's all over, man. You went to Nikki, didn't you? Bet you both had a real good laugh. Here's something for laughs." He kicked me hard in the small of my back. "This is for walking away." Another kick. "This is just for being an asshole." Another. He leaned down close to my face and said,

"Tell me a story. What did you say to Nikki?" He pointed the gun at my throat.

It took me a moment to get back my breath. When I could speak, all I could get out was, "—didn't tell Nikki anything about you."

"Don't lie to me, man. I know how it is. You have to have everything for yourself. All the fame, all the women, all the money. Nothing left for your partner. Nothing at all for the putz who got you down here."

By holding on to Virilio's shirt, I managed to get to my feet. Under the circumstances, I didn't point out that it was Lurie who actually got us here. "I didn't cut you out of anything," I said. I was able to stand, but there was something wrong with my side; I couldn't straighten up all the way. "Nikki's so out of it, she didn't even know I was there."

"Liar!"

"It's true. I give you my word."

A sad, angry smile appeared on Virilio's face. "No. I'll give you this."

He brought up the gun and shot me.

A punch from a steel fist. Searing pain. The whole left side of my body went numb, and I fell on my face. From somewhere far off I could hear Catherine's voice calling to Virilio. When the finishing shot didn't come, I crawled onto my knees and tried to move away, but my legs melted under me. I fell again. From where I lay, I got a grandstand view of Catherine and the old shaman screaming and advancing on Virilio. I tried to yell, tell them to get away from him, but nothing came out. Virilio was so preoccupied having Catherine and the old man in his face, that he didn't see Bronson, Nike, and a couple of other Xingaras swinging around behind him. I couldn't hear what Catherine and Virilio were screaming—my ears were full of the glittering noise of the sea. When Catherine got close, she lunged at Virilio's arm and hung on. He latched onto Catherine and punched her savagely before the Xingaras grabbed him. They brought him down fast, but when the shaman tried to pull Catherine away, Virilio got off one wild shot, hitting the old man right above his heart. The shaman's body seemed to collapse around the wound, and he fell hard. Catherine screamed. I sat up and yelled her name. But it was too late; when the Xingaras hauled Virilio to his feet, Catherine pulled her knife from its sheath and, in one flashing movement, slashed his throat.

The Indians let Virilio's body drop. I managed to get to my knees as Catherine came to me. She still had the knife in her hand, her forearm and vest spattered with Virilio's blood. I think she said something to me. Her mouth moved, but my hearing was gone. In a few seconds, the rest of my senses followed.

What's it like being dead? A reasonable question that I can't answer reasonably. Let's just say it's quiet there, and blacker than an entertainment lawyer's heart. And there was no city of light. The moment I felt the Big Sleep sucking the heat from my bones, the light in my head scattered like a swarm of nervous fireflies. Great. Something else I got wrong. The city of light wasn't death after all, but the edge of something vastly stranger, another *possibility,* an infinitely small zone of stability that exists at the frenzied heart of even the most turbulent systems—the eye of a fractal hurricane. It required will and presence to track down and learn from. If I died for keeps, the city of light would be lost forever.

So I didn't die.

I awoke to the familiar sound of rain. Opening my eyes, I made out a grid of acoustic tiles above me. I was on my back, and something moved by my feet. A young tamarin sat on the far arm of the sofa on which I was laid out, chewing intently on a large black beetle. I was back in the recording studio of the Capitol Records building. The sound of rain came again from the hall, echoing slightly from a broken window in the next office.

I rolled into a sitting position and immediately regretted it. A grinding, electric pain radiated from my ribs out through my body. Grabbing my side, I lay back down on the sofa. Several tamarins had gathered on the mixing console, and were watching me, checking out the invader who couldn't even stand up. Something thick and sticky hung in loose layers from the ribs on my left side. When my head stopped spinning and I could examine the wound, I was relieved to find that what felt like flayed skin was a dressing of some sticky brown Xingara ointment, wrapped in layers of anthurium leaf. Beneath the leaves, the skin was red and torn. But Virilio's shot had been off enough that the bullet just ripped up the skin on my side and maybe cracked a rib. Despite the ointment, and the bruised and swollen skin around it, the wound looked pretty clean.

I found a bottle of water on the floor and drank from it deeply. That made me feel considerably better. I closed my eyes and slowed my breathing, trying to relax all the muscles along both sides of my body. But I was out of practice and the breathing ritual only turned off the pain for a few seconds before I became aware of the pain's absence, bringing it right back to the center of my attention. In any case, I was too distracted to meditate properly. Some curious memory kept teasing me, floating right below the level of my consciousness. I went over the scene in the parking lot, letting the images play over and over in my mind until I was sure that what I remembered was, in fact, what happened. Catherine had killed Virilio in a way that had been even more blunt and painful than he might have deserved. But there was something else, and when I rubbed a stinging bead of sweat from my eye it all came back to me. I touched my face to make sure.

Yes, it was true.

A moment before I had thought Catherine a little excessive in the way she had taken care of Virilio. What must she think of me after seeing me cut out one of the dead man's eyes and replace it with my glass one?

Out of the corner of my remaining eye, I saw a bank of green and red LEDs glowing on a two-track mix-down deck next to the big console. I rolled carefully to the floor, holding the compress to my side while ruby dots of pain swarmed before me like video bees. Grabbing the padded edge of the mixing board, I pulled myself slowly into the swivel chair parked before it. An adult golden-lion tamarin sat on top of the two-track deck, idly gnawing the edge of a plastic cassette case. A partially chewed note lay at the tamarin's feet. The note said "Play Me," and when I checked, there was a tape already seated in the two-track. I hit the Play button.

Catherine's voice came from the overhead monitors, so clear, it was like she was standing right behind me. "Don't blame me if you wake up with a crick in your neck," she said. "When the Xingaras and I tried to take you back to their camp, you threw a fit. You'd only go to your studio, so there you are. If you're listening to this, I guess you're feeling better. I'll stop by with a new poultice and food and water until you're up and around. I'm glad you're nearby. I did miss you, you know. But I'm staying with the Xingara in their camp. This is my home now. The next few months ought to be exciting. We're all very sad about the death of Tiwa, the shaman, but after the mourning, there will be a long and complicated process to find a new shaman. Maybe I'll bring you here and you can see some of it. The Xingara wouldn't mind. Your name came up as a possible candidate. I think you impressed them with the eye trick."

When Catherine came for me, I had taken the knife from her and crawled over to Virilio's body. When I started cutting him, no one tried to stop me. They must have thought I'd gone insane. It took what seemed like a long time, surgery not being one of my strong suits (and doing it one-handed made me all the clumsier). After I stuck my false eye into Virilio's empty socket, I had a couple of the Xingara men drag the body to the entry of one of the nearby burning buildings. Maybe it would be Lurie himself who would identify the charred corpse. He could tell them that I was seen in the neighborhood, and that I had a glass eye. That could do it. My original mistake had been in playing cocktease with the world, not giving it a body. Now it would have one. Thanks to Lurie and Virilio, I would be found tragically expired in the tropics, just like Arthur Rimbaud. Hell of an exit. Rest in Peace.

There was a pause before Catherine's voice picked up again. "I wasn't sure, at first, how I'd feel if I saw you again. San Francisco was fun, but it would never have worked out, you know. Two crazy people can only make each other more crazy. If you decide to go back to New York or up north or someplace I'll be sad, but I'll understand. If you stay, though," another pause, "I'm still going to stay with the Xingara. L.A. is your place, not mine. I can still use the machines, just like you can still get food from the trees, but it's not where I should be and I can't live there.

"I hope you don't feel cheated, it's just that I don't need Clint Eastwood right now, just a friend.

"I found a studio in the basement of a house over in Echo Park and have been working on some new tunes. Let me know if you like them."

I went back to the sofa, shooed a couple of tamarins from the cushions and lay back down just as subtly modified night sounds of the rainforest came through the speakers. The light of the music was brighter and more complex than I remembered her San Francisco recordings. I liked Catherine's new music very much.

25. Helium in a Small Box

It took almost a month for the torn skin on my side to heal. When it did, Catherine brought me a nylon brace to wear while my ribs mended. This made it possible for me to work and get around by myself. In the weeks since Catherine and the Xingara brought me to Capitol Records I had slowly and painfully cobbled together a single functioning studio from bits and pieces of the others, plus some components I scrounged from electronics stores and pawn shops. The studio worked well enough, in fact, that I could probably have sold time in it, if there had been anyone to sell it to. Also, with Catherine's help, I registered for reclamation rights to the building (Nikki had been right about that option, at least), using an old pseudonym attached to a bank account in Toronto.

Catherine kept her word and came to see me every day for the first couple of weeks I was laid up. After I could move around a bit by myself, her visits dropped to every two or three days. Neither of us mentioned the change in her comings and goings. It was just the way things were. Now I see her, perhaps, every two or three weeks.

Sometimes she brings me gifts from the Xingara, woven necklaces and decorated arrows. Sometimes we make love in the little apartment I've set up in one of the old executive offices. She never stays very long; if she comes by in the evening, she's usually gone before I wake up in the morning. Sometimes I can talk her into staying for a day or two, but not often.

I've been pronounced officially dead by people who do that sort of thing for a living. I read that Lurie's film came out and is doing very well. I don't intend to see it. Apparently, he has lots of footage of me wandering through San Francisco collecting sounds, then Virilio and me coming down the coast, and my spirit walk. He must have had a crew on my tail from the moment we met. The film ends, appropriately, with the discovery of my body (He did make the identification, which is also in the film—the ham).

Although I haven't seen the film, I've heard the soundtrack music playing in a bars up and down Hollywood Boulevard. It never occurred to me that Lurie would have the balls to use the stolen tapes. What's wonderful, of course, is that all the music credited to me is by Catherine. Best of all, both the film and the album have been titled *Kamikaze L'Amour,* for the bar in which I was spotted meeting with my old manager, plotting my comeback, only to be cut down tragically in my prime, blah, blah. Nikki, if she's still alive, is probably having a grand old time, merchandising my demise. And Catherine has an album in the Top Ten, only she doesn't know it (not that she would care).

Tourists are starting to trickle back into the city, along with land speculators. But most of the prime property, the kind of stuff that attracted Nikki and would attract others looking for a ready-made empire, burned in the fires that went on for days after the quake. Even the tourists seem to have few expectations when they come here. Sometimes I'll be stopped by a group of Japanese teenagers who inform me that I look like the dead pop star. I explain to them how I hear that all the time, and we have a laugh together. Usually they want to take a few snapshots with me, and I almost always oblige them.

Despite my ribs, I'm feeling better than I have in years. What I'd been so sure was malaria turned out to be nothing more than a South American flu strain, filtered through a ketamine haze. The moment I stopped taking Virilio's spiked pills, the worst of the symptoms disappeared. Most of my time is taken with collecting the sounds of the city, the sounds that are inherent in any city even when it's mostly deserted—the sighs of convection currents hugging the downtown office buildings, the slap of feet moving across the different terrains of the city, the impressive silences locked in deserted libraries and warehouses.

Sometimes, I walk down Sunset to Echo Park, or wander into the rainforest in hopes of finding Catherine and her adopted tribe. During her long absences, our main method of communication has become what I call the Trinket Telegraph. Sometimes, when I return from a day of field recording, I'll find things in the studio: an old magazine with my picture in it, a plastic kaleidoscope, a bolo tie with a scorpion embedded in acrylic. The tamarins and I finally came to an understanding when I started giving them a share of the canned meats that would sometimes be waiting for me. When I go out, I leave behind blank ODR disks, fresh batteries for Catherine's recorder, tampons, and any useful looking medicines I find. I know that Catherine's been there when I return and find the items gone, and that's enough for now.

I have to admit that when I first heard about the release of Lurie's film, I was tempted to go back to New York, just to embarrass and shock him and the media. Play a set at CBGB's, do one or two quick interviews, and then disappear again, leaving them asking Who was That Masked Man? I didn't do it, of course. It's a characteristic of the dead that they remain quiet. I continue to record, to experiment with sound combinations. I even send tapes out to various small labels and magazines under the name of Joseph Kray. I have a wall of tiny fanzine reviews and polite rejection letters. It breaks me up every time I look at them.

New Indian tribes seem to wander in from the bush every few weeks. Some of the other Los Angelenos, people forced out by the original Amazonian invasion, have returned and blended in with the Indians, forming strange new tribes who are equally at home with the circuits of a digital sampler as they are with bamboo flutes. I've been visited a few times by MPs from the Army base over in Westwood. They seem suspicious of my wanderings and recordings, but really they're suspicious of anybody who made it through the fire.

Sometimes I want to tell them that I didn't make it, that I died and have the press clippings to prove it. Sometimes I want to tell them I'm mostly waiting. Even my work is a kind of waiting. When I work, spinning the lights in my head, looking for the perfect combination of sound that I saw above the burning city, I know that Catherine is doing something similar in a smaller studio across town. Sooner or later we'll both find the music we're after, and I know that when we do we'll be together again, able to finally know and teach each other the true dream shapes of both our hearts and homes.

KAD   Kadrey, Richard.

         Kamikaze l'amour.

7/29

$20.95